The Dark Matter Syndrome

The Awakening

Michael K. Drummer

Copyrighted material

Edited by Tina Winograd
Cover design by Stephen Campo
The Dark Matter Syndrome is an imprint of Kimball Publishing Group
ISBN 978-0989972215
Printed in the United States of America
Second Edition: September 5, 2014

The Dark Matter Syndrome is dedicated to Trinh, my wife and friend, for supporting my lifelong dream to become a writer. To my children: Isaiah, Rachael and Faith, I love you.

The Awakening

Chapter 1

Secret facility: Cascade Mountains, Oregon.
March 18, 2008

Drip... drip... drip... drip... the ever present sound outside Xiang's cell echoed through her drowsy seven-year-old mind. The only furniture was a thin naked mattress nearly as soft as the stone floor beneath. In the windowless space, she had no way of knowing whether it rained or snowed, or when day turned to night. She tried keeping track through the guards' shift changes and the stench of cheap cologne worn by one of them. However, before long, the forced drugs wiped away any coherency of time.

No matter what kind of trick she pulled to not swallow the pills, these bad people always caught her. Her eyelids closed, sending her to happy dreams.

When Xiang awakened, the *ping* droning in her ear made her head want to explode. The child had been so fatigued, she was not aware they had once again taken her from the cell to the lab. She had little strength left to move her arms or legs and she was thirsty. Her face scrunched from the sudden metallic aftertaste in her mouth, and her mind suppressed the urge to throw up. The last time she ate was a few hours ago and that was not food.

"What makes you think she's one of them? If there's any chance she's the person you've been looking for, why haven't you informed the boss?"

"Do not forget who you work for. If she isn't, perhaps *you* would like to be the one to explain to him we were mistaken—again."

The girl tried to open her eyelids, but the brightness in the room hurt from a drug-induced dilation. She remained lying still, waiting for the light sensitivity and queasiness to pass. Slowing her breathing, she tried to stop the spinning that made her feel impervious to gravity. Too late. Nausea washed over her and she gagged, vomiting over the side of the bed. The disgusting copper taste turned to bitter bile that burned her lungs and throat. If she could only have a drink of cool water.

"Wha'd you give her?" a man asked in a thick accent.

"Something to relax her mind and relieve her inhibitions," a female said.

"I'll relieve her inhibitions, all right." His laugh rolled the child's volatile insides and added chills. Peeking from one eye, the girl saw a tall white man wearing a black T-shirt and BDUs. He crossed his muscular arms as he stared at his military boots. With a twisted sneer, he glanced at the vomit between him and the bed, then smiled when certain none splattered on him.

"You're lucky you didn't hit me with that, you little snot." His hands balled in and out of clinched fists.

"This is not working," a female out of her sight said. "It's time to use stronger encouragement."

"Well, it's about time, don't you think?" The man laughed. A twinge of excitement growled in his deep, gritty voice. Xiang came fully awake, greeted by his compassionless smile and beady eyes glaring down at her. The hair on his chin reflected he had not shaven in days. His body odor confirmed he had not showered either.

"Ready to have some fun, runt?" His stained teeth and stale breath reeked of strong coffee and cheap cigarettes.

Xiang lay on a large hospital bed with white cotton sheets covering her from the waist down. A pair of long tubes ran to her arms. Steel chains and handcuffs secured her wrists and feet to the metal bedrails.

The man eyed the restraints. "Really, doc, this is overkill, don't you think?" the commando asked after taking a gulp from a tall steel thermos.

"Not if she's who we think," the female replied.

Xiang looked around hoping to find a familiar face, but there were none.

"Do not worry about your friends. They are safe." The Asian leaned over the girl and shined a painful beam of light into her eyes. "That should do it." She turned off the IV drip and removed the tubes from the girl's arms. "Do as instructed and you and your friends will go free. It's that simple."

This same woman frequently dragged Xiang from the cold cell and into this lab room, only to provoke the child with a never ending string of tests and questions. Her smooth, placid skin was as icy as her tone. The woman had made many promises, but after so many weeks, it became obvious she had no intention of releasing her.

A flash of light in the corner of her eye took her attention. Atop a metal table in the corner of the room rested an almost translucent amber chest, roughly the size of an infant's shoebox. It had never been there before and the magical essence of the glass-looking object held her attention. Ornate golden glyph etchings covered the outside. The container had no hinges or front lock. Were the glyphs instructions on how to open the box or a warning?

On the floor in front of the table sat a metal pail and a duffle bag large enough to hide a child. An Asian soldier in BDUs—gun on his belt, stood next to the table and noticed Xiang looking at the bag. He grinned.

Her gaze shifted to the full-length reflective mirror off to the side of the room. She knew someone watched beyond the glass. They always did.

Xiang knew of only one escape route. Her body relaxed on the hospital bed and her mind drifted, losing the soldiers, doctors, room, and oncoming pain. She imagined chasing a beautiful white butterfly in a huge green field with the warmth of the sun on her face—

The man snapped his fingers in her face. "Where did you go just now? Come back to me." Her head jerked as she left the daydream.

"All this time, the doc played nice and do you see where it got her? A bunch of head shrinking psychobabble, and guess what? You're right back where you started: with me. Well, I got news for you, kid. The whole mime routine may have worked with the lady doc, but by the time I'm done with you, you'll be singing like Mary Poppins."

Xiang had no idea who Mary Poppins was but doubted she would sing if she were here right now.

The doctor shifted her fist to her hip. "That would be a sight, since she doesn't speak English, moron."

A wide smile crossed his face. "English or no, she knows what the deal is. And if she doesn't, I'll enlighten her."

"We simply need her to open the box, nothing more. Do whatever you must to encourage her."

"And what if I determine she can't?"

"Then she's not who we think, and whatever happens to her after that will no longer be our concern."

The woman hurried to the door and shielded the keypad before entering a code. The door unlocked and she left.

"Whatever I need to do?" He leaned closer to the prone

4

child. "I'd say that gives a man a lot of latitude, wouldn't you?" He turned a sadistic grin toward the other soldier. "Get her up."

The second man unlocked the shackles anchoring her to the rails, then dragged her to a metal chair in the center of the room. The child lifted her bare feet onto the bottom rung of the chair to escape the cold floor.

The boss sauntered to the table and put down his coffee thermos before returning to her. He reached into his pocket and took out a small green box, pulling from it a stick of gum, and tossed the crumpled silver foil onto the floor.

"Can I offer you some gum?" The man held it under her nose. The sweet smell of peppermint made her mouth water and stomach groan. "No? Have it your way." He put the stick in his mouth. She stared him in the face but said nothing.

He stood directly in front of her, arms crossed. "After more than a month, there's been barely a word from you. Now, that's something." He pursed his lips and nodded as if impressed. "Right there...that's the reason I hate kids. When they should be quiet, they're the loudest thing around, but the instant they get into trouble, they got nothing to say. Is that funny, or is it just me?" The boss circled behind the chair. "Not you though. You're a cool one. You know I'm gonna' break you good and you're still not saying a word." His lips pursed, nodding in approval a second time.

He bent over, whispered into her ear, "You should know my first vacation in nine years was cut short for this, and I *really* need some time off. Turns out, they dragged me all the way out here to talk to a stinking kid. *Me.* As you might guess—I'm in a pretty foul mood right now. If you're as smart as you seem, little girl, you'd be wise to find your tongue before

5

I get too far into this whole thing."

"I don't think she heard you." The second soldier laughed.

"Apparently not." He smiled, stepping in front of the chair. "How many others are like you? These powers...how do you turn them on?" He let the question hang, expecting she would realize the seriousness of the situation and tell him what he wanted to know.

"Hey, kid, are you deaf?" Aggravated, he slapped her. She reeled from the jarring strike but did not scream. When she looked at him, an uneasy grin filled his face.

"Now that I have your attention, let's get down to it." He stepped away and leaned against the wall. "I'm told you have special abilities, but I'm not sold that you're anything more than one tough cookie. So, go ahead. Make a believer out of me." Spittle flew from his mouth. Then the man pointed at the thermos on the table.

"Let's start with something small. Knock that mug down." Her eyes flashed to the target before returning to him.

Overhead, a crackling noise from speakers interrupted. "Craven, just get her to open the chest and we can get out of here."

He spun to face the mirror. "Shut up, the commander shouted, irritated they'd referred to him by name. He paced the floor, circling Xiang. "Did Victor Kahng give you something that made these powers work? How do you turn them on?"

She remained quiet. His face flushed red. Veins rose from his neck.

"Well, did he?"

If she answered the question, her life would end. She

6

didn't know the reason behind her abilities, but dying in this chair couldn't be the plan.

The commander pointed at the pail by the table. "Grab the bucket. I'm tired of asking questions that aren't being answered."

The Asian soldier carried a bucket full of water across the room, setting it on the floor in front of the chair. He sank her shackled feet into the water.

Almost six and a half weeks of being drugged, probed, and questioned by the medical staff had felt like a hazy dream. Whatever the torture method, she could survive it by drifting away—

Craven slapped her face again, this time with such force, the chair tilted on two legs, nearly toppling. The sudden sharp pain made her yelp. Blood pooled in her eye.

The man reached into a pocket on the lower leg of his pants and pulled out a small hand-held device. When he clicked the trigger, a nerve-rattling sizzle filled the room as electricity arched between the two metal prongs at the tip of the weapon.

The child looked at her feet in the water and back to the device. Her breathing quickened. She reached her mind out to his.

Today doesn't have to end badly for you.

Craven stopped a few feet in front of her. "What? Did you say something?"

"I said, you don't have to die today," her young voice squeaked aloud.

"Whaddya' you know about that?" He turned to the other soldier. The subordinate chimed in, "Not only does she speak English, she's funny, too!"

7

The commanding soldier held a shooting line of blue electricity inches over the bucket. "This is the last time I'm going to tell you, kid. Knock that coffee jug off the table."

"Please, don't," she said, tears welling in her eyes. "I don't want to hurt you, it's not my nature."

He laughed. "Well, I am certainly thankful for that."

"But I will if I have to."

"Have it your way." The boss leaned to shock her with the device. This time, when he squeezed the trigger, a tremendous surge of energy rippled through the facility. The ground shook the building through its foundation. The walls and ceilings cracked and collapsed. Concrete slabs fell on top of the soldiers, crushing them. The building's lights went out and the door made a loud click as the lock released.

The handcuffs and shackles binding her fell away. Calmly, she rose from the seat and stepped over the chains with her wet feet and walked around debris to get the chest. Even in the total darkness, she had no problem seeing and moved quickly to escape.

In the corridor outside the room, a man blindly felt along the wall, working his way toward the room. Without a sound, she slipped around him. Reaching the lit exit sign at the end of the hall, she pushed the door's handle and crept to the other side. As she placed her foot on the second step up to the next floor, the click of another door closing sounded above her.

Descending echoes came toward her. Mouth dry, sweat covering her face, the girl tiptoed down the stairs to the landing. Wedging herself into a small nook beneath the stairs, the child crouched and waited for the person to pass.

The approaching footfalls slowed as they turned on the

half landing directly overhead. The heavy panting drew nearer and the sound of her muted breathing and racing heartbeat seemed to echo in the dead still.

The footsteps continued down and another door opened and shut. When the girl climbed out of the wedge, she saw him—crouching behind the door. He made a loud, shrill squeak and pounced. She kicked and fought, wildly clawing at his face and pounding her fists against him. In desperation, she fanned her hand around on the floor feeling for the box to smash against his head. Instead her hand found a pen, and she slammed it down into his eye as he was about to bite her neck.

He wailed in agony through the stairwell. She sprang from the floor, grabbed the box, and ran up the flight and down other stairs leading to outside. She exited the building into the chilly drizzle of the early evening sky. A thick mist hovered above the tree line, obscuring the surrounding mountain range. Men shouted in the distance, then the building's exterior lights flooded the area and a shrill siren blared. The rain intensified as she ran across the wet gravel parking lot in bare feet and into the forest.

Xiang had not gone far when blood-curdling howls pierced the night. They sounded like big dogs, but the unsettling yowls were none she had ever heard.

Chapter 2

Jonas lay on his stomach just inside the edge of the forest, watching the facility's rear entrance through night vision binoculars. For nearly ten years, he had scoured the news and town-talk for the telltale signs of a wraith presence cropping up. He'd then set out and tracked it down.

But after various local reports that people, right here in Oregon, suddenly began acting with erratic behavior: incessant scratching at sores no one else could see and extreme, dangerous paranoia, he returned and found wraiths operating in seclusion, deep within the heavy forests of the Cascades. They had established a base of operations to search for him, no doubt, less than a hundred miles south of his home. How had they discovered he was living in the Pacific Northwest?

Jonas had other plans. After wiring the building with explosives, he now looked on as he prepared to put a substantial crater in the center of their latest nest. His finger rested on the detonation switch.

A sudden tremor rumbled through the ground. It seemed to come from the building itself. He did not move, continuing to observe the panic stricken sentries milling around the facility, in obvious confusion.

When several others exited the building shouting, and the shriek of the alarm tore through the sky, Jonas knew he had been detected. Adrenaline raced through his aging body as he jumped up from the ground and sprinted through the woods. He climbed into his concealed truck and sped down the rural Oregon road.

Weeks of planning and surveillance and, just that fast, his entire plan came undone. He had been careful and too highly trained to be caught by the security and cameras surrounding the compound. He angrily slammed his fist against the wheel as his gaze fixed on his rear-view mirror for the pursuit that would certainly ensue.

A white flash on the road made him glance out the windshield. A child in a white hospital gown darted from the trees and into his path. "Whoa!"

Jonas mashed the brakes of his Ford F250 pickup. He slid on the wet blacktop, pulling the truck sideways in the road. He threw open the door and hurried onto the asphalt. Staring into the rain-filled darkness, he didn't see a body, but that didn't mean the truck hadn't clipped her, knocking her into a ditch.

"Hello? Are you okay?" He leaned roadside, peering between dark shadows. No response moved a queasy feeling through him. In the distance, he heard men shouting and strange barking, but he knew who and what they were.

From the sound, he gauged they would be here in minutes. He opened the rear door of the truck's super king cab and grabbed a pistol, tucked it into the small of his back under his jacket, and withdrew his compound bow and full quiver. He entered the tree line and set off down the hill, hoping to find a non-injured little girl.

His eyesight was as keen as ever in the eerie evening mist. Three uniformed men descended the hill to his left. He took cover behind a thick trunk. In one fluid motion, he notched and drew the arrow, waiting for an unobstructed shot. A smooth release, deadly accuracy. One man's chest caved. A second, pierced in the throat.

A third man in black gear, unaware that his team was no longer behind him, dashed to intercept movement at the base of the hill.

Jonas released the narrow spear. The man slipped to his knees as the missile slammed into a tree inches above his forehead.

"Someone's out here!" The distant shouts and cries silenced. In the darkness and wind, the soldier could only guess the direction of the arrow. When he backed against the wrong side of a boulder, his initial good fortune had turned. The arrow's impact sent the victim sprawling backwards, lifeless to the ground.

The resumed barking drew nearer. Jonas scanned the woods. In the rain-obscured sky, he saw her dodging trees toward the river. He slid down the slick, grassy embankment after her.

Traversing a shortcut of loose rocks, he was able to grab her arm. "Stop, kid, I can help you!"

The girl turned and kicked his knee. "Ow. Darn it! I said I can help you." Jonas rubbed his leg. The exhausted child panted, not taking her eyes off him. To her chest she clutched a box decorated with strange symbols.

He took her hand, "They'll be here in a minute. Come on," and led her away from the river.

On guard, she trailed him through the forest toward the road. The terrain was much steeper, forcing them to move slower as they worked through the densely wooded hill.

Halfway to the top of the ridge, Xiang's foot slipped on a mud swath and tore from the man's grip.

"No!" He whipped around to snag her, his extended hand missing her's as she part rolled, part slid down the muddy incline. Jonas watched helplessly as the child tumbled into the rain-swollen river and was swept downstream.

She clung to the chest as she fought to keep her head above the violent rolling waters that carried her toward a steep waterfall and certain death on the jagged boulders below. Her feet scraped over mossy bedrock and slammed her against debris. The water drove the dazed girl toward a large fallen tree with protruding branches forcing water to the underside. If she held on to the wrong limb, she'd be pulled under.

Jonas ran along the bank best he could without being swept in. He lost sight of the child, but picked up on her when she floated into a calmer side pool. Before he could reach her, overbearing currents ripped her body away. He was about to give up until he saw her draped among branches of a lodged tree.

Under normal conditions, he could have negotiated the wide tree trunk with little effort, but the mud on his boots, in addition to the rain-covered bark, made footing a far more difficult task.

"Hold on. Don't let go," he shouted. "I'm comin'—just hold on!"

The driving rain stung his eyes as he approached the child hanging on to the half sunken tree.

"Grab my hand, darlin', you can do it!"

As Xiang fought to remain afloat in the river's powerful current, she clung to the chest. She didn't know why but felt her young life revolved on its safety. Jonas leaned toward her but could not reach and knew any second she would be swept away. His footing slipped, almost sending him careening over the downriver side of the tree. He shimmied up a thicker branch.

"I can't come no closer, you gotta' help me." He stretched his long legs to the point of losing balance. "Let go of the box and grab my hand. Come on now...you don't got much time!"

She looked at him; panic filling her pale face, but squeezed the container under her arm—refusing to let go.

The water-logged branch groaned under Jonas's weight as he scooted the last two inches possible. His fingertips traced along her tiny hand. Xiang's grip slipped down the bending branch. In a burst, he snatched her wrist and pulled against the current. Supporting both their weights, the arm of the tree cracked.

Soaked with cold rain, numb hands, and a force pulling him to the water, Jonas's survival instincts screamed to stop this craziness and save himself. If he had listened to his gut feeling forty years ago, eleven men would still be alive.

Jonas wrapped a leg around the main trunk before the weaker limb broke away completely. "Careful now." He pulled the girl to him and navigated toward shore. Relief flooding his adrenaline-pumped muscles, he sat her next to him at the base of the wide trunk. She was shaken, bruised, and dazed, but still had the chest in her arm.

Under the passing clouds, the sudden rain relented, and he scanned the forest for movement. The faint light of the waxing crescent moon reflecting off the icy black water was the only light he had, but more than enough to see her face was bloody, particularly the right side. A deep gash crossed her right thigh above the knee, numerous lacerations covered both arms, and a swollen right eye so bruised, it could hardly open.

"You okay?" he asked, knowing full well she was not. "Can you walk?" His eyes traced the river's edge. The suffocating murkiness encroached upon them as if an intelligent corporeal entity from an alien world. It left him with the feeling that something inside the tree line watched them.

"Ow!" Xiang screamed when she put pressure on the ankle.

"Shhh now, okay, this ain't gonna' work." He repositioned his bow around his neck. "I'm going to carry you." He was a large, strapping man for his sixties and had little concern about the added weight. The challenge would be navigating the poor footing along the steep embankment.

"All righty, let's do this," he muttered under his breath, hoisting the girl in the crook of his left arm. "Put your arms around my neck." They climbed the hill a second time and reached the roadside.

It was quiet—too quiet. No shouting, no beastly barking or howls. His intuition told him they were walking into a trap but would be caught if they stayed put. The man stopped short of the pavement, knelt, and set the girl in the muddy brush beside him. He placed his finger in front of his mouth indicating she needed to be silent and pointed at his truck some ninety feet up the road.

"Stay quiet and keep your eyes open."

She nodded as he picked her up again.

He scoped the area as they emerged from the trees. Seeing nothing immediate, he made a full sprint toward the truck. They were fewer than twenty feet from the vehicle when a large beast on two legs stepped out from behind it. The wolf-like creature growled, revealing a mouth of Bowie knife fangs, and unleashed a spine-tingling roar.

The man set the girl on the ground. "Easy now, stay behind me." He removed the compound bow from his shoulder and reached for an arrow. When the creature saw

15

him readying the weapon, it rushed forward on all fours. The hunter stood tall and nocked an arrow. Jonas sucked in a deep breath, and slowly let it out, waiting . . .

Ten feet away, the lupine beast launched into the air. Xiang screamed. He released the arrow and nailed the beast in the ribs. With a high-pitched yelp, it fell to the ground in front of them. He fired another arrow, ensuring it would not get up.

The man scooped up the girl and ran the last length to the truck. He flung open the door and tossed her into the cab. On his climb in, a second creature bowled him over. His bow bounced on the road, skidding into the woods. The animal lunged for his throat as Jonas hammered his fists against its skull. He grabbed the animal's demon head. The mass of wet fur slipped in his hold and snapped powerful jaws onto his right hand.

Chapter 3

The rain-slick mountain road shimmered in the passing moonlight. Dense woods on both sides squeezed the lanes to a path barely wide enough for two small cars, much less a full-size diesel truck. Fortunately, perhaps not for Jonas, the road was seldom traveled.

Pain from the creature's bite pierced Jonas's hand, killing the nerves and feeling in his arm. It whipped its head back and forth, violently dragging him. He punched the beast in the rib cage, over and over. The animal yelped, releasing its vice bite long enough for Jonas to regain his feet. He backed until he felt the truck behind him, pulled himself inside, and shut the door.

"Get my keys. Front pocket!"

Frothy saliva fell from the monster's face as it

16

continued its ferocious barking outside the driver door.

"Hurry!" he shouted as the child pulled the keys free. He fumbled before getting them into the ignition and winced in pain as he turned the modified super diesel engine to life.

"Get your seatbelt on!" The truck pulled into a lane while the creature leapt into the truck bed and rammed its cranium into the sliding windows at the back of the cab. The opening was too small, but hell bent on eating them, the beast tore into the window until the rear glass gave way. The dog, halfway inside, lurched forward, seized Jonas's headrest and ripped it off. It turned, snapping at Xiang as it pulled its body through the rapidly deteriorating rear window frame.

The Ford fishtailed and Jonas nearly lost control over the steep embankment. He stomped the brake with one foot and then punched the accelerator with the other, sending the beast hurling back against the tailgate. The animal clawed its way to the cab. With his uninjured hand, Jonas reached under the seat and pulled out his double barrel sawed off shotgun. He flipped up the barrel to rest on his right shoulder, handle up, muzzle pointed at the gaping hole behind the second row of seats.

Jonas watched in the rearview mirror as the creature dove through the rear opening, its mouth stretched for attack. He pulled the trigger. The 3 ½ inch magnum slugs eviscerated the dog's face. It turned to a pile of dust, dispersing behind them as the man red lined the engine and escaped down the dark mountain road.

Several hours later, he pulled off the highway onto an isolated gravel road. The exhausted man climbed out of the cab and lumbered to the long iron gate blocking the path. Fifteen minutes later, they arrived at a large cabin.

With his last remaining strength, he carried the sleeping, shivering child still clutching the box, up the porch stairs, into his home. Inside, he wrapped her in a blanket. Child in his arms, he slumped into his recliner. Still filled with adrenaline, he reached for the Colt on the coffee table. With his piece in his good hand, and the girl leaning against his other shoulder, he settled deeper into the chair and rocked, humming, until she fell asleep. All the while, his weary, bloodshot eyes lingered on the front entrance. His finger tapped against the trigger, waiting for the second they blasted through his door.

Chapter 4

Cascade Mountains, Oregon, March 22

Her sneeze woke her from a deep sleep. She sat up with a start. Sunlight filtered into the room through the two large windows at the head of the bed. A fluffy blue and white goose down comforter covered her on the bed, the foot and head rails made of rod.

From where she sat, she looked around the room. On the nightstand sat a framed, very dated color photo of a black woman fishing alongside a young black child she presumed was the woman's son.

At the foot of the bed stood a large, light brown wooden dresser with a mirror, and a much smaller dresser next to the bed on her left.

The smell of food wafted into the room, causing her stomach to churn loudly. It made her ravenous and, almost on cue, she felt faint and began to shake. She had been so preoccupied with the smell she did not notice the hospital clothes she wore had been replaced with children's jeans and white cotton shirt. When she didn't see the chest in the room, panic immediately consumed her.

Her eyes raced to every corner, every shadow, but she didn't see it. Without a sound, she climbed out of the bed and opened drawer after drawer in the large dresser looking for it, but they were empty.

"How you feelin'?" A coarse male voice from another room startled her. A minute later a tall, black, older man walked in carrying a plate and small tea cup.

"I hope you don't mind but your clothes were so wet I had to change you out of em'. What you're wearing was the

19

best I could do on short notice, but if you prefer the smocks, they're clean and dry now. I placed them in the drawer over there. The chest you was carrying is in there too." He gestured with his head, toward the smaller dresser next to her bed.

She darted toward the dresser and opened the top drawer. When she saw it inside, she snatched the box from the hiding place and backed away from him.

He grimaced when he placed the large plate on the dresser next to her. "I'll bet you're pretty hungry so I got you an apple, rice, and some eggs. An', here's some tea. You're probably much too young to have a likin' for tea, but this is herbal tea and will help you relax."

She grabbed the apple from the plate and took several quick bites.

"Take your time, no one's gonna' take it from you. I promise. 'Sides... if you eat too fast, you'll get sick."

She regarded him with curiosity as she tore through the fruit before devouring the bowl of rice. The man wore a white tank top and a sterling silver necklace with a cross. An old, pencil-length scar looking like he'd been slashed by something sharp—a knife or a pick—was etched into the top of his chest. She was halfway finished with the scrambled eggs before she noticed the man's hand. Through the wrap she saw dried blood spots. He caught the remorseful look on her face.

"Oh, no, don't worry about me. I had bigger mosquito bites in 'Nam." He smiled. "I took antibiotics for the bite, I'll be fine. You slept so sound, I had to keep checking on you to see if you were still breathing. I gotta' admit, for a time I wondered if you was a goner." The man stood next to the bed watching as she finished the last of the breakfast.

20

"You seem to be feeling much better now. I'll bet you don't speak any English do you? I spent two tours overseas and I'd bet the ranch you're Chinese. I can't speak a lick of it and since my Vietnamese is pretty rusty, I guess we're in a pickle. Anyway, where are my manners? My name's Jonas Montgomery." He patted his chest with his good hand. "What's your name?"

The question was ridiculous if she didn't understand.

"It's okay. I'll just call you Katie if that's fine with you. I've always liked that name.

"Anyway, I'll let you get some rest. I should probably change my bandage again. I'll be right down the hall if you need me, okay?" He smiled and closed the door behind him.

She listened to his footsteps as they faded down the hall. When she believed he was gone, she slipped across the room and poked her head into the hallway.

The walls, floors, and stairs of the beautiful split level cabin were made of yellow cedar that reflected natural light throughout the two-story foyer below.

He had gone down the upper level hallway. She tiptoed down the stairs in bare feet and through the main level of the cabin. Lining both sides of the walls were black and white, as well as color photographs of various types of war planes. The hall opened into a two-story den with large glass windows. On the adjacent wall, there was a large cast iron wood-burning stove built into the fireplace. A decades-old reclining chair sat in front of the TV. Most of the rest of the room's furniture was simple and also unassuming.

Resting on a small stand to the right of the TV was a dated color-framed photo. In the picture's background, several men, she thought soldiers, wore tank tops and camouflage BDU pants rather than uniforms.

At the forefront of the picture were two men—a casually dressed black man wearing sixties style clothes and a fedora, his arm draped around the shoulder of the white man, both forever immortalized with laughter on their faces. She smiled, wondering what it was that made the two men laugh so hard.

She opened the front door and went onto the porch. The home sat high atop a range surrounded by magnificent mature trees jutting up from the expanse below, spanning the range for countless miles, as far as she could see. A gentle breeze lifted the unmistakable fragrance of honeysuckle from within the forest.

After a month and a half in a cold, dark cell, the sun seemed brighter than she had remembered.

She found a wooden oak chair on the front porch but when she leaned back in the chair, it rocked backwards, at first, startling her. When she got the hang of the motion, she relaxed into the chair, looking down over the beauty of the mountain range.

Jonas stepped onto the porch, walked toward the edge, and closing his eyes, inhaled a deep lungful of air.

"Magnificent, isn't it?" He lit a cigarette and leaned forward to rest his elbows on the rail.

"I've been all around a time or two in my life, and for me, this is still as good as it gets."

The girl continued rocking but cocked her head to the side. "Don't those things make you die?"

"Everyone dies, kid."

He spun around to face her. "What? Wait! You speak English after all!"

"Yes." She stretched her arms and yawned. "How long have I been here?"

He pushed back the brim of his cowboy hat as he stared at the child in puzzled amazement.

"Young lady, you are full of surprises, I'll tell you that for nothing. Shoot—what? Four days ago I found you in the forest in a bad way, blood in your eye, scratches all over your face and much of your body.

"Now, that ain't even to mention your leg. It was so busted up, anyone with any sense would have sworn up and down it was broke. I would have taken you to the hospital but they got spies everywhere, so I decided not to risk it and brought you here.

"Now look at you! Seems like you all healed up just that fast, sitting out here enjoying the mornin', just lookin' as pretty as the day you was made."

"I guess I was lucky." She smiled.

"Lucky?" He scratched down the side of his arm. "You had one full foot and three more toes in the grave, baby girl. Fact you're sitting here with me right now, well I'd say, that ain't nothing short of a miracle."

She stared at the chest in her lap. "Why were you out there that night?"

"I've been following a wraith cell for several weeks and tracked them back to their secret facility. Problem is, the building is heavily guarded and they're armed to the teeth. If I went in guns blazing, I would've been dead before I made it to the gate.

"So I'd been watching them come and go for the past few days, getting down their schedules and routines, and that night was my final walkthrough before I went in. When the

23

alarms sounded, I was certain they were on to me so I hightailed it out of there.

"Seems like all hell broke loose and you pop onto the road and over the side. That's what led me to the forest. It's still hard to believe you happened to come right to that very spot where I was on the road." Recalling the incident made him pause in a moment of reflection. "Boy, I'm glad I didn't run you over."

"Me too." She giggled for the first time in a very long time.

"I am Xiang, but you can call me Katie."

"Katie it is." He chuckled. "Man, I need a drink. You prefer pop or lemonade?"

"I'll have the thing you call a pop, Mr. Montgomery," she replied.

"Mr. Montgomery? He's here? Mr. Montgomery was my father. You can just call me Jonas."

"Ok, Mr. Jonas." She smiled.

He chuckled. "Thing you call a pop."

***

Fifteen minutes later, Jonas returned to the porch with a pop and a bottle of whiskey. To his surprise she was nowhere to be seen.

"Katie?" he called. Jonas listened for her response but it did not come. "Katie?" He would have shouted louder but had no idea who might be in the range far below. Though the secret facility was more than eighty miles away, he would remain cautious.

Thinking she might have gone up to her room or the bath, he popped his head inside.

"Where are you?" He pulled the door shut and returned to the front porch, scanning the forest surrounding his home but no sign of her.

Jonas tried to remain calm but worried she might have wandered off or worse. Where could she have disappeared to so fast?

He raised beefalo and sheep, most of which were completely tame. They could be dangerous but very seldom posed any problems to people. He was very concerned about the bear tracks he'd seen down range a week ago. None of his cattle had been killed but it was unlike bears to enter the expansive wooden fence built along the eastern edge of his ranch. It was beautiful country but had the potential to be a very dangerous place, especially for a child her age.

His imagination raced as he descended the path that ran along the side of the cabin, down a steep hill into the woods. At the entrance of the forest, he saw her right away and stopped.

His heart pounded and his mouth ran dry. Down the path, Xiang knelt, petting a small black bear cub. His first thought was to run to the cabin for his gun, but there was not enough time.

Instead, he hurried toward her and acutely zoned in on the trees around her, ready for the confrontation with the cub's mother.

"Xia—uh—Katie!" he stuttered. "Move away from him. Do it now." He did not want to startle her or the cub, but this was a life-threatening situation.

"Katie. Listen to me! Stand up and back away from that cub. Do what I say and do it right now." He urged her, nearing the edge of panic.

Even in the pleasant cool of the morning shade, he was sweating through his clothes. The thought of a pissed off momma bear protecting her cub scared him far more than the encounter with the strange wolf-like creatures.

"Shoo!" He waved his hands, motioning for the bear cub to run away. "Go on now, git." He ran in full stride and was about twenty-five feet away from the little girl when the second bear come into the clearing behind her.

The female black bear, at least 350 pounds, stood on her hind legs, growling in the distance. Jonas emptied the whiskey bottle onto the ground, and slammed it against the side of a tree. When the base of the bottle shattered, he changed his grip on the bottle's neck, letting the jagged edges protrude from his hand.

"Katie, listen carefully to every word I tell you. If you're listenin', say yes."

She nodded.

"Very good, now don't panic but the bear's mother is right behind you. I need you to turn around and face her. Listen now—whatever you do, it's very important you don't run. Just turn toward her, then slowly back your way to me, okay?"

Katie turned when the bear dropped to all fours and raced full speed toward her. She backed away not seeing the log on the ground and tripped over it, landing hard on her back.

Within seconds, the female bear had reached the fallen child, lying on the ground. The bear rose up over her, paws slashing the air, teeth bared.

"Look at me! Over here!" Jonas screamed and jumped up and down to draw its attention from her. The huge black bear dropped on top of her.

"Nooo!"

Running all out, he closed the final few yards, then slid to a stop. To his amazement, the mother bear was licking Katie's face. She reached out and gently touched the adult female's snout and then scratched the bear under her neck.

Jonas, now within striking distance of the enormous animal, approached her with extreme caution, unable to comprehend what he was seeing. The bear looked up at him and with a ferocious growl froze him in his tracks. He jutted out the bottle.

"No. No!" Katie shouted, admonishing the full-grown female bear as if a terrier pup. The mother growled to its cub, and both bears quickly walked toward the clearing before disappearing around the bend.

As they returned up the trail to his cabin, Katie said nothing, afraid that Jonas's silence was because he was angry with her.

"For more years than I'm willing to admit, I've found myself moving back and forth between faith and doubt. I really wondered if I'd lost my mind. Until this very moment, when I saw the truth—the holy man knew."

"What do you mean?" she asked.

"I'll tell you everything I know, soon enough, but now I've got to start getting you ready," he replied as they made their way up the trail. "And about that nickname I gave you earlier."

"Yes?" She looked up toward the towering man's squinted eyes.

27

"I got a better one." He smiled. "Katie bear."

"I like that too." And with a smile, she placed her tiny hand in his.

Chapter 5

Fierce lightning and peels of thunder vibrated the cabin's wooden planks. Every explosion from the sky felt like a direct hit on the house. Katie tried to sleep, but she kept imagining the terrifying storm ripping off the roof and hurling her from the peak to her death.

She clung to her pillow, clinching her eyes shut, trying not to see the flashes that kept her room ablaze. She dashed from the bed, grabbed the chest from the dresser, and knelt with it on the floor. She prayed as Jonas had done with her many times when she was afraid.

"Our Father in Heaven, Hallowed is your name. Your Kingdom comes and your will be done, on Earth, as it is in Heaven. Give us this day, our daily bread, and forgive our debts as we forgive our debtors. Lead us not into temptation, but deliver us from evil. Yours is the kingdom, and the power, and the glory. Amen."

Feeling braver, Katie returned to bed and put the chest next to her pillow. She closed her eyes and imagined the thunder as a beautiful blue ocean, waves crashing along the shore. She had never seen the ocean but always smiled whenever Jonas spoke of it. He promised to take her to see it one day.

She began to calm when, downstairs, she heard something that sounded like furniture sliding along the wooden floor, and then footfalls across the cabin.

Katie slipped from her bed, peered out, and saw the front door wide open. Lightning flashed and the rumbling thunder continued. She crept down the stairs and peeked down the lower level hall. Out the front entrance she saw the wind slamming the open barn door against the sides.

"Jonas! Jonas! Help!" Katie dashed through the cabin. The TV was on, full whiskey glass, but he was nowhere. She returned to the porch and stared out. It was up to her.

On the bench behind the door, she pulled on her boots and jacket and tore off into the gale winds. The rain pelted her face. In flashes of lightning, her eyes searched the dark building. Katie didn't see Jonas and grabbed the door to pull it shut. The gusts were too strong. She scampered across the hay-covered floor to the livestock.

"It's me. I'm here now."

Storms, particularly loud ones, always made them skittish, but she had never seen them this worked up. She slipped through the flock of sheep and stooped to pet them, speaking in a soft voice to calm them.

"Shhhh. Don't be scared, it's just a storm." She kept assuring but the clamor and braying of the beefalo made the herd nervous. With sudden panic, they bolted within the confined space, trampling her.

Through the throng of desperate animals, she saw three huge black wolves at the stable entrance. They cut through the huddled mass of fleece, mauling everything in their path. Hair-raising screams, sounding like distressed infants, filled the barn, drowning the thunder outside.

An aura of fear filled the air, and the livestock retreated as far back as they could. In a crazed frenzy, several bulls rammed against the pens until the wood splintered and gave way. The cattle closest to the broken end of the pen fled. The wolves continued to murder the unfortunate that could not make it to the opening.

Katie stumbled backward against a storage bin. She lifted the lid and climbed inside. Pulling it closed, she remained still.

Outside the crate, she heard the creatures lapping, shredding, and the sickening sound of crunching of bones. Perspiration beaded on her face as the suffocating stagnant air inside made her feel trapped in a tiny coffin with walls closing in.

Then, as sudden as the screaming began, the barn fell into silence.

With caution, she lifted the top of the crate to see the wolves feeding on the nearly two dozen sheep and beefalo unable to escape. When she saw the entrails and bloody wool that filled the barn, she nearly vomited. She let out a gasp and hurried to close the lid.

Did they see me?

Heavy breathing panted directly overhead. In an instant, the lid flew away. A wolf seized her wrist and ripped her from the container. Behind its glowing red eyes, she felt a primal rage—intelligence unlike any ordinary animal.

Another grabbed her free arm. She was snatched from her feet as the powerful beasts yanked her side to side. Shoulders separating, she screamed.

"Katie! Katie! It's okay. It's okay." She heard Jonas's voice. Her eyes opened and he sat next to her in the bed. "I'm here. It was just another nightmare."

Confused, she looked around the room, unsure of her surroundings. For reasons she could not immediately recognize, the room *felt* different to her, and a strong odor of sulfur filled the room. It made her uneasy and she needed the chest near her. Her eyes went to the nightstand but it wasn't there.

"Everything is fine. You're fine," he assured her.

"It's not fine, it's gone!" the girl shouted. When an urgent pounding sounded at the front door, she jumped.

Jonas frowned. "Who can that be this time of night? Stay here, I'll be right back." The drunken man got up from the floor and staggered toward the stairs.

When he left, Katie tossed the room for the chest but could not find it.

"You ain't got no business here!" Jonas yelled from below. After hearing how upset he sounded, she hurried from the room to see about the commotion. When she saw him peering out the window, she leaned over the banister to see out the pane.

A reflection of Jonas's face showed on the window, but it wasn't right. Imposed onto his image, another man's face melted, like they were one person. Jonas stepped away, removing his visage, but the other man came into full view, then vanished.

Katie covered her mouth to dampen a scream and dropped to the stair tread. Whoever he was, Jonas wanted him gone, and so did she. Jonas reached for the knob and she yelled to him, "Don't! Everything's wrong! Don't let him in." He ignored her, opening the door a crack. He glanced up at her, then back outside. "You heard me. Get off my property! You got no business here." Jonas wagged his finger in anger and slammed it shut. Then, he turned with a vexed look clouding his face.

"Jonas, who's out there?"

He was about to answer when a black wolf crashed through the door, landing on top of him. She screamed, falling backwards up the stairs.

"Katie! Wake up! It's me. I'm here."

When she opened her eyes, she lay on the floor, tangled in bed sheets. He pulled them away from her and put his arms around her as she sobbed into his shoulder.

"It's okay, Katie bear, I promise, everything's going to be all right."

Chapter 6

"One of the first things I'm gonna' have to learn you is how to defend yourself." Jonas adjusted the gun holster on his belt.

"You mean how to fight?" the seven-year-old asked.

"Yeah, well, something like that." He had lined up three large mason jars on log stumps roughly ten yards away. When the ranch hands, Oscar and Hector, saw him setting up the makeshift targets, they became curious. The two men stopped mending the fence and climbed onto the top rail to watch. Jonas, unaware of his spectators, drew his old Colt and took aim at the jar on the far left.

"Go on and cover your ears now, it's gonna' be real loud."

She nodded and obediently stuck her fingers in her ears as hard as she could.

"Have you done this before?" Katie asked with a loud voice. He passed her an irritated glare.

"Lil' girl, you should know back in the day, I was a

32

marksman and one of the best shots in my unit. It's not exactly the kind of thing you unlearn because you ain't done it in a little while. Just remember, when firing a weapon, you gotta' set your feet toward your target, and don't forget to breathe when you squeeze the trigger."

She involuntarily flinched from the series of loud bangs as he fired three quick shots—one at each of the three jars.

None twitched.

Oscar elbowed Hector and both men snickered to themselves. When Jonas heard them chortling, he looked their way.

"Ain't you fellas got' some work to do?"

"Don't mind us, Jonas. We're all finished." Oscar smiled.

"Fantastic," he mumbled. Jonas walked to the stumps, repositioned the jars ever so slightly, as if that had been the reason for the misses, and then returned to where he stood. He took aim, focusing on the one in the middle. He lined up his sights and squeezed the trigger three more times.

A shot ricocheted harmlessly off the side of the fat, woody stump. But no containers moved.

"Are you supposed to hit the jars or the tree?" Katie shouted with her fingertips planted into her ears.

"Sights must be off." Jonas stared at the gun in disbelief.

"It's okay. Maybe you'll do better if you move closer." Katie smiled innocently.

Hector elbowed Oscar and both men fell off the fence, laughing.

Chapter 7

Late April rolled around before the bitter cold began releasing hold of the Pacific Northwest and, albeit slowly, giving way to spring.

Jonas didn't seem to mind the ever present Oregon rain which, even after five years of living there, still made Katie's teeth chatter and chilled her to the bone. And undeterred by weather—rain, wind, or snow—they woke every day at the precise time of 5:00 a.m. without fail. If he was affected by the cold, or the pre-dawn rigors of their work, he never let it show. What your body feels is nothing more than a state of mind, he always said.

All the days were long. He was unrelenting and unapologetic. They would spend the early pre-dawn hours tending to cattle, mending fences, and bailing hay. She loved working with the animals and didn't mind the ranch work, hard as it was. Afterwards, at 8:00, Jonas sent her into the house to practice her English and other online studies while he continued working in the fields. Ninety minutes later, he would join her inside where they began the day's instruction on his military specialties: communications and surveillance.

Immediately thereafter, they were outside for the balance of the day for survival training in the wild, finding water, and scrounging for food. Then they spent another four hours in physical, hand-to-hand fighting and Aikido, advanced combat training—which included setting pyrotechnic ambushes, tactics with a variety of weapons, and how to make weapons when there were none.

Katie was exuberant when he announced that next month they were ready to move on to something new. She did not know what endurance training meant, but she was sure it had to be easier than this.

***

May 5, Katie's twelfth birthday. Half asleep, she eyed the digital clock on her nightstand. 4:57 a.m. She reached over and turned off the alarm before it uttered the rude offensive buzz that shocked her senses. She lay there, trying to mentally prepare herself for the doldrums of another long, hard day of training.

Rain pinged on the cabin's roof as she peered out her bedroom window into the early morning darkness. It seemed a bleak day for a birthday—if it was her birthday. As far as she recalled through slivered fractures of her memories, there had never been balloons, or a cake, no children singing songs, or games played in her honor. Since no one could tell her what day she was born, she did what any child would do: picked one for herself.

She was sore, fatigued, and irritable. And the dreary rain added to the malaise of her self-pity-soaked, sullen mood. She pulled the covers over her head, wishing more than anything to be left alone.

"If he has any compassion at all, he'll let me sleep, for once."

Minutes passed as she nodded in and out before again glancing at the clock that read 5:30 a.m.

A miracle! He's never ever late. I guess he read my mind. She settled deeper into the bed. Before long, she closed her eyes and dozed.

"It's gettin' late and we got much work to do." His voice bellowed from the other room.

Katie woke with a start. "Oh, come on!" she groaned

35

from the toasty depths of the blue and white goose down comforter. "Let me sleep in, just this once?"

"I did. I gave you an extra half hour and now we're behind. See you outside, front and center in ten minutes."

"Whatever," she grumbled.

Day five of another challenging, stamina-building regimen began with an early morning four-mile run uphill through the dense forest surrounding his home; sword and Bo staff training to the point of exhaustion; and a fifteen minute break with a meager snack masquerading as lunch. Before she recovered from the harsh morning routine, they were outside and at it again.

When he was feeling gracious, they would break early at 4:00 p.m. No matter when training finished, she would will herself into the cabin where she'd fall onto either the sofa or her bed. Her reward at the conclusion of the exhausting activity filled day: her choice of one of the myriad of the frozen dinners that filled every inch of his freezer. So repetitive were the minutiae of their routines that, were it not for the red Xs on the non-descript calendar hanging from the fridge, one day would have been indistinguishable from the next.

***

The heavy rain that pelted the western range during the predawn morning tapered off. She dashed the final leg of the uphill hike, reaching the clearing at the top of the peak before Jonas. A smile broke on her face when she reached the summit. And through a small crease in the cloudy gray skies, only for a few moments, she saw the sun's amber rays flirt with the heavens. It was the first time she had beaten him to the top. She was stronger and faster with every passing month.

"See you later, crocagator!" She waved, passing him on her way to the bottom.

A few minutes later, he emerged from the path.

"It's getting easier!" Katie beamed as he came into her view.

Jonas turned a poker face to her. "Good! I don't have to carry you anymore. No more vacation." He went inside and returned carrying a tattered green canvas backpack. He put the pack over her shoulders and tightly adjusted the straps.

"No problem," she smiled with a confident defiance. When he let go of the bag, the unexpected weight made her fall backwards.

"Now—let's do it again," he said.

She turned to face him, waiting for him to bail her out and say he was only kidding.

He trotted toward the woods a second time. "See you at the top. And by the way, it's see you later, *alligator*," he yelled, disappearing into the trail.

"What vacation, Jonas?" she called out in irritation. "When have we ever gone on vacation?"

When they returned to the cabin after the second run,

37

Katie was physically spent. Out of breath, she panted, resting her hands on her knees.

He nodded in approval. "You were less than awful today."

It was a rare near compliment that caught her by surprise and with the prideful smile of accomplishment still on her face, he swept her leg from behind. Katie landed on the ground still hard from the brutal deep winter frost.

"What did you do that for? That hurt!" Angry tears filled her large hazel eyes. He reached down, extending his hand to her up.

She waved him off. "No, thank you. Are you such a sore loser you can't let me win even once?"

"Pride always goes before the fall. When you are most satisfied with what you've accomplished, you're most prone to an attack from the enemy. You always gotta' be ready. One can come for you anytime, anywhere, and usually happens when least expected."

"That wasn't fair and not very nice either! All we do is train every day and I don't even know what for. I'm sick of it. I hate it here."

He found himself shocked that the mild mannered child reacted in such a strong way and recognized he'd taken things too far and extended his hand a second time to help her from the ground.

As she stood to her feet, she rubbed her backside, which stung nearly as much as her pride. "Sometimes I don't like you very much, Mr. Montgomery." Katie called him by his last name when she was angry.

"Everything I've taught you from the first day may be important soon. Don't you understand, I'm just doin' my best to protect you?"

"I never asked you to protect me—I didn't ask for any of this. All I want are friends. To be a normal girl...I want my family."

Jonas understood the lonely frustration she must feel, but her words still penetrated his tough veneer like a double-edged blade.

He didn't have the courage to tell her, the creatures hunting her were resourceful and tireless. From his numerous encounters with them, he knew Katie's life would never be normal.

"You'll get used to being here, just give it some more time."

"I don't want to get used to it. This isn't much better than the place I escaped. After five years, my life's still a prison, it's just a new one. The only good part of being stuck here with you is the animals. I hate everything else about it."

Jonas turned toward the house, no words on his tongue. Filled with dejection and shame, he looked at the ground to avoid her gaze. "Dinner in forty minutes, you should go on and clean up."

Forty-five minutes later, Katie emerged from the bathroom, still not over her annoyance with his sneaky leg sweep. She crossed the landing, brushing her wet, long black hair, then made her way down the stairs. Her curiosity grew as she followed the delicious, somewhat familiar aroma wafting throughout the house. The smell triggered spotty flashes of memories, filling her with nostalgia of a life she couldn't remember.

When she joined Jonas in the kitchen, he stood over a large black skillet of fried rice and a second skillet of sizzling barbecued steaks on the stove. The combined aromas were a symphony of music to her nose. Katie had never seen him cook anything that didn't require a microwave or toaster.

As a rancher of both sheep and beefalo, she didn't know why daily meals were limited to either grits or oatmeal for breakfast, sandwiches of either canned wieners or Spam for lunch—both of which Katie loathed, and extra low budget, frozen meals for dinner. She could have asked, but chose not to, chalking it up as one of the oddities about the man she would never quite understand.

On the counter to the right of the stove was a large, comically uneven, very over-done, yellow cake with one large lit candle in the middle. At the center of his kitchen table, four fresh cut long stemmed wild flowers protruded from a large glass mason jar.

"This is a surprise!" She gasped. "What's the occasion?"

With an awkward smile on his face, he handed her a brown leather book. "Happy birthday, Katie bear. I know it ain't much, but I hope you like it."

She ran her hands over the soft leather, then opened the cover and flipped through the blank pages.

"It's a journal, but most girls call them diaries. Not sure I can much tell the difference, but you can write down your thoughts each day. You know—private stuff and the like. There's one more thing." He held out a tiny cardboard box.

She took it and removed the lid. Inside lay a gold ring with a small blue sapphire stone.

"I gave that to a very special woman a long time ago. It's all I have of her but it seems only right that you have it. I gave it my best getting it refit to your size, hopefully it's close."

Katie slipped the oversized ring onto her finger, smiling

wider than seemed possible.

"This is all for me—for my birthday?" she asked in astonishment, a tear creeping into her eye.

"Mmmhmm." He nodded. "Sorry about the cake. Didn't turn out the way I planned."

Instantly, guilt washed over her in waves. A deep blush burned through her so intense, she felt heat on her face that made her little ears turn red. Only an hour ago, the most awful words she had spoken to anyone fell from her lips. And afterwards, all the time she sulked and stewed in the bath, he had been downstairs happily working to put everything together for her.

"It's perfect!" She threw her arms around his neck, kissing him on his stubbly cheek.

Jonas blushed. "Now, don't go gettin' all sappy on me. It weren't nothing.'"

So, maybe today was not exactly the same as the others, she thought with an inward smile.

Chapter 8

Los Angeles, May 28

For over an hour, Dorian waited behind the dark tinted windshield for a group of females to make their way through the line of the most exclusive night club in L.A.

When he saw the doorman wave the group inside, he pulled the car around and found a dark parking lot on the next block. After returning to the front of the building, he strode past the people in line and approached the entrance. The 6'6, 285-pound bouncer glanced up from the IDs in his hand with an angry scowl.

"Your invisibility must be off, prick, because I can see you. Don't know where you think you're going but the line starts back there." The bouncer pointed down the block.

With a smirk, Dorian pushed the man's mind. "Let me in." To the displeasure of the patrons, the doorman stepped aside and unlatched the rope.

The rhythmic pulse of high-energy music reverberated through the bowels of the underground. Virtually blind, Dorian's echolocation guided him across the gothic catwalk and through the throng of people dancing to a hypnotic cocktail of intoxicatingly sensuous sounds and oscillating strobes that pulsed throughout the club. Many danced on the floor below while others, perched atop the catwalk arches, overlooked them like gargoyles ready to pounce.

Even among the energized crowd, Dorian's acute animal sense made ease of finding his quarry, needing only to focus on the distinct electromagnetic current of her beating heart. He squeezed past a pair of blondes and found an empty booth near the bar. He raised his hand, flagging a hostess, and ordered three shots of expensive Cognac.

The hostess returned with his drinks and set the glasses on the table just as the two blondes slipped into his booth on both sides of him.

"You want to party?" one of them asked as he gazed past her to the floor and the same group of women he had been watching outside.

"Get lost." He took another shot, paying the woman no mind. When the women would not leave, he stared one in the eyes. She was overcome with fear and both women hurried from the table never knowing how lucky they were to get away.

Dorian lit a cigarette, exhaling an unbroken, thick plume of bluish white smoke that curled back to his nostrils. His eyes moved across the crowd, and a crooked smile made its way to his face. The savory essence of so many people in this confined space made his stomach churn with hunger, but he pushed thoughts of feeding aside. As he watched, he marveled at what meaningless creations humans were. Even the best among them were simple-minded sheep, brooding over any number of trivial pursuits in their rudderless existences.

His eyes returned to Angela, the one who had cleverly eluded him for months.

Did you really think you could escape me? He laughed to himself. Have your fun now, because tonight, you're going to die.

He motioned to the hostess again, and placed an order for their table.

"These are courtesy of the gentleman in the black jacket, past the bar." The cocktail waitress placed napkins and a drink in front of them.

"Now that is one beautiful man," one of Angela's friends

43

said.

"Whoowoo! You know it's gonna be a good night!" The most intoxicated woman of the group took off her heels and climbed onto her chair and began to dance.

"Girl, you are out of control!" All five laughed.

One of the ladies motioned to the man to join them. "Tell him to bring his fine self over here! Come here, yeah, you!" she yelled near the top of her voice. Before any of them could restrain the wild woman, she jumped from her chair, and sprinted barefoot across the crowded floor to his table.

"Come over and sit with us."

Dorian smiled, holding up his hand as if timid. "Thank you, but really I couldn't impose."

"Sure you can. I insist you join us!" Angela's friend grabbed him by the arm, trying to drag him to their table, but he would not move.

"You're not my type." He looked past her toward Angela.

"Really, loverboy?" A stunned look found her face. "Your loss!"

The annoyed woman left and rejoined her friends. "He's shy, I hate shy guys!"

And then to the astonishment of her friends the quiet, low key Angela who hated dancing, walked onto the floor. Sipping her mojito, she continued gazing across the room at the man and then the otherwise demure woman did the previously unthinkable and motioned for him to come to her.

As her friends watched with open-mouthed incredulity, the man smiled back, sliding out of his booth, and with certain coolness, crossed the floor to their homely friend. He wrapped his arm around the backside of her waist. The two began a slow, sensuous dance without regard for the high-energy music that filled the room. Angela stared into his eyes and touched her finger to his mouth.

He leaned close to her ear, brushing aside Angela's auburn hair.

"Where you been beautiful? I've been looking for you for quite a long time."

"You think I'm hot?" Angela smiled.

The man looked deeper into her eyes. "You betcha'—tastiest woman in the place tonight, by far. Let's get out of here."

Her face lit with anticipation. "Sure. Where should we go?"

"I'm not from around here. Take me back to your place," he said, exerting a powerful mental influence over her. With a soft giggle and submissive nod, she waved goodbye to the others and he led her toward the exit before they could interfere.

When they were out of eyesight from anyone near the club, he tightened his hold. Every now and then, Dorian glanced back to Angela, but never spoke. She followed him, seemingly compelled to go wherever he was headed.

Several blocks from the nightclub, they turned down the dark alley to his car. When safely in the concealment of the darker shadows, he stopped and turned so abruptly, it startled her.

Holding her by the wrist, the man drew her closer. The corner of his mouth pressed gently to the left side of her neck. The smell of her essence kindled an ancient hunger deep inside—an intense affliction that stirred within, day and night. Once he recovered the Artifact and the child, he would appease

45

his primal desire to suck her essence clean until nothing remained but a soulless husk.

She shivered as he pressed close to her. His body brimmed with a scintillating eagerness.

No more running, Angela. No more hiding—it will all be over soon enough.

***

They pulled into the parking garage of her condo. He followed her as they exited the elevator on the twenty-seventh floor.

A seducing grin on her face, she motioned for him. "Come on inside."

He glanced around the apartment. "Do you live alone?"

"Sure do. Why do you ask?" She smiled.

"I just want to be considerate and not wake anyone when you scream." He grinned with anticipation.

"I like the sound of that," she replied.

He walked behind her and she turned to him, running her hand along the side of his strikingly handsome face.

"Can I get you anything to drink?"

"There is no need," he replied, growing more ravenous by the minute.

"Well then, make yourself at home for a few minutes while I slip into something a little more comfortable." She put her purse on the dinette and disappeared into her bedroom.

As soon as she was out of sight, he searched through her cabinets and drawers for the Artifact but found nothing. He slumped on the couch as his hunger overtook him and his energy waned.

"Angela, come to me," he summoned. "I command you to come to me."

Seconds passed and he grew impatient. Pain from his extreme hunger tore through his limbs, demanding he feast without further delay. He was about to go to the bedroom when the corner of his eye caught light from a glint of steel. The tip of a sword gashed the side of his throat, and saved by supernatural reaction, he narrowly avoided being decapitated. When the second strike fell, he dove across the coffee table, rolling to his feet.

"I know who you are, Dorian—do you think I'm stupid? I lured you here!" Angela screamed. "You look stunned. What? Did you think you'd come in here and charm me? You have no power over me."

He touched the deep lateral slash on his neck and looked at his fingertips. The sight of his own black blood enraged him. Fangs protruded from his mouth. He withdrew a retractable sword and a blade snapped from its handle.

"Knowing who I am won't stop me from devouring you, Angela. Give me what I want and I promise you a quick death."

"You can't turn me and what you're looking for is not here. You've wasted your time hunting me. I have no idea where it is!" She was careful to keep her sword between them.

He glanced at her weapon, laughing with both amused surprise and annoyance that Lighthouse thought an inexperienced person had any chance against him.

"I smell the lie on your lips, but when I consume you and steal your memories, I'll know everything I need to."

"Good luck with that."

Angela attacked in a swift flurry of strikes. With uncanny agility, he parried. The sound of violently clashing steel filled the apartment. His blade gashed her hand, disarming her. She fell away, avoiding another hit. As she back

47

peddled, she crashed into the lamp on the table, the room becoming pitch-black. She scurried along the floor to the table, feeling in the dark for her purse. She reached inside and grabbed her gun, firing wildly in the direction he had been. A third shot to her left, a fourth to the right, then the fifth. When she fired the last one, he howled in pain, and the room fell silent.

Angela tossed the empty weapon and scurried into the kitchen for a knife. With no sound, he was upon her. Dorian plunged his fangs into her throat and she struggled, trying to break free but his extraordinary strength easily held the young woman on the floor as he drank, passing her memories into him.

Her life flashes past him. The image of a woman referring to herself as Jane, befriending Angela in the park.

Jane escorting a blindfolded Angela to a chair surrounded by sixteen men and women. Dorian did not recognize all the individuals, but three he had already killed.

At the head of the table is a man. Their purpose is to protect the Artifact, as they had done for centuries. Dorian sees the multi-colored chest covered in symbols. The only artifact remaining that could destroy their god.

These people instruct Angela, give her insight, teach her to be undetected, to identify the wraith living among them, to combat them.

A ring is placed on her finger. The same worn by Jane and all others in the room. A raised lighthouse with rays projecting every direction.

A flash to one of Angela's final recollections. *The man Cameron. His demeanor of worry and concern clouds his face. He lays a small photo of a young Chinese girl on the*

table in front of her. Written under the image: Xiang Shi.
  Having obtained all of the information he needed, Dorian took the ring from the dead woman's hand and left the apartment.

Chapter 9

Standing high atop the raised deck on the backside of his cabin, Jonas was still. As the sun set on the mid-July evening, he lingered and watched it inch down from its reign over the western range of the Oregon Cascades. Even in a momentary rapture of the sun's final beautiful moments, he could not ignore the ill-omened, deep crimson-tinged clouds looming in the distance. The ever expanding hostility from an adjacent world, descended from the horizon like a mantle cloaked in darkness.

Pluming through unseen vents in the atmosphere, the corporeal black smoke that suffocated the sun, and shortened the light of day in other parts of the world, now made its presence known here. Seeming to possess an almost other worldly intelligence—the towering cloud moved wherever it willed—swallowing the skies. Only something this evil could overshadow the "plague" spreading across the globe.

Katie joined him on the second-story deck and stood to his left, leaning her elbows on the wooden rail. Jonas glanced to the child, filled with disquieting thoughts about the uncertainty her generation would face.

"What is that?" she asked.

"The tempest is coming," his voice portended doom.

"What do you mean?" An expression of perplexity fell across her face.

Jonas took a deep breath, and released with it a troubled sigh. "I've never told you about the wraiths because you weren't ready, but it looks like it's time."

"What is a wraith?"

"As far as I know, there are three different kinds. I've

50

heard teens call them Dead Enders and Creepers. The ones called Dead Enders were regular folks bitten repeatedly by the Creepers, then the darkness takes hold of them. Kids took to calling them that because of how they just seem to wander. With no cure to the virus, their life is at a dead end.

"Most of those are more danger to themselves than anyone else, walking in front of cars and off the side of bridges. However, the worst of them—the most depraved, well, their hearts become so dark, they turn to feeding on humans.

"Those—Creepers, are the dangerous ones because they bite their victims and drain the life out of them, then leave behind a body with a heartbeat and not much else. Other than that, they got no special abilities far as I can tell."

"I don't understand. Why would they do that?"

"I suppose, in some misguided way, the creepers—once human, are trying to replace the life they lost. Maybe, feeding temporarily comforts their pain. Truth is, no one knows for sure. I guess evil don't really need a reason."

Katie swallowed her fear. "You said three kinds."

"Thoughts of the third kind of wraith keep me awake at night. I call those Agents, and they're something different altogether. They're not from our world and are the ones that started the plague. Those are real nasty sons of guns. They're cunning, highly evolved creatures that utilize weapons, advanced fighting, and many even possess special powers. I've seen this kind take on the form of people as well as animals."

"Is that what attacked us on the road that night?"

"Heck no." He blushed. "Pardon my language. Those things on the road were Gwyllgi. They're similar to the legends about werewolves with the difference they don't need the moon, on account they change forms at will.

51

"They're pretty weak compared to the wraiths. Wraiths treat them as slaves or keep them as pets. Now that I think about it, I'm probably one of the very few that's managed to survive multiple encounters with both Agents and the Gwyllgi. Trust me though, both are wicked strong and faster than you know."

Katie might have been convinced he was putting her on if she had not seen them for herself that night.

"Where do they come from and how many are there?" she asked.

"I don't know. Right now, I still got more questions than I got answers. I came across my first Agent nearly ten years ago, and I've been hunting them ever since.

"Once humans are infected, it takes some folks longer to change than others--one bite, could be two, at times even three...I reckon that depends on the constitution of the person and the power of the wraith that bit em'. Really, there don't seem to be any rhyme or reason. No matter what, it ain't never more than three bites before the person gives way to the darkness inside."

"How do you find them?"

He reached into his pocket and pulled out a small crystal vial and held it eye level.

"What is that?" Her curiosity compelled her to step closer and examine it.

"It's water. A holy man gave it to me a long, long time ago."

"Water? What good is that?"

"When those monsters are close, I see sparkles of light inside. Sometimes it's one, sometimes it's a few. They're so good at hiding their form, many times the water is the only

52

way I can tell when I find them. Sometimes though . . ." he trailed off.

Her dollish eyes instantly grew wide with suspense. "Sometimes what?" she asked.

"Sometimes, they find me."

Nearly five years since her last nightmare of being killed by the wolf like Gwyllgi, and even longer since she had pushed thoughts of the hellish roadside attack from her mind, Katie wished desperately that she could rewind the conversation twenty minutes, and keep the door tightly shut on this very unpleasant topic.

Though smart enough to know better, it seemed the very discussion of the soul-devouring creatures might once again invoke and lead them here.

"There's one more thing, Katie."

"What?" A tight knot of anxiety welled in her chest.

"They usually come at night," he said.

"Usually?"

"As the skies continue to darken and the line between day and night blurs, their insatiable appetites have led them to roam free."

"What do you do when you run up against one?" she asked.

"Whatever I have to."

Deep concern etched her typically placid face. "How will we live?"

He turned his gaze toward her. "We remain ever vigilant and always prepared to run."

"I know but what if we run and they keep coming?"

"Then you fight until you can't," he said plainly. "They can come as anyone and at any time. No matter what, never

ever let your guard down, and be wary of everyone."

Katie took a deep breath. "Even you?"

After a long pause, Jonas answered, "Let's hope for both our sakes it never comes to that."

***

Returning home, Katie smiled as they neared the dusty turn-off to the cabin. The weekend had been peaceful and turned out much better than she had anticipated.

Convincing Jonas to take a day off to relax had not been the easiest of things but she finally coaxed him into it. Fishing hadn't exactly been the getaway she'd hoped for, but she had been so restless at the ranch and desperate for a day off and change of scenery. After much failed pleading, when she justified that technically fishing was an essential part of survival training, he gave in.
They packed a tent, fishing poles and sleeping bags, several changes of clothes, food and water. They each carried pistols— just in case. And even though Jonas teased it would be cumbersome and unnecessary to carry through the woods, Katie took the Artifact. Even in her dreams, she never left home without it.

Nearly a mile from the long, private gravel road that led up to the cabin, sheep and beefalo strolled along the side of the road. Jonas was no longer a happy camper.

They continued up the rural road approaching the driveway to see the gate open and steer everywhere.

Katie glanced at him. "What do you think?"

He killed the vehicle's headlights as they came to a stop. "I don't know."

"Hang tight." He took his pistol from under the seat and got out.

Katie ignored him and followed onto the grounds. The few cattle remaining were in a crazed, highly agitated state, galloping around in the darkness. Hector and Oscar were nowhere to be seen. Both were thorough, conscientious men and neither of them would have been careless enough to leave the gate open.

Katie walked closer, sawed off shotgun in hand. Foreboding flooded her. She couldn't shake the feeling something horrible happened. She touched Jonas on the arm.

"We should get out of here," she said quietly.

"Not yet, we've got to get our stuff from the house."

She grabbed him by the sleeve. "Forget it. We can't go back in there."

"Katie, all of our equipment including the laptop, our IDs, our cash—everything's inside. We won't make it very far without it."

"The most important thing is the Artifact and it's here. What good is any of that other stuff if we're dead?"

Jonas looked toward the barn, and then his eyes shifted up the hill toward the dark cabin.

"All right, let's go," he said.

They returned to the truck and backed out of the driveway, before speeding down the road.

**

As the black Ford headed south on Interstate 5, Katie turned to face Jonas. Below the brim of his cowboy hat, his face was distant and solemn.

"Where will we go?"

"I guess we'll head south to New Mexico or Texas perhaps."

"Then what will we do? Who do you know there?" Her

frustration was apparent in her tone.

"Wish I knew, little lady, but I don't."

Chapter 10

In the years that followed, they rested their heads in sixteen—maybe eighteen, towns between Oregon and Montrose, Colorado. They moved like gypsies, seldom remaining longer than a few months.

The road was lonely and their existence harsh; the luxury of comfort, trust and peace, they could not afford. And ever since ditching the truck and running out of cash, life had become unimaginable. They slept in forests when warm out, and as the weather turned, took shelter in abandoned warehouses and under railroad trestles.

Though he did his best to conceal it from Katie, he had grown weary. Life on the run had stacked hard miles on him and was taking a toll. The fact the wraiths could change their appearance to any living thing made virtually every person they encountered highly suspect.

Jonas was convinced everyone was out to kill them, capture them, turn them in, or take advantage in one way or another. He became increasingly withdrawn and paranoid with each passing day, all the while his judgment became erratic.

Still, he got them by. He was humble and took employment anywhere he could find; work included everything from handyman to stable hand.

Katie, sixteen years old, tried to contribute, but finding legitimate work for a teen from out of town, with no skills beyond that of cleanly removing a head with her sword, proved nearly as challenging as staying undetected. The places changed, the faces changed, but the outcomes remained the same. Small towns, large cities, remote farmland, no matter where they hid, eventually the wraiths came.

They always came.

A shootout in Colorado left three wraiths dead, along with two unfortunate deputies caught in the cross fire.

Now, the police had a nationwide APB on them for murders they did not commit.

**

Katie's watch read 1:05 a.m. as she wearily stood lookout while Jonas rifled inside the alley dumpster for their dinner. This one, behind a Denver bar and grille, proved successful when Jonas scored a white paper bag full of discarded burgers. He shoved that bag inside a larger shopping bag with other items.

"What's taking so long?" Katie grew antsier by the minute.

He ignored her, continuing to sift through the refuse for what he was really looking for. Five minutes later, standing knee deep in the rubbish, his face brightened. Jonas was about to toss the bounty to her when she spun around.

"Cops!" Katie yelled and dashed to the doorway of the bar's rear entrance. She melted into the shadows for cover.

Jonas jumped out the rear side, just as the car wheeled into sight and turned their way.

No way to tell if they'd been seen, but obviously something made the two-man squad car detour down the dark back street. As the vehicle rolled toward them, its bright floodlight tearing away the alley's concealment, she saw the panicked whites of Jonas's eyes peering behind the bin.

"Wait." She motioned for him to stay put.

Katie took a step deeper into the shadows and tried the door behind her. It was open. They had their way out of the long alley—but only if Jonas could make it to her without being seen.

When he saw the thin sliver of light in the doorway and realized she could get inside, he animatedly pointed for her to go. But she would not leave him.

Less than twenty feet away, the vehicle abruptly stopped and directed the blinding beam to the dumpster. Both officers left the car and walked in Jonas's direction. The driver had his hand on his weapon, remaining holstered. The second officer leaned to the side, using the beam from his own flashlight to illuminate the open area between the trash bin and the corridor where Katie hid.

Neither cop spoke as they drew nearer, all the while both Katie and Jonas thought about what they should do. Jonas decided to give himself up, in doing so, planned to provide such a huge distraction, Katie would be able to slip away.

"Unit 53," the male dispatch crackled over walkie-talkies.

Still holding the light in their direction, the second officer stopped his advance.

"Go for 53," the second officer replied with a low voice.

"Respond code 3 to an apartment fire in Rochester Heights: Washington St. and 55th Avenue."

The man looked toward his partner. "Ten-four," he replied.

Immediately, both men doubled back to the cruiser. Lights and sirens came to life. The car quickly reversed and disappeared into the night.

***

Jonas and Katie cautiously worked their way back to the abandoned bottling plant where they had been living the last month. They'd been lucky in the alley but it was obvious the danger had not passed. If anyone recognized them, they were finished. During the relatively short walk, they were repeatedly forced to duck away to avoid any attention of the flurry of emergency vehicles that seemed to race past nearly every city block they crossed.

When they reached the grounds of the long-ago vacated warehouse, Jonas peeled back a concealed flap of broken chain-link fence that served as their door, allowing Katie to step through.

Five blocks away, endless sirens wailed through the city sky. There would be no relaxing until they were safely inside. It had been yet another close call they would not soon forget. They sat on the floor and Katie looked on as Jonas rummaged through the contents of the large shopping bag he'd carried from the alley. A bottle of water, a palm-sized working flashlight, a thin acrylic blanket, four soggy hamburgers and a box of petrified fries. At the bottom was the prize he had been looking for—a liter of cheap whiskey recovered from the dumpster.

She hadn't eaten in days, but with fixated disgust she gazed at the bottle in his hand. None of it, not even the food, was worth the risk they'd just taken. And now, she fully understood his insistence on going there.

"Take as much chow as you want," he said with the first smile she'd seen in weeks. Immediately, he turned the drink to his lips.

She shot a disappointed glance. Without speaking, she grabbed her pack and the sword and got up from the concrete slab that doubled as their living room and beds.

"That blanket is for you too," Jonas said, still unsure why she seemed so annoyed.

Katie stepped over it and went into a higher area of the structure overlooking the block. Wanting to be as far away from him as she could, she settled into the dusty shadows for the night. For long hours, Katie stared across the city toward the high-rise fire, hoping for survivors as the fire department fought to contain blaze.

Jonas sat alone on the floor, drinking until he passed out. Heavily intoxicated, he slept through the clamor of shouting and persistent emergency sirens that carried on during the night. Somehow over all of it, he thought he'd heard someone come through the corridor just outside his room.

Half out of it, with one eye, he glanced toward the corridor. It seemed Katie had finally gotten over her sulking mood and came back for her blanket.

The rear and main entrances to the building as well as both sets of stairs were rigged with makeshift anti-personnel devices assembled from items they'd scavenged from various dumps. Crude, but effective contraptions intended to deter intruders and give the early warning he'd need to be ready to deal with them.

He drifted off again.

When an inadvertently kicked bottle rolled across hallway, his eyes popped open. Someone was here. In an alcohol-induced haze, Jonas lost track of his pistol. He sprang from the concrete rushing to take cover behind a metal bureau along the wall of the door. His eyes searched the floor but he didn't see the gun. He grabbed a three-foot shelving brace lying nearby.

A second or two later, Jonas saw a long shadow fall across the moonlit room. With no way of knowing if it was the police, he readied himself. The metal in his clammy palm, he waited...

When he heard Katie's sudden, distressed, muffled scream down the hall, he instantly bolted from his hiding place. As soon as Jonas rushed forward, he saw him. As Jonas lurched from the dark wall, the startled man spun to face him and fired twice.

Wielding the metal as if it were a sword, Jonas struck him. The first blow to the wrist disarmed the assassin. With three more slashes to the enormous man's torso, the man dropped to his knees and fell onto the ground. Jonas turned to confront a second attacker rushing toward him.

Jonas saw a glint of a knife's steel in his hand as the nimble killer cut him on the forearm and then gashed his side. While Jonas focused on him, something smashed over his head.

***

With the continued sounds of shouting and sirens from the fire a few blocks away, Katie, in her sleep, never heard anyone enter her room. Before she realized she was not alone, a man seized her, cupping her face with a chemical-covered kerchief.

Katie managed a short, muffled scream, until the cloth came across her mouth, dampening her cry. With panicked desperation, she thrashed around the floor as the man tried to subdue her. She turned onto her side. His face loomed just over her left shoulder. Fingers from one hand were wrapped under her jaw as he forced the rag under her nose with the other.

Katie drew her face away from the rag and the powerful, sweet solvent chemical it had been soaked with and reached back, raking her nails across the man's cheek.

Her awareness slipped away.

The man hoisted her from the ground and over his shoulder, carrying the semi-conscious woman down the stairs to his car. When he tossed her into the trunk she came to.

"Nooo!" Katie screamed.

He went to shut the trunk but she threw up her hand, blocking its closure. The enraged man leaned over her, punching her in the gut. She gasped with pain but kept fighting him. The man then slammed the trunk so hard it did not catch. This time, when he reached to close it, she leapt from the car and tackled him.

In a half-crazed delirium, she tussled with the man on the pavement. All she knew was if he got her into that car, there was no telling what awaited her.

Creating distance, he scrambled to his feet and faced her. With a flick of his wrist, a two-foot length baton opened in his hand.

Glancing at the iron, Katie tried to shake off the dizzying effects of the sedative. He rushed in. With agility designed to disrupt his attack before it gained momentum, she entered his aggression. In a single seamless action, she secured the wrist holding the baton and spun directly into him. As his feet left the ground from the perfectly executed throw, she drove him to the pavement. The impact knocked him unconscious. Her eyes flashed to the fourth-floor window as she ran back into the building.

Katie recovered her sword from the room she'd been sleeping in and raced through the hall. When she burst into the room, she saw Jonas and the cuts on his body. He walked around the room, trying to keep a safe distance between himself and an enforcer with knives in both hands.

The man's eyes shifted between them and the door, and then he rushed her. Katie side stepped safely past his reach and twice cut him. When he fell to the floor, he released one of the blades. Jonas recovered his gun from the floor and rushed over and kicked him in the ribs. With his Colt aimed at the man, he stood on his wrist allowing Katie to secure the second knife.

Jonas pulled the holy water from his pocket and glanced into it.

No lights. He returned the vial to his pocket.

"Who sent you?" he asked.

Katie's sword tip loomed inches from the man's face as she glanced at the body of the man's partner across the room.

"Why have you come?" Jonas shouted.

When the man spied Katie, the corner of the man's mouth rose in an almost imperceptible smile.

Jonas leaned down and grabbed the much smaller man by his shoulder-length hair, and dragged him across the room. The man screamed when he yanked him from the ground and forced him into a rolling office chair.

"Watch him," Jonas said, crossing the room to a pair of desks to find something to bind the man with.

"What are you going to do?" Katie asked.

Jonas returned and bound the man to the chair with two short extension cords.

"You should go." Sweat covered Jonas's face.

Katie walked over and stood between him and the sitting man.

"Do this and we're no better than they are."

"It ain't up for discussion."

"Jonas, I'm begging you!"

He walked around her and stood in front of the man. Before she could protest further, he punched the man in the face.

Seeing the man confined in the chair at the hands of someone willing to do anything to force him to talk was eerily reminiscent of her own ordeal in the Oregon compound so many years earlier. With angry revulsion, Katie left the room. She slammed the door behind her and returned to the room where she'd slept. Over the sound of the distant sirens and with her ears covered, nothing could drown out the sound of the man's tormented screams.

"Who do you work for?" Jonas asked him time and again.

"InGene Biotechnologies," the captive screamed.

"What does InGene want with her?"

Refusing to say more, the seated man peering at him through his unbruised eye, looked away.

Jonas stared at him, filled with unpleasant memories of a war long ago and how he'd dealt with enemy combatants trying to withhold vital intel. He knew how to make men talk, but would have to return to a very dark place to do it.

He left the man to retrieve one of the two knives from the floor.

Katie burst back into the room, immediately glancing to the blade gripped tightly his hand. Her eyes went to his with appalling dismay. The steely distant-eyed look on his face seemed like he was someone else.

"What are you going to do with that?" she asked.

Jonas turned away without an answer.

She grabbed him by the arm. "What's wrong with you? This isn't okay!"

"What do you think is happening here, Katie? Do you understand what these men would have done to us—to you?"

"I'm not going to let you do this!"

Jonas snatched his arm away from her. He turned to see the man, whose hands were still bound to the chair, bolt for the window and jump from the fourth floor.

They ran to the edge and gazed down into the night. The assassin was dead, impaled on a fence post.

Chapter 11

Vaughn, New Mexico, May 5, 2019

They walked down the isolated stretch of highway, both trying not to think about the heat. A large white tractor trailer with a blue cab approached and slowed. Their third lift since Colorado Springs, Jonas was exhausted and hoped for a much longer haul.

"Where you headed?" Jonas called up to the driver.

"San Antonio," the sandy-haired man yelled back.

Better than Jonas had hoped—trying, for reasons he had not explained, to get to Beaumont. Katie had never been to Texas but guessed that city was as good as any other.

"Got room for two? We won't be any trouble."

"My pleasure, hop in." The man motioned for them to climb aboard.

"The seat's kind of small so your friend may need to sit in the middle. I don't mean any harm in sayin' that." He smiled, holding up his hands to indicate no offense. Katie easily climbed upon the truck's chrome foot rail then slid into the cab next to him. Jonas climbed in beside her, placing his bag on the floor between his feet.

The air-conditioned cab was a welcomed relief from the inferno desert temperature, but it took her a minute to get used to the cold leather bench seat.

The first thing she noticed was the half dozen or so pictures of women around his truck. None were naked, but most wore swim suits or stood in provocative poses.

"Rick Barnes. Pleased to meet you both." The man extended his muscular right hand. "Friends call me Rickey."

She was fixed on the pictures and did not see his extended hand.

"Good to meet you." Jonas reached across her to shake. He too couldn't help noticing the photographs proudly displayed around the cab.

"We're pretty tired so if it's all the same to you, we'd prefer to keep the chat to a minimum."

"I respect that." Rickey nodded his head.

Three minutes later he broke silence.

"Where you guys from?"

"All over," Jonas replied. *So much for minimal chat,* he thought.

His eyes were dry; the lids felt as though someone was pulling them, forcing them shut. There'd be no harm in resting for a little while.

She guessed the annoying music playing on the radio was not Jonas's preference of music either but he managed to sleep through it.

"You're listening to WXJR 102.1 Colorado's Best Classic Rock," the obnoxious voice blared over the speakers. Rick, his truck, the music, everything about the situation, made her feel uneasy. Without thinking about it, she scooted closer to Jonas, already in deep sleep. Katie knew they had little choice. They were nearly out of water and a good ninety miles from the next town and desperate to escape the intense heat that sought to grind them to dust.

Every few minutes, Rickey turned his head. His lips wore a devious smile and she didn't need to see beyond the polarized auto-darkening glasses to know his eyes passed over her. She also noticed his head beaded with sweat, even in the cold AC.

The back of the man's hand brushed her leg but, believing it could've been inadvertent in the small cab, she said nothing.

The man glanced at her. "How old are you? I'm guessin' what...nineteen, maybe twenty? You're a real knockout and they sure don't make them like you where I'm from."

Katie turned a worried glance to Jonas in a dead sleep.

"I don't know about you but it sure gets lonely out here on the road all the time. Know what I'm sayin'?"

She pretended not to hear him, hoping in earnest she was simply misinterpreting what he said. But when the man, once again, brushed against her left leg with the back of his hand, she knew it was no accident.

"Very lonely in fact."

She pushed his disgusting hand away, then the corner of her eye caught a glint of steel and realized he was holding a large hunting knife. He pressed the flat side of the blade along her leg and traced it along her smooth skin.

"Out of the goodness of my heart, I gave you nice folks a ride. It would be really great if you would show your appreciation."

She tensed as the flat side of the cold blade moved slowly toward her inner thigh.

"Shhhhh...if you wake your friend over there, I'm going to cut his throat. Just be a good little girl and I promise I won't hurt either of you."

"Get off me." Katie said. Her eyes moved from the knife to the road, all the while considering the prospect of overpowering him, but quickly decided against it out of fear they would career across the highway's dividing line directly into oncoming traffic.

69

Again, she glanced toward the sleeping Jonas and fixed her thoughts on him in a desperate attempt to wake him from his slumber. He stirred slightly but did not awaken.

"I'm just saying you should be a little more thankful is all. Why don't you come a little closer to me?"

"Mister, I'd suggest you take your hand off her, right now." Jonas's coarse voice bellowed through the cab. Leaning against his door, he peered at the trucker from under the brim of his hat—gun poised just above Katie's other thigh.

"What the heck man! I think you misunderstood me on this." While Rick was talking he slipped the knife out of sight, figuring Jonas had not seen it.

Jonas adjusted his grip on the pistol. "I reckon I understood you just fine. Drop it on the floor."

Rick released the large buck knife onto the floor, partially between Katie's feet. She stepped on the butt of the knife and, using her foot, slid the weapon toward Jonas. Her boot snagged on something sticking out from under her seat. When Jonas leaned to pick up the knife, he saw a length of long white nylon rope and a roll of duct tape.

"At the next clearing, we'll be getting out."

On a double lane stretch of road winding through a pass in the Rocky Mountains, they drove another eighteen miles before they reached a clearing safe enough to pull onto.

"Here's good enough. Stop the truck," Jonas said.

The angry trucker pulled to the shoulder and slammed on the brakes, causing the truck to skid in the gravel.

Rick laughed. "You're a long way from anyplace out here."

Jonas opened the door. "Don't worry about us. We'll get along just fine." Standing on the side rail, he kept his eyes on the dangerous man as Katie exited the cab.

When she was on the ground, Jonas slammed the door shut and jumped down.

"Good riddance and screw both of you." Rick revved the truck's engine. "I hope the coyotes and the buzzards tear you limb from limb!"

The diesel re-entered the road, its tires spitting loose gravel and brown dirt at them. A minute later, the truck was out of sight and they were on foot again.

Three miles later, they saw a sign on the road: Ruidoso, New Mexico - 12 miles.

Jonas reached into his backpack to inventory their rations. They carried between them roughly eight ounces of water, two small teacakes, and a corn muffin wrapped in a napkin.

"Here." He handed her a half bottle of water.

She took a tiny sip before giving it back. "Thank you."

They were both parched, but too selfless to indulge. He needed it more than she did but she didn't bother asking him to drink because she knew he wouldn't.

He returned the water to his bag. "You hungry?"

"No," she lied. Her stomach panged viciously at the very mention of food.

Jonas handed her a whole teacake. "Eat anyway."

When she saw the cake in his hand, she thought of many desperate times they were left to begging for food, or worse—rifling through dumpsters foraging for scraps.

She smiled in gratitude.

Jonas took a bite of the sweet cookie-like dessert in his hand before wrapping the other half in the napkin and

71

returning it to his sack.

"Everything's going to be just fine." His favorite expression came out of the blue.

Funny thing was, in retrospect that had basically been true. Things had never been easy but even in their most difficult times, for the most part, everything had worked out. However, this time: no ride, food, or friends, and worst of all— no plan, she was not so sure.

Chapter 12

The weight of the unseasonably hot, ninety-one degree May day pressed as they made the final stretch of the twelve-mile walk into Ruidoso. Every step along the hot asphalt had been a force of will for both.

Up ahead, they saw a roadside diner with several vehicles parked in the gravel lot. A large white sign with orange neon lights read: Margie & enny's. The bulbs in the sign's letter K flashed in and out.

"Those are the most beautiful words I've seen in a very long time."

Katie nodded her head in solemn agreement.

After walking in the direct sun for hours, which felt like days, they were relieved.

The clouds, carried along the prevailing winds, obscured the sun, and for several long minutes, the air became noticeably cooler.

What, now the relief? Jonas shook his head. The sudden coolness made him look up. He expected to see a few random clouds drifting through the sky. Instead, a massive portentous shelf cloud approached from the western horizon.

Katie glanced to the skies. "Pretty lucky we got here when we did."

"You got that right." They quickened their pace.

***

"Welcome to Margie and Kenny's." A caged, green and yellow Naped Amazon Parrot bobbed up and down on its perch. The eccentric bird cocked its head, eyeing Katie with interest as they entered the diner. The delicious smell of bacon and cheap grease filled the room.

Like Jonas, over the years, she had conditioned herself to push thoughts of food from her mind and go for longer periods of time without it, but the pungent aroma of grilled meat, fried potatoes, and scrambled eggs made her ravenous.

She looked around the diner and found all eight of the patrons staring at her.

Two men sitting at the bar watching baseball glanced at her, then returned their attention to the game. Several others, including a couple in their mid-thirties, whispered under their breath as Jonas and Katie strolled through.

Numerous pictures lined the walls of the establishment, which proudly displayed black and white portraits and old photographs of famous cowboys and lawmen including Wyatt Earp and Pat Garrett. Among them, several pictures of a man named Clint Eastwood, including a life-sized poster of him entitled *The Good, the Bad and the Ugly*. Amidst the myriad of black and white pictures of famous men and women of the old West, her eyes were drawn to a picture that seemed out of place: mounted above the bar, a black man wore a helmet and a uniform with a large number on the front. Printed in gold letters at the top of the picture read: A real American Outlaw. Across the bottom: Mean Joe Greene.

"Welcome." A thin middle-aged brunette balanced three huge white plates on her left arm and a carafe of coffee in her right hand. "I'm Margie James, and I see you've already met Polamalu." The woman grinned, nodding to the parrot.

"That's a curious name for a bird." Katie smiled, sticking the tip of her finger between the cage bars.

"Careful, he may look harmless, but when he hits you, you'll know it."

Katie withdrew her finger from the cage.

The woman laughed. "I'm just messin' with you. He's gentle and wouldn't harm a hair on a quarterback's head. Go on, grab a seat anywhere you like. I'll be right with you."

The pungent aroma of food wafted to their noses as the waitress walked by; the tormenting smell caused their stomachs to growl at the same time. One of the plates held a stack of pancakes so high, they wobbled as the woman placed the plate in front of a large balding man.

Jonas pointed to a booth toward the rear of the diner, next to the window—as usual, his back facing the wall. He always chose seats that gave him a clear vantage point of doors and angles of approach.

He plopped heavily onto the seat, and, though he did not mention it, Katie knew his knees bothered him. He would not complain, just sighed as he leaned back into the worn, faux green leather cushion.

"Welcome to Margie and Kenny's," the bird squawked again, as the door chimed and a new patron entered.

"Afternoon, Margie." The man waved from the door as he placed a stack of newspapers inside the entrance.

"Thanks, Jesse." She smiled.

"No problem at all, ma'am." He waved, trotting down the stairs.

Jonas gazed across the table at Katie.

"Happy birthday, kiddo. Not the ideal place for a young lady to spend such a special day."

"You've got to stop beating yourself up every year. You know me and birthdays, all that fuss is overrated."

"All the same, I'm sorry you ain't never had a real kid's birthday."

"That might matter if I were still a kid but I'm not. And

75

like I said, it's no big deal. Besides, you got me this." She smiled, holding the cell phone for him to see.

"That's my *old* phone which only plays music. That doesn't quite count."

The waitress came to their table, placing two colorful laminated menus in front of them.

"Good afternoon. I'll be your server. What can I get you folks?"

Jonas tipped his hat. "Service by the one and only Mrs. Margie."

"In the flesh." The woman smiled and bowed.

"Pleasure. ma'am. You mind if we just rest for a few moments?"

"Not at all, take your time, make yourself comfortable and stay a while. I'll give you a few minutes to decide. Before I go, might I offer a recommendation?"

Jonas nodded in respect, even though they wouldn't be able to afford it.

"Kenny's fried catfish and etoufee platter is out of this world."

The very mention of fried catfish made him homesick for his mother and his childhood home in Mississippi. "I have no doubt about that, ma'am," Jonas replied.

"If you're into sweets, and who isn't—I'd also recommend the pecan pralines: Cocoa or Blondies. Take your pick.

"Don't be deceived by the diner here in New Mexico. No disrespect to the wonderful food in this state but Kenny's not from here. He grew up in Baton Rouge and there is simply nothing like his food for hundreds of miles. Trust me on that."

"I'm guessin' Kenny's the owner as well as chef," Jonas

asked.

"Co-owner, chef, husband; he wears many hats. He probably doesn't have the best business sense in the world but he's an outstanding cook and husband. I guess two out of three ain't too bad, right?" She smiled. "Anyway, I'll get out of your hair for a few minutes and let you think about it."

Katie touched the woman's arm just as she turned away. "Excuse me. What did that man with the all the plates order?"

"Oh yeah—that's a classic here. It's called the Sunrise Platter. Chocolate chip pancakes, scrambled eggs, pork sausage links, hash browns, hominy grits, and hickory-smoked bacon."

"Pancakes?" she repeated with wonder. "They sound heavenly."

"Cutie, you're putting me on, now. Where you from, that you've never had pancakes?" The woman put a hand on her hip, cocking her head in disbelief.

Katie smiled out of politeness but she knew better than to answer.

"How much is the platter?" he asked.

"Guaranteed to be the best pancakes this side of the Mississippi." She smiled with confidence.

"Let me guess—another specialty?" Jonas ribbed her. "Is there anything Kenny doesn't make well?"

"Ha! Since you mentioned it," she covered her mouth, as if trying to avoid being heard in the kitchen, "if I were you, I'd stay far away from the enchiladas. He always goes way overboard with those forsaken avocados! I'm just sayin.'"

And then she laughed. When the woman said *enchiladas*, her southwest accent was more pronounced, which made Katie laugh, too.

Jonas hated Mexican food with a passion but was so hungry, he'd happily eat it now.

"Good to know." He smiled.

"Anyway, like I said, take your time. I'll check up on you again in a few," the waitress said.

Katie sat with one leg curled comfortably under her on the seat and studied the pictures hung around the diner. Jonas made sure she wasn't watching when he pulled out his wallet. There were three singles and another dollar thirteen cents in change in his pocket. That was the last of their money but he hated seeing Katie disappointed. He was not aware behind the counter, Margie watched him count his change. And she guessed by his expression he was short.

Katie had noticed too. She avoided eye contact with him, so as not to embarrass him. "I'm not hungry."

"Come on now, we got enough for pancakes," Jonas replied.

She was about to refuse when Margie returned. "So, what can I get for you folks?"

"Just some water please, that's all." Katie smiled.

"What, nothing to eat? You can't come all the way across the desert into Margie and Kenny's and not eat! I'm pretty sure that's against the law." As the woman talked, she tapped the pencil on the table, feigning insult.

Jonas looked across the table at Katie. "She'll have a short stack of the pancakes, with hickory bacon. I'll take a cup of coffee—black."

Coffee was the cheapest thing on the menu and was about all he could afford after paying for Katie's lunch.

Margie stared at him with a displeased frown.

"Everything sounds good but my stomach's been acting up," he lied.

"All righty then, one short stack, one black coffee...coming right up," and she returned to the kitchen.

"I'm worried about you old man." A gentle smile crossed Katie's face.

"Don't worry about me, kiddo. I'll be—"

"—just fine." Katie finished his sentence. "Jonas, you are the most predictable person I have ever met. I guess in a world of so much uncertainty, I should be glad I can at least count on that."

He laughed. "Oh, you think you got the old man all figured out, is that it?"

She touched the back of his scarred, rough hand. "Yeah, I pretty much do."

Margie returned to the table in what seemed only a few moments later, placing the large platter in front of the girl.

"Wow! That was fast!" Katie stared wide eyed at the plate in front of her.

"Hope you enjoy it, sweet thing," Margie replied, putting a plastic shopping bag with four large red apples and two pecan pralines wrapped in cellophane on the table between them. She slid a huge pecan covered honey bun, and a large bowl of steaming hot grits in front of Jonas before pouring him a brimming hot cup of black coffee.

"And for your reading enjoyment..." She placed a current edition of the USA Today on the seat beside him.

Jonas panicked at the sight of all the food. He barely had enough for Katie's meal, let alone the rest of it.

"What's all of this, ma'am?" he stammered. "I'm afraid there's been a mistake. We didn't order this."

"Don't be offended. I couldn't help but overhear you both talking, and if I heard you right, I believe you said something about it being the young lady's birthday? Well as luck would have it, birthday guests eat free." Margie lied this time.

"Thank you, ma'am, that's mighty kind, and I'm much obliged but I can't take your charity," he blushed with injured pride.

"The only offense would be if you didn't. Most of this won't travel well, but pralines and apples are great for the road."

"Thank you." Katie grinned.

"You're very welcome, young lady. By the way, how young are you today?"

"Nineteen."

"Nineteen? Isn't that just wonderful! Happy birthday, I sure hope it's a memorable one." Margie waved and skittered off, leaving them to themselves.

Katie moaned with delight when bacon grease glistened on her lips and fingertips. The small globs of ketchup on her cheek made her look like she had been the unsuspecting victim of a food fight.

He reached in his bag and removed a half empty bottle of whiskey, and topped off his cup.

He smiled sipping the hot coffee. Seeing her eat like that reminded him of the first meal he brought to her after rescuing her from the river as a child. "How's the grub?"

"Oh my gosh—my manners. Did you want some?" She giggled with embarrassment.

"I'm good. Keep on it." He chuckled. He was thankful for the unexpected provision. More than either of them had eaten in a really long time.

***

Jonas sat enjoying his coffee; Margie never allowing him to get to the bottom before she was there to refill. He picked up the newspaper.

Splashed across the front page, a picture of people on the streets of Asia and India, in their ignorance about the plague, wearing ineffectual surgical masks in hopes of preventing infection. The headline at the top read: International concerns over the 'Black Flu.'

He read the entire article before flipping to the section that showed a state-by-state chart to get a snapshot of how localized or widespread the virus had become.

In Dallas, several cases of individuals admitted to local area hospitals for excessive scratching on their skin, leading to their injuries. In Los Angeles, Oregon, and sporadically throughout New England and New York: more of the same.

In Washington D.C. and Maryland, random outbreaks of hysterics and dangerous paranoia dominated, and news about an investigation into a mysterious murder where bite marks were found on a postal service mail carrier near a wealthy suburb of Chicago.

Those locations were significant only in that the wraiths had been there, searching for anyone to lead them the Artifact. Until recently, their activity in the U.S. had ceased, or they kept a very discreet profile. Their days of quietly walking among us had passed.

Outside the diner, black, crimson-tinged clouds crawled across the horizon like fingers stretching forth their baleful grasp. As the storm approached, random downdrafts spun dust devils twirling through the hot, sunbaked New Mexico desert. The thunderhead would've been welcome had they delivered much needed rain, but these brought only darkness that suffocated the sun's light.

"I'll be right back." Jonas excused himself from the table, on his way to the restroom.

Katie gazed at the sky, sucked into the display of slowly unfolding clouds, stretching out high above the plains for as far as the eye could see. She jumped when a sudden ping from her phone startled her. Perplexed, she glanced at the phone before looking around the room.

Jonas was still in the men's room and everyone else gazed outside. Creeping anxiety wrapped around her insides as she pulled the inoperable phone across the table and glanced at the screen.

It displayed the words: *Text Message.*

Her hand trembled as she unlocked the phone and read the note. Jonas returned and slid into the booth. He saw the bizarre look on her face.

"You look like you just saw a ghost."

She gazed up at him from the phone. "I thought you said other than music and apps, all calling features were disabled."

"They are. There's no phone service on it."

"All right, explain this." She turned the phone to face him. Jonas gazed upon the device with the look of worried bewilderment.

The text message read: ***You are in danger.***

Chapter 13

Katie and Jonas found refuge in the wayside diner, until the foreboding clouds and cryptic text message on her phone shattered the brevity of their solace. In a matter of minutes, all comfort vanished. Like ethereal vapor escaping between their fingers, peace departed.

A commotion at the bar began. "Aw...you gotta be kidding me," the thinner of the two men groaned. "Not now, for Pete's sake! We're in the top of the ninth inning, for cryin' out loud."

"Ronnie, turn that up!" Margie yelled across the room, referring to the television.

We interrupt this regularly scheduled program to bring you a press conference from the president of the United States...

"The timing of this guy is unbelievable!" The second man slammed his fist on the bar.

"Ronnie Jacobs and Justin Lloyd, for the love of all that breathes, do you mind? We'd like to hear this!"

The press agent said, "The president would like to give an update on the current state of events surrounding the virus. He will give a brief update before leaving for a meeting with the chiefs of staff. There will be no questions at this time."

The man stepped aside and the president took his position in front of the podium.

"As you are all aware, the world has been wrestling with two calamities of global proportions. First, I begin with the so-called Dark Matter. Just over four and a half years ago, the world experienced the first in a series of catastrophic earthquakes around the globe.

"A short while thereafter, a mysterious black smoke began pumping into the atmosphere, as if coming through vents in the sky. Albeit slowly, this physical cloud of darkness has continued to spread throughout the world, carrying with it heightening concerns.

"While the long-term effects of this current situation on our planet's ecosystem are still being assessed, no negative effects have been determined. All speculation to the contrary has no scientific basis or merit, and is therefore highly sensational and counterproductive.

"The second catastrophe is the viral infection known by the World Health Organization as Cotard's Syndrome, popularly referred to as the Black Flu. Initially, the situation was localized to regions; the spread was very slow and somewhat easy to contain.

"Now, however, because several uncooperative citizens in these areas have disobeyed the World Health Organization's advisory for affected locales to remain indoors, officials have struggled to keep the areas contained.

"The WHO has not yet confirmed the source of the initial outbreak, however the first reported cases were in the Middle East, South East Asia, and Western China. While these are the same regions first experiencing the atmospheric conditions of black fog in the sky, I hasten to add that it would be very premature to make definitive connections between the two situations.

"Here, in the United States, while the presence of the clouds has also been noted over portions of the southwest and the west coast, there are no confirmed cases of the virus.

"Specifically relating to the virus itself, what we *can* say is that the severity of this condition is unlike any ordinary sickness. Dr. Mark Bradley, chief of the World Health Organization, has indicated at present, all treatments have proven ineffective. However, Dr. Bradley assures us that his teams continue to work with all diligence to identify the specific causes of this epidemic and find a treatment.

"The darkness at hand has created pervasive fear and despair around the world. Even so, as Americans, we are steadfast in our resolve to patiently stand united and unafraid. We will not allow this calamity to rob humanity of its hope, and welcome all other nations to join us in solidarity. I am convinced with a collective partnership of the world's governments and the WHO, fortune will smile upon us. Within twelve to eighteen months, leaders in the scientific and medical communities will develop a cure for this disease.

"Thank you." The president smiled confidently. Moments later, he disappeared into his cadre of Secret Service.

"Caused *a degree of overblown concern*?" Kenny shouted. "Are you kidding me?" With disgust, he took off his apron and threw it at the TV.

"We're gonna die. We're gonna die." Polamalu squawked in the background.

"You get all of that, Ronnie?" Justin elbowed his friend. "Whaddya' say you translate all that presidential mumbo jumbo for the rest of us?"

"My dimwitted friend," Ron took a long sip from his mug, "you heard the bird. We're all gonna' die."

***

When a large flock of sparrows flew overhead, Polamalu crashed into the side of the cage as if trying to escape and join them in flight.

"What's gotten into you?" Margie asked.

"Trouble comes! Trouble comes!" the bird crowed. He landed on his perch and began shuffling side to side again. Margie peered through the windows, toward the looming dark skies.

"Darned crazy bird, it's just the storm!"

Jonas looked out the window as a car raced toward the diner. The black '67 GTO pulled into the gravel lot. This was the first time they had seen the GTO, but his gut told him its presence ushered in malignity. Moments later, a man got out of the car and strode up the stairs.

The bell on the front door chimed. Jonas peered over the top of the newspaper in his hands, eyeballing the long-haired, sandy blond stranger sashaying through the entrance. The large, muscular man wore deep brown leather cowboy boots, dark blue jeans, and a long black duster that was completely unnecessary in the hot New Mexico sun.

"Whooweeee! MMMMmmmm...hmmm. Something smells absolutely de-light-ful!" He grinned, slapping his hands together and rubbing them back and forth.

Polamalu fluttered, slamming into the bars of the cage. The man ignored the frightened bird, peering around the room, as if looking for no one in particular.

An uncomfortable tension filled the diner as he meandered down the aisle toward the bar. As he passed their booth, he glanced at Katie, and then his gaze fell to the backpack on the bench beside her.

Jonas eyed him with quiet suspicion as he walked by.

The man took a seat on the padded red swivel bar stool.

"What'll it be, hon'?" a second waitress asked with a flirtatious smile.

The stranger tapped all of his fingers on the countertop. "Coffee."

She placed the cup on the bar and filled it for him. "What's your name, darlin'?"

"Dorian," he replied in a flat tone.

"What? Like that book, Dorian Gray?"

"One and the same, you've read it?" His smile feigned intrigue.

"Gosh no," she snorted. "Are you kiddin' me? Do I look like the reading type to you? Well, actually, I tried but like fifteen pages in, I was bored to tears. No offense."

"None taken." He glanced to Katie and Jonas for the second time.

"My name is Vicki, and I'm just as pleased as punch to see that the mysterious Dorian is so much finer in the flesh." She smiled, after blowing a small bubble with her gum.

"Baby girl, I'm the one your momma warned you about and I'm evil, through and through."

She smiled propping her elbows across the counter in front of him. "So what's up, if I'm a girl who just so happens to like bad?"

He leaned forward in his seat.

"Trust me—you don't know the meaning of the word." And then, with disinterest, he sat back in his chair and flipped through the cheap laminated menu. "What's good in this dump?"

"It's all good," she replied.

"Is that a fact?" He passed still another glance at Katie in a nearby booth, before inhaling, as though food was already before him.

"That's a fact."

"Well then, bring me something delicious."

"I'll be right back." She smiled and went to put in an order.

Since his entrance, the room had fallen as silent as a mausoleum and, other than his exchange with the hostess, remained so.

An impish smile filled his face. "What kind of good, clean, wholesome fun can a stranger get into in this one donkey town, or will I have to make my own?"

Like a child, he spun slowly on the swivel bar stool and sang in a flat melody:

Oranges and lemons, Say the bells of St. Clement's.
You owe me five farthings, Say the bells of St. Martin's.
When will you pay me? Say the bells of Old Bailey.
When I grow rich, Say the bells of Shoreditch.
When will that be? Say the bells of Stepney.
I do not know, Says the great bell of Bow.
Here comes a candle to light you to bed,
And here comes a chopper to chop off your head!

The hypnotically spinning chair slowed as he reached the end of the rhyme. When it came to a complete stop, he leaned against the counter behind him, and once again, his eyes fell across Katie.

"If it's not too much to ask, we'd appreciate it if you were your best behavior here," Margie warned, still hopeful she could preempt any bad intentions he had in mind.

A wicked bend formed on his thin lips. "My best behavior? You can be sure of it." He rose and walked toward Katie and Jonas. The stranger stopped next to Jonas, snatched the cowboy hat from him, placing it on his own head. "I smell something on you, old man."

"Mister, I'm mindin' my own and suggest you do the same." Jonas opened his hand for his hat.

The man smiled when he looked down at Katie. "Does the youngling even know?"

"Know what?" Jonas snapped, looking at the man in

88

confusion.

In that instant, the jukebox against the wall made several loud clicks before switching tracks to a Britney Spears song.

"What... is that abysmal noise?" Dorian covered his ears as though the music caused him literal physical pain. "Garbaaaage!"

He crossed the checkered black and white tile floor to the machine.

Katie looked at Margie, trying desperately to get her attention without him noticing, but the woman was locked on the man leaning over the jukebox in the back of the room.

Margie, it's me. Please don't panic.

The woman turned her attention toward Katie, now gazing at her from across the room.

Do you have a car here?

Margie stared back at her in disbelief as she fished the keys of the Chevy Impala from her pocket and set them on the counter top. Then, she started toward the unwanted patron. It was time for him to leave.

Vicki placed the man's hamburger on the table beside the machine. "Where'd you go?"

When he looked at the food on the plate, his face contorted.

"I tell you I'm hungry and you serve me this slop?" He whipped the plate across the room with such force it smashed against the wall, sending shards of porcelain everywhere. "I wouldn't feed that to my hound!"

Terrified, Vicki cowered away from him. Then, as if nothing had happened, he returned his attention to the jukebox and continued perusing the song listings, voicing his disapproval of the artists in the lineup, calling them out one after the next.

"Dylan!" he said in final satisfaction. "That's what I'm talking about. Music of a conflicted and tormented soul!" He hit the machine with his fist and the track changed to that song. When the music started, he spun around and faced the room.

"Uh huh." He swayed his shoulders back and forth as he mimicked playing an air guitar. After a few moments, he tipped the Stetson, beckoning Vicki to dance with him. The same waitress, who only moments before stood paralyzed with fear, now enchanted, crossed the diner and danced with the mysterious stranger. The whole time, he sang.

"...It may be the devil or it may be the Lord...

"but you're gonna' have to serve somebody...and this time—it's me."

Margie stomped across the room. "I swear I don't know what's gotten into you woman, but you need to get a hold of yourself, right this instant!"

Vicki ignored her and kept dancing with Dorian as he adlibbed the song, twirling her over and over again.

"Can you check on table three? He'd like some pie." Margie persisted, pointing to one of the tables on the other side of the diner.

"I'm busy. You take care of it." A glazed look filled her eyes.

Margie noticed the gossipy couple on the other side of the restaurant making a commotion. Then, they stood and slinked out the door. A moment later, she saw what they had been chattering about. At the crest of the road leading to the diner, five motorcycles headed their direction.

"Oh shoot. Shoot, shoot, shoot! This is bad. This is very bad!" She grabbed Vicki by the arm. "Girl, Sean's coming. He's right outside!"

Spellbound, she continued to glide across the floor with her body pressed against Dorian's.

Margie left her side and hurried through the swinging doors, into the kitchen.

"Kenny! Kenny! Where are you? Call the sheriff's department ...now!"

Chapter 14

"Now that's what I'm talking about," Dorian shouted, and with every obnoxious twirl of the waitress, he moved closer to Katie.

"MMMMmmmm." He moaned over the music, clearly for her benefit, even as he pressed his lips on Vicki's neck.

Katie felt him staring past the waitress at her and turned up her phone's volume to drown out his repulsive comments.

"You don't have to play shy with me, little momma," he teased, tracing the brim of Jonas's hat.

With a sudden flick of the wrist, he sent the hat hurling through the paper into Jonas's chest.

Jonas picked it up and put it back on. "You got a problem, mister?"

The enigmatic stranger continued to dance to a new song, paying Jonas no attention. Holding Vicki's hand high, he spun her away and then pulled her into him. The smile disappeared from his face as sharp fangs emerged. Before she could retreat, he pressed his mouth against the exposed left side of her neck.

He continued staring at Katie. "When I said I was hungry, I wanted her!"

With amazing speed, Dorian pulled a pistol concealed behind his jacket, and took aim at Katie. With her own agility, she had already sprang to her feet and drawn on him as well; she stood sideways—her Sig trained on him, as the music in her ear buds continued to play.

"Katie, be cool," Jonas warned. He pulled his .45 from his pack, keeping it under the table.

As Katie and Dorian stood feet apart, face to face, handguns drawn, five bikers from the Outlaws motorcycle club walked through the entrance, all brandishing firearms—save one. Four men filed into the room and spread out, pistols pointing the direction of Vicki and Dorian. The sole unarmed man, the leader, wore a black bandana pulled over his head.

"So, is this how you act when I'm not around?" The man picked up a gumball machine and smashed it into the floor. The glass dome shattered, sending a rainbow of dozens of colored candy bouncing across the floor.

Startled by the noise, and as if choreographed, Katie and Dorian simultaneously turned their attention and weapons toward the armed biker gang blocking the door, then flashed their aims toward each other.

The boss withdrew a box of cigarettes from his front pocket and removed one from the pouch. He lit it and took a long deep drag.

"Sean...baby, I know what you must be thinking but I promise you it's not at all what it looks like." Vicki cowered. She squirmed and broke Dorian's embrace, stepping away from him.

"You see!" Sean bent down, scooping up a large handful of gumballs. "And there it is! It's just like on TV...that's exactly the first thing the guilty always say."

He shook his head in disbelief that she actually used that one—perhaps the mother of all clichés.

Ronnie looked at Justin and motioned with his head toward the door. Justin laid cash on the counter and both men made their way toward the entrance blocked by one of the larger bikers.

"Junior, tell them boys ain't nobody else leavin'." Sean

93

motioned to the goliath with him.

"Have a seat." Junior pushed Justin so hard that the 147-pound man tumbled backwards. The man recovered and cowered back to his bar stool. The biker leader walked into the center of the dining area, and headed down the left side of the room toward his girlfriend.

Sean took another drag from his cigarette.

"Open your mouth, Vicki."

"Sean, please don't. I'm sorry," she pled with him.

"Don't make me tell you twice!"

She began to cry as she opened her mouth. One by one, he pushed fifteen large gumballs into her mouth.

"I've always been real good to you but if you want to act like a cheap, up-to-no-good floozy, then you better believe I'm goan' treat you like one."

The humiliated woman sobbed intensely before the on-looking patrons.

"And as for you, pretty boy, it's for plain sure that you ain't from around here else you'd know me."

Dorian smiled. "I have no problems with you; I came for the girl. She's my reward. Leave me to my business, and I'll let you and the boys here get back to your leather and lace pajama party."

"Pajama party, he says. Now that's just fantastic!" Sean laughed for a few seconds but when his laughter cut off, he pulled his gun, aiming at Dorian.

"I'm passing through my town, mindin' my business only to see you through the window, kissing all up on my girl, and you got the nerve to have jokes, too?"

"Friend, let me offer my sincere apology." Dorian bowed his head. "I meant you no offense. I wished only to

94

dance, just this once, with the queen of the trailer park."

Sean laughed again, turning to look at his crew.

"Are you fellas getting all this?" Then he stepped up to Dorian, stopping inches from his face.

"Cat—I simply cannot tell you how much I love jokes. Will you tell me something though? When I cut that stinkin' smile off your face, do you think you could still make me laugh?"

Jonas, still seated, was about to raise his weapon from under the table when another biker walked up behind him and shoved a pistol into his back.

"Stay down," the man said, unaware of the gun Jonas was holding.

"Margie! Margie, tsk, tsk, tsk, woman," the biker boss said in a voice loud enough to carry into the kitchen. "I gotta' tell you. I'm pretty disappointed in you, too."

"Looks like you and Kenbo will serve darn near anybody these days."

Ken peeked through the small crack between the doors at the armed group in the lobby. He turned and slipped into the storeroom closet. He came out holding a shotgun, checking it to be sure it was loaded.

Margie put her hand on his arm trying to hold him back.

"Kenny, please let the police handle it."

"Go on out back, mother, just in case things get rough out there."

Tears welled in her eyes, and she shook her head. "No, I will not."

"Woman, I love you. Just once, will you please listen to me?"

"I love you too, Kenny, and I'm not leaving."

"All right. Stay here and keep down."

Ken took several deep breaths before kicking the doors outward as he emerged into the dining area. *Tchick Tchick...* the unmistakable sound of him pumping the shotgun caught everyone's attention, though no one took their eyes off one another.

"Everybody settle down!" he yelled, shotgun propped against his shoulder. "Sean and whoever the heck you are. You can kill each other as far as I'm concerned but you're going to have to do it somewhere else."

Sean glanced at him with disinterest, as he exhaled smoke through his nostrils.

"Adults are talking, Ken. You should go put that thing away before you get hurt. And besides, don't you got some cakes to bake?"

The boss faced Katie and Jonas for the first time.

"Now, I know the two of you ain't from around here," he pursed his lips and breathed a stream of noxious white smoke directly into Jonas's face. "What's your beef, spook?"

"We just came to rest our feet and get some chow. Not looking for trouble."

Katie kept her gaze and pistol locked on Dorian who she considered, without question, the most significant threat in the room.

Sean sized her up, glancing from her to Jonas. "Who's this? Your old lady?"

His men laughed.

"She's my niece," Jonas replied, knowing nothing he said mattered.

"The resemblance is striking." Sean circled the

motionless woman, still looking her up and down.

"We get that a lot," Jonas said.

"Judging by the way you handle yourself, sweetness, I'm thinkin' maybe, you should be *my* old lady." When Sean said this, he turned a disgusted glance to Vicki. "Rumor has it, there's a new vacancy and I'm presently accepting applications."

The overworked bell at the door chimed again. A sheriff's deputy, responding to what had been dispatched as a disorderly conduct call, strolled with complacency through the door. He was not prepared for the wasp nest he walked into.

In a fluster, the officer pulled his service revolver and aimed in the general direction of the large group of armed individuals.

"What in the name? Everybody drop your weapons!" the man shouted with a hoarse voice.

Dorian howled with laughter. "My-my-my; how the plot thickens! So what do we all do now—shall we walk twelve paces and draw?"

"Shut your face, slick," Sean shouted. "I've about had it with you."

"See, officer? Everybody's just fine," Dorian said.

"I think it's time you all get moving along." The cop's voice faltered and his weapon hand trembled.

Sean glanced at the law official. "Nobody's going anywhere 'til I sort all this out."

Less than four feet separated Katie and the man who had relentlessly pursued them across three states with the singular purpose of ending her. She ignored everything in the bar, unwilling to take her eyes from him. As she watched his hand, she perceived his finger moving as he squeezed the

97

trigger.

The instant Dorian fired, time slowed in her eyes—almost to a standstill. In the microsecond that followed, his weapon malfunctioned and jammed. The pistol exploded, wounding his hand as a sulfurous mixture of volatile gunpowder and hot shrapnel burned his face. Blinded, he wailed in agony. Katie crouched to the floor and perfectly executed a spinning sweep, kicking Dorian's legs out from beneath him. The speed and rough force of her roundabout sent him crashing onto his back.

"That wench burned my face!" He flailed on the floor in pain, cupping his face in his hands.

His gunshot ignited the fuse of the tense standoff, and a cacophony of gunfire erupted, bullets flying every direction. Countless shards of glass were airborne as the TV, pictures, jukebox, and the diner's windows exploded under violent impact.

Katie completed a front shoulder roll and came up on her right knee, taking cover behind another bench. Her Sig Sauer spit two rounds at Sean, just as he ducked behind an adjacent row of benches. The deputy crouched, crawling rapidly backwards past the dead bodies of Ronnie and Vicki. Nothing remained of the glass door except the aluminum frame and he climbed through it, firing his revolver in no particular direction as he ran from the diner, shooting behind him until he jumped in his cruiser and fled.

Jonas ducked behind a table and fired, hitting Junior, the largest of the five bikers. The man clutched his leg and fell to the floor.

Enraged, Sean pulled a .44 Magnum from his

waistband. "You killed Vicki!"

He fired several times before hitting Ken in the left shoulder. Ken returned fire and the shotgun blast blew Sean backwards against the wall.

"Let's go!" Katie screamed. She grabbed Margie's key ring as they ran past the counter.

Jonas sprang from the table and grabbed her pack, firing as he backed out the door and down the stairs. They climbed into the Impala, and he gunned the car's engine as they sped away.

Chapter 15

They traveled east, heading along the rural interstate. Several hours after leaving the diner, the darkening sky did what it had only teased for countless months—it rained.

At first, only a sprinkling, then heavier. Katie rested her head against the door, and as she watched the long water drops race across her window, they reminded her of the bleak reality of her life.

They were forever on the run, and carried forward as if by the wind, with seemingly no control over the forces that wisped them along. They were as insignificant as the tiny droplets of rain that hurriedly trailed down the glass.

Amidst those thoughts, she wondered what was going on with Jonas. There was an unexplainable ever-present cloud of wrenched-up emotions concerning him that had troubled her for years. Though they did not keep secrets from each other, there was something he was not telling her.

In minutes, the misting gave way to a torrential rain, and before long standing water puddled on the highway. Through the large, unavoidable pockets of water, the worn tread on the tires had Jonas frequently fighting for control as he pulled against the wheel to keep the car from gliding toward the edge of the road. With no good place to stop, he drove until he saw a Quickie Mart off to the side of the highway.

"We may not see another station for many miles so we'll stop for gas. We'll hold up here for a few minutes or so. Hopefully this thing will blow over quickly."

He pulled the car into the fuel plaza and stopped at a pump. They were both thankful the station was covered because the rain only intensified.

"I need to go to the bathroom, back in a few," Katie

said, pulling her hood over her head and zipping her jacket.

After she came out, she milled around the store.

She was keenly aware of the clerk's stare closely following her every move as she meandered through the aisles. Among the overpriced groceries, automotive supplies, and so called collectibles, light glinted off a round object on the top shelf. Filled with curiosity, she picked up the object.

Paying no attention to the clerk and her suspicious glare, Katie palmed the large snow globe. She shook it and watched in fascination as the fake snow drifted around the beautiful park inside the glass. She stared at the delicately hand-painted flowers and blue stream that ran through the park, passing through the mouth of a garden. Behind the garden was an intricate labyrinth of meticulously painted green hedges, accentuated by a small grove of trees at its center.

The strange familiarity of the foreign place beckoned to her.

Beautiful.

Katie heard a distant call. Mesmerized, the globe continued to draw her in, as an ever so faint milky white trail swirled around the waters inside. Little by little, the globe grew warmer. Then she thought she noticed movement inside. She squinted, leaning closer. A miniscule woman emerged from behind a tree. She blinked, disbelievingly as the globe illuminated a spellbinding white glow that held her transfixed.

"Beautiful," a voice said again, in a near whisper.

The globe made a sound, barely audible at first, a slight *twang* that sounded like the reverb of a large rubber band rapidly vacillating back and forth. The noise gradually became louder, then, ceased. A clamorous droning of wings filled the store. As the noise crescendoed, a blood red fluid swirled into the clear water in the toy.

"I see you," a voice echoed around her.

Afraid, she tried to put the globe on the shelf but her hands stayed affixed to the object. She felt herself being physically snatched into the snow globe by an unseen pair of spectral hands.

"No! No!" Katie shouted in the full throes of panic.

Inside the tiny world, a huge red serpent eye opened. She screamed and smashed the globe against the edge of the shelf to free herself from its grasp. The globe shattered, sending sharp slivers of glass and blood everywhere.

Horrified she screamed again.

"It's okay, it was an accident and it was totally my fault for startling you." A man she had not seen enter the store stood next to her. "I am so sorry." The middle-aged Indian blushed profusely. "I was just asking if you had ever seen such a beautiful globe."

He bent down and carefully picked up the sharp glass fragments. "I am so embarrassed. Are you okay?"

She looked over her hands and arms to see if she was cut, but she was not.

"The wings...did you hear them?" Katie asked in fear.

"I didn't hear anything other than your scream and this glass when it broke." Concern filled the man's face as he glanced to the angry cashier.

"I really didn't mean to scare you. Don't worry, I'll pay for it. It's the least I can do."

"No worries," the rattled woman replied. She looked at the floor, covered with nothing but broken glass, porcelain, and water. The only blood was a drop from a tiny piece of glass stuck in her hand.

The door chimed as Jonas entered the convenience store.

"My wife collected snow globes from all the places we'd visited. I've never seen one like that. I'd say it's kind of funny having one in a place where it never snows, if you ask me."

She forced a smile.

When Jonas saw the stranger talking to Katie, he became suspicious. Immediately, he proceeded down the aisle and stood beside her.

"Good evening." The crouching man smiled, still picking up shattered glass.

Jonas nodded to him "You okay?" he asked her.

"Yes," she replied. "I am truly very sorry," she said as she walked away.

"You have nothing to apologize for. This was my fault. I'll take care of it."

"Thank you," Katie said politely. They turned and walked toward the front of the store.

"Bye, now." The stranger waved. "See you around."

Jonas picked up a pouch of tobacco on the side counter. The cashier smiled politely, though regarding him and his traveling partner with a suspicion.

"Pretty please." Katie smiled as she placed the yellow package of M&Ms on the counter next to his chew pouch.

He smiled, shaking his head.

"All this together?" the clerk asked.

"Yes, ma'am, that and the gas."

"That'll be twenty-seven dollars, eighteen cents."

Jonas paid from the eighty-five dollars they found in Margie's car, sliding the cash under the Plexiglas window between them and the clerk. Behind her, a small TV showed a weatherman in front of a map as he gave the regional forecast.

When the report concluded, the station recapped an earlier report that showed video of the exterior of Ken and Margie's bullet-riddled diner. Black soot marks surrounded the outer edges of all of the windows and doors as if a fire had burned, chasing the trail of oxygen. On the right pane of the screen, a poorly done composite sketch that didn't vaguely resemble either her or Jonas displayed.

A police investigation continues surrounding today's shootout and explosion at a diner in Ruidoso, New Mexico. A composite sketch has been done of these two suspects: an elderly black man and a young Asian female, approximately twenty to twenty-two years old. They are being sought for questioning in relation to the crime. The police have advised to be on the lookout for these two individuals, both of whom are armed and considered highly dangerous.

The clerk's back was to the TV as she tended to the register. She looked up, her eyes shifted from Jonas to Katie before she yelled something in a foreign language.

Jonas was anxious, and wondered if she'd seen the story.

After a number of long seconds, a tall, bearded man came out of the office and stood beside her. His eyes passed over all three customers. He handed a roll of quarters to the clerk and with his finger extended, he briefly scolded her in the same language she had spoken before returning to the office and shutting the door.

She cracked the new roll of quarters into the drawer and slid Jonas the change. She bagged the candy and his tobacco, and placed it on the counter.

"Thanks," he said before exiting the convenience store. "Hard to tell if she noticed the report."

"I don't know if she heard it either but she definitely recognized us."

"Are you sure?" Jonas asked.

"Positive. She told her husband to get the gun. He told her we were not worth dying over, that she'd better let the police handle it."

"Shoot, I was worried about that," he said as they approached their car.

A mammoth recreational vehicle had parked beside them. Inside, a large white Akita sat on the passenger seat, barking.

Jonas asked as they backed out and quickly drove from the plaza, "So it seems my 'ever intriguing sidekick' also speaks fluent Arabic?"

Katie glanced at him. "It was Farsi."

"When did you learn Farsi?" he asked with astonishment.

She shrugged. "Just now."

***

Anxious to put as much distance as possible between them and the diner and Quickie Mart, Jonas led them up the interstate. All the while, the wipers on the Chevy shuffled frenetically, slapping rain from their windshield as they cautiously navigated their way through water-saturated sections of the highway.

The thought of Margie, Ken, and the others in the diner, dead, left Jonas with emptiness and wrestling with his guilt for stopping there in the first place. If he and Katie had passed by, all of them would still be alive. Maybe, if they had walked on a bit longer; maybe, if they rode with Rick a little longer; maybe, if they had hitched a ride with someone else altogether. In the end, it was Margie's selfless gesture that saved their lives and ultimately cost her own.

More and more blood on my hands, Jonas thought. The whole thing was so senseless, so much death and heartache, good, innocent people falling everywhere, and for what? He was weary and had long since stopped fearing his own death. Now he faced it head on and was ready, and it could not come soon enough, as far as he was concerned.

"Darn it!" Jonas snapped back to the present.

"What?" Katie asked. She understood when the alternating red and blue lights of a police car pierced the moonless jet black sky behind them. Neither of them had seen the deputy lying in wait behind the trees on the side of the highway.

"Just what I was afraid of," Jonas said

"Were you speeding?"

"Of course not, I'm careful. The clerk probably changed her mind and tipped them off."

"Maybe you should keep going." Katie peered back from her mirror.

The cruiser closed the distance behind them within seconds.

"Keep going, eh?" His heart pounded as he considered their options. They were both armed fugitives on the run. No way of knowing whether they were being stopped as a result of the state wide all-points bulletin or just for a moving violation.

He ran a number of scenarios through his mind, but all of them resulted in either being detained or killed. As an honest man, the thought of seriously injuring a law enforcement officer never once crossed his mind. Of course the feeling wouldn't be mutual if the cop searched the vehicle and found any of the numerous weapons stashed inside.

He considered running full bore to try and get away, but they wouldn't get very far. He scanned the terrain ahead looking for any roads they might quickly jump onto but this was a straight stretch of highway through Texas, and as far as he could see in the driving rain, there were no places to hide. He would have to let this play out.

"Runnin' ain't no good. It wouldn't be long before support arrived and then we'd have no chance," he answered.

"What are you going to do then?"

"I'm going to pull over." He slowed. Leaning to the side, he slid his pistol under the bench seat of the Impala. Katie's gun remained in her backpack.

"Stay in the car and don't say anything unless I say so," he said.

His ensuing actions would be dictated largely by his assessment of the officer himself. The brilliant spotlight from the cruiser behind them blinded Jonas as the intense beam reflected off his mirrors and shielded the officer's approach.

The deputy sheriff advanced toward their vehicle with caution. Jonas faintly saw his silhouette in the backlight. Rain bounced off his yellow slicker as he shone his flashlight in the rear of their vehicle and behind the seat, before directing the light to the front seats of the car. And even though they were expecting him, the hard sound of the baton rapping on the glass startled him. Jonas rolled down the window and squinted at the officer through the unrelenting rain.

"Good evening, sir. What seems to be the problem?" he asked.

"Driver's license and registration." The man's demeanor was stern, and his palm rested on the handle of his weapon.

Jonas knew full well his politeness gave no assurance of getting off with only a warning, but then again being courteous never hurt. If the polite tact didn't help him talk his way out of the citation, he was at a total loss for what to do.

It was obvious the dangerous situation could easily turn bad in a hurry. He decided to play it cool and avoid giving the cop any reason to escalate, at least for now.

"Driver's license and registration," the veteran officer repeated, disregarding his pleasantries.

"Yessir, of course." Jonas reached across Katie's leg for the glove box. "Here's my license but I seem to have misplaced the registration. I bought the car from a woman named Margie a few days ago but she probably hasn't had time to change the registration over to my name yet."

"You got a proof of sale?" the deputy asked with a pronounced, southwestern Texas accent.

"No, sir. I gave her five hundred dollars and she said she'd take care of the paperwork."

"Did she, now?" he asked dubiously.

"Yessir, that's correct."

"Where you folks headed this evening?"

"We're on our way to Mississippi to visit kin," Jonas said.

"Mississippi? Whereabouts?"

"Jackson sir, my sister's sick."

"Sorry to hear that." The officer nodded. "Do either of you have any weapons, drugs, or anything else in the car I should be aware of?"

"No, sir. We're just tired and trying to get to Mississippi

as soon as possible."

"Where y'all comin' from?"

Jonas fidgeted nervously. Since shootouts in Colorado and New Mexico had left a trail of bodies in their wake, the less the man knew the better.

"East from California," he said. "Just trying to make some good time before we break for rest, speaking of which, can you recommend any good places to get some shut eye around here?"

"No, sir," the officer responded, still regarding him with suspicion.

"If you don't mind me asking, who's the young lady?"

And there it was. Jonas froze. What plausible story could he provide that would explain why an old black man was on an isolated stretch of country interstate with a young Asian woman? What reasonable explanation could he offer that would appease the curiosity of even the dumbest of backwoods cops? He kept stories ready for times like this in the various 'what if' scenarios he rehearsed in his mind. This time, however, for inexplicable reasons, as he searched for an answer that might satisfy the man, he only drew a blank.

Concerned for her safety, the deputy shifted the beam of the heavy duty mag light to Katie in the passenger seat. She had been feigning sleep the entire time, now pretending to wake up.

"Everything okay, ma'am?" the deputy asked.

"Evening, officer, Yes sir—I'm fine," she said, sounding groggy.

"So, you were telling me who this is. I need to inform you that transportation of a woman across state lines for immoral purposes is a federal offense." The cop's stature and tone were more authoritative and accusatory than before.

"No, sir! She's older than she looks and this ain't nothing like that," Jonas said. The mere thought of the scenario the deputy conjured up in his mind appalled him.

"She's my daughter."

"The resemblance is uncanny," the man mocked him.

"It's the truth. I swear."

"You know that will be easy enough for me to confirm, but for the moment, I'll take you at your word," the man said. "Do you know why I stopped you, sir?"

"No, sir, I do not."

"Your taillight is out."

Innocuous enough under a different set of circumstances, the minor infraction would at most amount to little more than a small fine. Tonight however, the mere triviality would lead to the deputy running his license. It would be a few short minutes before his entire story came apart and the authorities would happily conjure one of their own. When they ran it, they'd discover his prior criminal record, find no record of Katie in their systems, search the vehicle and find the concealed, unregistered weapons that no former convict is allowed to possess.

If still alive, the kindly waitress Margie would certainly confirm that she had given him the car. However, if dead, Jonas would get the electric chair for her, Ken, and the litany of others' deaths. He'd never be able to explain the vehicle they would allege he stole, and with the young lady they'd charge him with trafficking. To be certain, anything more than being released with a warning, right here and right now, would result in a catastrophic chain of events.

A fine mess, he thought to himself, fidgeting nervously

as he considered the next move.

The cop was nearly as old as he was but not in near as good condition. Jonas figured if he could get the drop on him, he'd knock him out, without doing the man any significant harm—that is if the opportunity presented itself.

"Imma' go run this info. You folks just go ahead and stay righ'tcheer," the deputy said.

Jonas watched in his mirror as the man returned to the cruiser.

"Katie, what are we going to do? He didn't believe a word I told him."

"No, he didn't," she agreed. "Will you let me talk to him?"

"You? And say what exactly?"

"I don't know yet, but let me see if I can reason with him."

"I don't feel comfortable with that, Katie."

"If you have any better ideas, I'd love to hear them," she said.

Jonas shook his head.

"Okay then." She opened her door to get out. Immediately the interior light came on.

"Remain in the vehicle!" the man's voice bellowed over the cruiser's PA system.

Katie ignored his command and continued walking, arms raised, toward him.

"Get back in the car!" he exclaimed again.

In the distance, a second set of headlights rapidly approached and she froze in her tracks.

He called for backup. That plan's out the window.

Adrenalin flooded the deputy as he exited his vehicle

with his firearm drawn.

"Young lady, put your hands on the car! Driver, step out of the vehicle!"

Jonas abandoned his thoughts of overpowering the man now that a second cruiser was en route. Any resistance offered at this point would result in the certainty of death.

"No problem. Okay. No problem!" Jonas complied with the lawman's commands, keeping his hands high in the air.

"Walk backwards until you get to me," the man shouted.

Jonas took fifteen paces backwards and then the cop patted him down. The headlights of the second vehicle stopped behind the first police cruiser.

"There's a female suspect over there," the officer yelled when he heard the sound of a car door slam behind him. He cuffed Jonas's wrist and pulled it behind his back. As the cop was about to secure the second cuff, he wailed.

Jonas hazarded a glimpse over his shoulder to see the deputy being mauled by Dorian—the hunter from the diner. The badly bitten deputy discharged five wild shots at the wraith boss.

"Get in!" Jonas screamed. Loose gravel shot from the car's tires as he fishtailed onto Interstate 80. Dorian fired as they drove away. The rear window imploded glass around them and several rounds struck the Impala.

"You okay?" Jonas asked with great concern.

"I'm all right," Katie said taking inventory of herself. But then, she touched the place on her left arm where she felt a stinging sensation. She held up her hand to see blood on her middle and index finger.

A worried glanced filled his face when he saw the blood

on her hand. "You're hurt."

Movement on the road ahead of them caught Katie's eye. "Look out!" she screamed.

Jonas looked back to the road and saw a woman standing in their lane. The dark-haired apparition wore black and scarlet, and tall, black leather boots. He slammed on the brakes, causing the Chevy to skid on the slippery pavement, veering into the wrong lane and the path of an oncoming tractor trailer. The truck driver yanked hard to the right as he jammed his brakes.

The mammoth steel vehicle skidded momentarily, then the man lost complete control, sending the flammable truck directly toward them. The rig's headlights loomed above them as Jonas yanked hard to his right. The truck sheered the driver's side, sending them airborne. Jonas was thrown from the car as it catapulted, spinning through the air.

The sickening shriek of grinding steel filled the air as the driver of the trailer overcorrected, causing the fuel-filled tractor trailer to fishtail. The truck then, in a sideways roll, careened into the police cruiser, engulfing the truck and the other cars in a reddish-orange fireball.

The white-hot fingers of the flame danced high into the sky, brightening the previously ink black desert night. Even at a distance of two hundred yards, intense heat emanated from the tanker. Another explosion ignited the long gasoline trail that traced back to them. The fire angrily lapped up the gas-covered road, whisking toward two more victims.

Jonas lay unconscious, face down in the ditch, and Katie—semiconscious, was pinned by her own seatbelt upside down in the Impala.

In a daze, her eyes followed the leading edge of the

flame racing towards her. She frantically pushed the belt release, tugging as hard as she could against the restraint. Finally, the buckle unlatched and she grabbed her things, crawling onto the street as the car was engulfed in flames.

"The woman...did I—" Jonas was unable to complete the nauseating thought.

"I don't know!" Katie screamed. "It all happened so fast."

"She's got to be here, somewhere." For the moment he ignored the nasty gash above his right eye, where he had bounced off the asphalt. He limped to the opposite side of the road and searched for her body.

A pair of headlights approaching the wreckage caught their attention. The vehicle slowed before coming to a halt. A minute or so later, it drove around the blaze then quickly continued in their direction.

"Get off the highway." Jonas winced with pain. They left the road and ran for the safety of the tree line.

Chapter 16

A quarter mile inside the Louisiana state line, a vehicle slowed near the portion of the highway where they left the road. A flashlight scanned the tree-lined darkness. They ducked into the woods as the beam moved over the area. In the distance, a dog, Jonas assumed was a police K9 unit, barked wildly as the vehicle approached. To escape dogs, their only choice would be retreating through the perils of the murky swamp that lay behind them.

They watched as the vehicle drove slowly up the road before coming to a sudden stop. Jonas recognized the RV as the one from the Quickie Mart.

Through the open passenger window, the man yelled, "Come on! Hurry!"

Jonas and Katie peered at each other in the darkness.

"We don't have many options. We won't last long out here in the middle of nowhere," Katie said.

"Agreed." Jonas nodded.

When they saw a new set of headlights appear, they ran toward the vehicle with caution. Just outside the RV, Jonas slowed and removed his pack from his back. The huge white Akita barked from the passenger seat. "Come on! Get in!" the driver yelled over the barking.

Jonas watched the headlights closing in the distance as he retrieved the glass crystal of holy water. He looked for the telltale glimmer but the water did not sparkle. Of course, that only meant the RV driver wasn't a wraith. Jonas wished the supernatural power of the water also gave him a foolproof method of detecting psychopaths as well.

"You sure about this, Katie bear?"

"Like I said, we don't have much choice. We'll have to

115

be more careful this time."

He nodded again and boarded the vehicle. He tipped his hat obliging the driver, but having learned from their experience several states back with Rick Barnes, he stayed prepared.

"Thank you," Katie said as she boarded the RV.

As soon as they were inside, they were immediately greeted by the dog. Though Jonas had never said, he was deathly afraid of dogs—even the tiny ones. As it sized him up, he wasn't sure if he should pet the 130-pound goliath or brace for an attack. It came to him wagging its tail, and licked his hand. Jonas side stepped backwards trying to avoid the frisky dog as it stood on its hind legs and licked him in the face.

"Good enough for me." The man put the vehicle in drive, leaving the twisted mass of wreckage behind.

"Uhm, no—don't." Jonas squirmed, recoiling from the animal's kisses.

"This here's Chance." The man patted the huge dog on the back. "Don't mind him."

Jonas was relieved when the ultra-frisky animal left to introduce itself to Katie. She knelt and his huge tongue lapped her in the face. The man smiled at her through his rear-view mirror. "He's obviously taken to both of you and believe it or not, if Chance likes you, that says quite a bit."

"Yeah?" She smiled, scratching the dog between the ears.

"Let's just say that my instincts are good, but his are even better."

"The name's Herman Dhaliwal," he said offering his hand.

"Jonas." He shook the driver's hand.

116

"Good to meet you, Jonas. Please, make yourselves comfortable. Have a seat."

Jonas quickly glanced around and, when he saw nothing out of the ordinary, sat in the front passenger seat.

"What's your name, miss?"

Jonas nodded giving her his approval to give the man her real name.

"Katie," she replied.

"Pleasure to have you aboard, Miss Katie."

She surveyed her surroundings. "Herman, this place is wonderful."

It had a fully functional deluxe kitchen, a dinette section, and a full bath. She peered into the room in the aft section. For a mobile home, the bedroom was nothing short of extraordinary, having a queen-size bed, with cabinets overhead and a floor-to-ceiling closet concealed behind mirrored doors.

"It's like a house on wheels," she said.

"I'll take it you've never had the pleasure of riding in an RV before, is that right?"

"I can't say that I have." She emerged from the room.

"Now that's just not right. You haven't lived until you've enjoyed the open road in one of these babies," he said as he proudly traced his hands around the wheel. "It wouldn't be an exaggeration to say I've lived in lesser homes than this ride. Anyway, like I said, make yourselves at home and I mean that. Anything I have is yours so don't be bashful—take whatever you need, friends." He smiled, and then leaned forward to get a good look at Jonas's eye.

"Looks like you're pretty cut up. There's a first aid kit under the sink. You should patch yourself."

"Thanks," Jonas responded but remained seated.

Herman smiled again. "If you're hungry, there's food in the fridge. Heck, I even have ice cold beer if it suits you. Where you headed, friend?"

"Far east as you'll take us." Jonas shot a glance at Katie.

Herman said, "I'm making my way from Colorado to Sanibel Island in Florida."

"I understand it's out of your way, so if you could just get us as close to northern Georgia as possible," Jonas said. "We don't want to burden you."

"I'm retired, friend, so I'm in no hurry; if you're not in a rush, and don't mind stopping at some camp sites along the way, I'll happily take you right to your friend's door." He grinned as he slapped his knee.

"That sounds just fine," Jonas said. "I'd be forever indebted to you."

"Don't mention it, man. It's actually great to have company. I've been on the road for a long time. Don't get me wrong, Chance is great but the conversation tends to be a bit one sided." He laughed.

"I'd imagine so. Seems like a big rig just for you and the pup."

"The missus passed, three years ago, June 28th." The man scratched his chest.

"I'm very sorry." Jonas nodded with respect.

"Thank you. Claire was a remarkable woman. This RV was our life dream. We've been saving for this thing since we got married twenty-two years ago. We planned on spending our retirement seeing all the places we've dreamed about.

"A few months after we bought it she was diagnosed with breast cancer. By that time, it was too late. It had already gotten into her lymph nodes and fully metastasized within her lungs.

"I promised her that Chance and I would carry out our plans and visit all the places we talked about. Claire's fantasy was to spend a week in Sanibel, getting pampered in the spa. I guess Chance is gonna' have one mean doggie facial and pedicure in her memory." Herman smiled again. "So, that's it. You know everything worth knowing about me now. Tell me something about yourself. Where are you folks from?"

And there it was, Jonas thought to himself. It never took long before people got a little too inquisitive for his own liking.

"Long way from here." He stared into the darkness.

"Oh come on, now, man. I practically bore my soul to you, and that's all you got?" Herman chuckled. "You're going to have to trust somebody."

"Trustin' ain't something I'm much accustomed to," Jonas answered.

"I hear you, brother, but I'm not sure life is even worth living if you don't have anyone you can rely on. Know what I'm saying?"

Jonas regarded the talkative man. "Historically, that ain't worked out so well for me."

Herman, still laughing, shook his head. "Man, you are jaded! The world's actually a pretty good place. You really should get out and see it sometime."

"Yeah? I've seen a lot of death, evil, and sadness in my life, but one thing I ain't seen much of in the world is good."

"All the same, brother, there's always hope," Herman said.

"I'll take your word for it," Jonas replied.

Herman was unsure if he had offended his new acquaintance and decided not to say anything more. When they drove on unspeaking, for nearly twenty minutes, Jonas's silence confirmed his annoyance.

"Oregon," Jonas said out of nowhere.

"Oregon! Now, we're talking! That's some beautiful country up there. What would ever make you leave that place?"

Again, he did not answer.

Herman peeked at Jonas from the corner of his eye. "Where can a man run to escape the shadow of troubles so determined to follow?"

Jonas frowned. "Who said anything about running?"

"Like I said, I was born with great instincts. I'm seldom wrong about people but on the rare occasion I'm off, Chance here keeps me honest."

"Speaking of the dog, doesn't he need to go out soon?" Jonas said in a transparent attempt at changing the subject.

Herman smiled, letting him off the hook. "Don't worry about Chance. He loves travel but hates being cooped up too long. I tend to stop pretty frequently to let him stretch. Besides, if he really needs to go that badly, he usually just let's himself out. He's really quite self-sufficient that way."

"What do you mean he just let's himself out? How does a dog do that?"

"Just that...he'll literally open the door if he needs a break."

Jonas turned to look at the door.

"How is that safe? What if he got out in traffic?"

"We've been together a very long time." Herman smiled. "Chance is a man's dog and knows how to handle himself."

120

"Now, don't that just beat all." Jonas shook his head in sincere amazement.

"So," Herman glanced at him, "it wouldn't be me if I didn't ask. Did you do it?"

"Mister, my soul is as black as sackcloth and I'm in need of absolution for a great many things. Lord knows I ain't no angel, but I certainly ain't done what they say I've done."

"What exactly is it they say you've done?"

Jonas passed a subtle glance to Katie, who sat on the bench seat behind the man.

Oddly enough, for once he seemed to be searching her face for consent to speak candidly.

"What are you, a priest?" Jonas scoffed, and this time— he really was offended.

"Me? No—hardly. I just think everybody needs to clear their conscience and put down their burdens."

"For an Indian, you sure sound like a home-grown, tree-lovin' hippie."

"I was born in the U.S. and am just as American as you, friend. And, just like everyone else, wishes the world was a better place."

"Wishin' don't make anything so," Jonas said flatly. "I believe you mentioned having beer?"

"Yep, right in the fridge. Naturally, I'll pass but go ahead and help yourself."

"Thanks." Jonas stood and limped to the fridge. He took out the first aid kit, then cleaned and bandaged his eye. A few minutes later, returned with a cold six pack in his hand.

"There you go, man!" Herman cheered.

Katie sat with one leg under her and the Akita's head across her thigh. She patted the giant head softly, watching as her friend returned to his seat and plopped down.

She wondered how much he would actually confide in the man. Figuratively, Jonas took it upon himself to carry the weight of the world on his shoulders, and it was apparent. It was unhealthy to always remain so keyed up, burying his emotions the way he did. After so long on the road together she knew Jonas well, but in many senses, he still internalized most things, as if trying to shield her from their bleak outlook.

Maybe more than anything, right now, he needed a real buddy. She smiled inwardly, happy to see someone he could really relate to. It was cute the way the two of them talked away, bouncing seamlessly from one topic to the next, like school boys with no real cares.

She knew he liked Herman if for no other reason than his light-hearted, positive view of things. She liked him, too. He seemed like the type of friend Jonas needed—a friend they both needed. No reason to believe he was anything other than the person he came off as—a lonely, kind man looking for some good conversation.

Still, they had been wrong before.

***

A third six pack later, Jonas had completely forgotten about his bruised eye and no longer felt soreness in his leg.

"As it turns out, we were one hundred-twenty klicks behind enemy lines, doing recon for a large offensive. We hadn't slept in days and our unit was exhausted. Me and my buddy Frank were on watch that night. I dozed off for what couldn't have been more than a minute, but I came to just in time to see him disappear into the jungle.

"He got spooked and went off chasin' ghosts. I knew it was only in his head. Problem was, the Viet Cong really was

122

out there just lying in wait. Inadvertently, Frank stumbled right through them and gave away our camp's position. By the time he and I circled back, they had cut us off and hit our base camp. A firefight broke out, but our men never had a chance.

"It was my fault because I knew he needed help in the head and didn't tell anyone. I was the only one who saw it, but Frank hadn't been right for weeks. Comin' in, he had always been the cut up, always upbeat and darn near always poking fun at someone—so much so, we gave him the call sign Joker. He was a good-natured cat and very little ever got to him, but in the weeks leading up to that night, everything changed.

"He started getting irritable and jumpy and not only that, but was having nightmares all the time. With the horrible stuff we saw, I suppose we all had them, but when Frank started seeing things that no one else saw, I finally decided to speak to him. He begged me to not say anything to anyone because he didn't want to get sent home. He was married but the unit was his life."

Herman glanced at him. "That's horrible, brother, did they all die?"

"All accept one." Jonas took a long swig. "My best friend Richard Trask."

"When's the last time you saw him?"

"We haven't spoken since that day, forty-three years ago. I haven't been able to face him."

"What about your buddy Frank? Did he have family?" Herman asked.

Jonas was quiet for several long moments. "He had a wife and a baby on the way."

"Oh no." Herman shook his head. "I don't know much about the military but from what I understand, at that time,

123

dishonorable discharge in death was probably the end of his benefits for his widow."

"Yep—if the military had known the truth."

"What do you mean?" Herman looked at him, brow drawn down.

"Rather than letting his name be dishonored and have his family endure that shame, I took the heat. The price of my sins was eight years in Ft. Leavenworth, and as far as I am concerned I deserved every day of it. If I had just told somebody that Frank was coming unglued, he would have made it home, and none of the others would have died, so it's all on me."

At this, Herman shook his head with sorrow. "You gotta clear it, talk to him, man. Don't carry something like this for the rest of your days. You owe it to yourself to lay down your burden."

Jonas's eyes began misting up, and he quickly turned toward his window.

Katie was stunned by his painful revelation. As close as they were, this was a part of him she did not know. A shade of a troubled past that he never shared with anyone before now. For the first time, she realized his fear of letting someone down was the reason he never let anyone get close. And more, she understood the tremendous guilt this poor man bore and why he felt he would never live down his mistakes—he genuinely felt there was blood on his hands.

She was broken hearted for him, and tears welled in her eyes. She experienced anguish so deeply, she had to resist the overwhelming urge to throw her arms around his neck and hug him. Katie knew, among other things, he was a deeply prideful man. She would not embarrass him further, so she let him be, alone in his sorrow.

Chapter 17

Herman, forever the gentlemen, insisted that Katie take the bedroom in the back. She tried to protest but he said it was simply an offense for her not to accept. When Jonas joined in the discussion, she grudgingly obliged him. He assured her that the sofa and the pull out bed were equally as comfortable. He and Jonas flipped for the pullout, which Jonas won, but to his dismay, was apparently Chance's favorite spot, too.

Every night, as soon as Jonas lay down, before his head was comfortably on the pillow, Chance jumped in and slept beside him. With every instance, Jonas showed his genuine lack of affinity for dogs, complained incessantly about the 'doggone' mutt. His displeasure was always met with laughter from Katie and Herman.

This continued for weeks, but over time, Jonas got used to it, and though he would never openly admit it, he grew fond of Chance.

They took their time as they made their way through Louisiana. During those weeks, they stopped at numerous campsites and did quite a bit of fishing. Katie held Jonas to the promise made long ago to take her to the ocean, and they also spent several days taking in the gulf coast.

Jonas and Herman quickly formed a deep bond as if they had been lifelong friends. The brooding countenance that had perpetually clouded his face since he rescued her, amazingly lifted, and for the first time, she saw a lighter, much less burdened side of him.

Still, the many years on the run were catching up with him and she saw him physically age in front of her eyes. Of course, she never called attention to it, but she noticed how often he massaged his joints or clawed at his muscles as if trying to get to a deep-rooted itch. Though he never complained, it became more obvious over the passing weeks and she could not help being concerned.

Anytime she asked Jonas how he was doing, he said in a dismissive demeanor that he was fine, and that would be the end of it.

***

Katie said good night, and politely excused herself for the evening. She left them, Jonas taking his turn at the wheel and Herman in the passenger seat, deeply engaged in another one of their never ending philosophical conversations. This one had something to do with U.S. foreign affairs. She had little knowledge or interest of American politics and decidedly little substantive opinion either way.

Working on the third consecutive day of a nasty migraine, she made her way into the back room, locked the door, and turned off all the lights. She lay down in the quiet, dark room as the dizzying disorientation triggered by the migraine washed over her in pounding waves. The motion of the RV made her nauseous, but the feeling subsided and she drifted into sleep.

***

In the still of the dark room, a white light pulsated in the corner, a few feet from where she slept. As the gleam dissipated, a bird-like apparition materialized on the dresser, then silently transformed into a woman dressed in black and scarlet. The woman, crouching atop the stand, watched the sleeping girl from the shadows. Without a sound, she slipped from the stand and moved across the small space before creeping onto the sheets.

In the front cab section, Chance whimpered and paced, but Herman, engaged in a deep debate, did not notice the dog's agitation.

"Jonas, I think Chance needs to make a pit stop." Herman said finally. "Will you pull over at the next place it's safe to do so?"

"Absolutely, think he can hold it for a few more minutes? There's not enough of a shoulder here for me to get over."

"You're going to have to hold on a little while longer, buddy boy." Herman said, reaching out to pat him, but the dog drew away.

Chance, half whining, half howling—began pacing circles between him and the bedroom door.

The woman slithered along the bed and straddled Katie. With both hands, she grabbed her throat. The attack woke Katie and she flailed, thrashing back and forth, fighting the woman's grip. Her strong, icy grasp held steadfastly unmovable around Katie's neck.

Then she tightened her powerful vice and leaned within

inches of her face, and began to inhale. As she breathed in, Katie felt her soul, her essence, slip away.

The girl tried to scream but a nearly inaudible gurgle was all that left her lips. In panic, she tried to extend her thoughts to Jonas.

Assyria smiled, tightening her grasp even more. The woman spoke to her mentally, assaulting her with her own wraith telepathic abilities. *He can't hear you, insufferably foolish child. You're going to die and I will have the Artifact.*

"What's gotten into you?" Herman asked. He reached out again to pet the dog. Chance growled and began barking animatedly.

"Jonas, I think he isn't too pleased with having to wait."

The canine grabbed Herman's sleeve and dragged him from his seat. "That's enough! Bad dog! What in the world is going on with you? Sit!"

Chance barked again, before dashing through the RV, and scratched at the bedroom door.

"Everything okay back there?" Jonas asked with worry. He glanced in the side mirror at the car behind them and stuck his arm out the window, motioning for the driver to pass. Herman walked to the back of the RV and rapped firmly on the door.

"Katie, are you okay?" he shouted over Chance's frenzied barking.

"Settle down!" Herman tried pulling the dog away from the door and knocked again. "You okay in there?" He jiggled the doorknob.

"What's wrong?" Jonas called.

"Katie!" Herman pounded on the door repeatedly.

"Katie!"

Jonas turned on the flashing hazard lights and having no shoulder, slowed the vehicle in the middle of the highway. He noticed a narrow service road barely wide enough for the RV to fit through.

Herman took a step back from the door and kicked it three times before the frame collapsed. He saw the woman wearing black straddled over Katie. The woman hovered inches from her face when he dove into her and stripped her from the bed. They crashed into the mirrored glass closet door.

Katie gasped for air as Herman fought to keep the writhing woman subdued. When he pinned her shoulders to the ground, he became captivated by an alluring, otherworldly beauty and found himself unable to look away from her. Asian features and long, chest-length black hair, perfect eyebrows framed a strong, round face that held him seductively transfixed by her lifeless Cimmerian almond-shaped eyes.

Bewitched by her sirenic gaze, he leaned down to kiss her as she raised her head from the floor to meet him. Movement in the mirror caught his attention. He turned his gaze toward the broken glass on the door and paused.

His hands appeared to be grasping only air, and the woman's reflection showed her standing on the opposite side of the bed—watching him wrestle with an invisible entity.

His mouth fell agape. *How is that possible?*

She grabbed him under the armpit and dug her claws behind his pectoral. He screamed and in pain, dipped to his side. In a flash, she flipped him onto the floor. The woman lunged at his throat as he tried to hold her at bay. She easily broke free of his grasp and plunged her fangs into the side of his neck.

Chance seized her by the wrist just as Jonas hurried into the bedroom. He raised his weapon to shoot and instantly the woman dematerialized and was gone.

Katie gagged and wretched onto the floor. On the other side of the bed, Herman lay in a huddled mass on the shattered mirrored glass that covered the floor.

Jonas sat on the side of Katie's bed. "You all right?" He observed the conspicuous handprints that marred her throat.

She sobbed, shaking her head.

"We're gonna' be okay. She's gone." He assured her, putting his arm around her shoulder. "Hold tight, I gotta' check on Herman."

He kneeled to put Herman's arm around his shoulders and lift him.

"Please get Chance out of here, he'll get glass stuck in his paws," Herman said, holding his neck.

"The dog will be fine. It's not him I'm worried about. Let's get you some room and fresh air."

Jonas led him to the forward section of the RV and placed him on the couch.

"I'll be right back," he said, and went back to check on Katie again. While he was helping her from the bedroom, the vehicle's door opened, and their friend stumbled down the stairs.

They exited the RV. Outside, Herman sat against a tree in front of the vehicle with the alert dog beside him.

Jonas crouched on one knee next to his friend.

"How many times have you been bit?"

Herman coughed painfully, and blood dripped from his mouth.

"Three, now," he responded.

Jonas looked away in disgust. "Why the hell didn't you tell us you'd been infected?"

"I was lonely and desperate for a friend and I didn't want you to be afraid. I'm very sorry I wasn't completely honest with you." He coughed again. "It's not exactly the kind of thing you volunteer up to people."

"How did you keep it from us, Herman?" Jonas asked with an angry tone.

"What do you mean?" he asked, genuinely confused.

"Don't play me. You know exactly what I mean. I know the symptoms of this thing. The paranoia—sweats—shaking hands. I've seen it too many times. I mean I was suspicious when I saw you scratch your arm a few times, but it wasn't that bad so I gave you the benefit of the doubt. Somehow you were able to hide all of this from me and I want to know how."

"Jonas, he doesn't know," Katie said. "Doesn't matter, anyway."

"It does matter! There's always a sign, something's not right," Jonas snapped.

He patted the man's pockets and pulled out a pill bottle.

"What's that?" she asked.

Jonas strained his eyes to read the label under the flashing hazards.

"It's Clozapine, an antipsychotic. I'd bet that's why he wasn't caught up with the paranoia and hallucinations."

"The doc gave that to me to help me cope with Claire's death." Herman winced. All the while, Chance continued barking.

"I can't hear myself think over that darn dog!" Jonas snapped. "Katie, take him inside and keep him there!"

She took the dog by the leash and opened the door.

"Come on, boy," she called.

Chance turned, looking at Herman.

"Go on." He motioned for him to follow her.

The dog obediently trotted in front of her and jumped inside the RV. Once inside, Katie closed the door. Her ears rattled with the thunderous *BOOM BOOM* of deafening gun shots just outside the vehicle.

Katie drew her gun and raced through the door. Arms listless at his side, pistol in his right hand, Jonas stood over Herman in the amber glow of the flashing hazards.

"What did you do?" Katie screamed. She lowered her gun, sobbing in heaving waves. "Oh God, Jonas, what did you do?"

"Don't ever lose sight of the monsters this sickness turns people into," he replied. "We had no choice."

"That's bull! There's always a choice! He saved my life, Jonas—he was our friend!" she screamed with angry tears streaming down her face.

"No matter who it is—no mercy, you hear me? No mercy," Jonas said with a dispassionate facial expression that matched the coldness of his voice.

"Keep an eye out." He shuffled back into the RV and closed the door. She stared at the man in pity. Inside, she heard the sound of cabinet doors slamming shut and things thrown around. He returned a few minutes later with a large plastic bottle of lighter fluid.

"Please, don't do this. We need to bury him!" she pleaded. Jonas pulled the man into the center of a clearing, away from the trees and underbrush. He doused the body in lighter fluid and without hesitation, set it aflame.

"I know it's hard to believe but trust me—the killin' will

133

get easier over time."

She sobbed, forlorn of comfort. "Not for me, it won't."

They stood in silence as the flames consumed their friend. Jonas came to stand next to her, but Katie turned away and went back inside.

Chapter 18

Journal Entry: June 25, 2019

I tried to talk to Jonas about the incident two days ago in the RV, but he got really angry, so I let it go. I am really bothered with the thoughts of the woman who attacked me that night. She was the same person we saw on the road in Texas. How is it possible that hundreds of miles later in Louisiana, she ends up in the vehicle with us?

She is not the same as the other wraiths. Her powers are different—they are much stronger. When she fought with Herman, she cast no reflection and when she attacked me, her dead, black eyes pierced me, raping my mind.

When she pinned me down and tried to kiss me, I think she was actually stealing my breath. Since then, day and night, I am filled with dark thoughts, and I'm sure it's because of what she tried to do to me. I know if she had completed the kiss, something horrible would have happened. Even with all my abilities—I felt completely powerless against her.

We have no real hope of standing against something so evil. I am very scared.

Journal Entry: June 26, 2019
*Jonas talks less and less now. He has become distant
and short tempered, growing more paranoid by the day. I
have no doubt the incident in the RV is weighing on him, but I
feel there's more he's not telling me.*

*A long time ago, he warned me to be suspicious of
everyone, and I challenged the notion that he, himself, would
ever be someone I could not trust. But the night he ended
Herman's life, I saw a side of him I had never seen. That
night, Jonas was cold and calculating—his judgment was
swift and indiscriminate. I love him like a father and nothing
will ever change that. Even so, he has changed, and I will
never see him the same again.*

*Herman has so many of the critical things we need. We
were out of water and food. The RV has unlimited water and
enough food to last a month. We were broker than broke.
Three hundred fifty-seven dollars were in his nightstand.
Some of his clothes were close enough to Jonas's size for him
to get by. That sweet Herman even still had some of his wife's
clothes in the closet!*

*Lucky for me I guess, some of them actually fit, but all
of it, even the food, makes me feel wretched inside and
reminds me of what happened out there. I am still angry at
burning his body instead of burying him. I understand the
risk of Herman's transformation but he was a kind, gentle
man, and a burial would have been far more respectful.*

*Jonas said we had to burn him, because cremation
was the only way to be sure.*

*I know I should be thankful. Out of this evil, there was
a blessing. Still—poor Herman deserved better than that, and
no matter how I look at it, I find myself at an unspeakable*

loss.

Chapter 19

Over the twelve long years since Jonas rescued Katie from the river, the days had quickly turned to months. He took every possible opportunity to teach her the critical skills she would need to stay alive. When it came to survival, he'd been an open book, instructing her on every tactic he had ever learned from his early boot camp days to his combat tours in two wars. Even things he picked up in prison.

Jonas prepared her for life in the wilderness, including hunting and foraging for food, guerilla warfare strategy and tactics, firearms training, and hand-to-hand combat, with the sword, staff, and knife. With little effort, she easily mastered everything he taught.

Katie possessed the most amazing total recall he had ever seen. Her attention to detail and execution were virtually flawless. She was an amazing student, and in a different set of circumstances, would have been considered the perfect soldier. Jonas would continue to protect her as long as he was able, but the day would come and she would be on her own, and he needed to prepare her for that eventual certainty.

***

They'd driven in an uncomfortable silence for 140 miles. She felt his eyes shift toward her several times as if he had something to say but didn't speak. Katie was as sick of the played out songs on her phone as she hid behind the music to kill the chasm of awkwardness that had become normal between them. She fidgeted with the drawstrings of her backpack before pulling out her journal. She started to write, and then slammed the book shut.

"All right, I'm tired of being your emotional tampon, so what gives?"

"What would ever make you think it is okay to speak to me like this?" Jonas asked.

"Now, that's funny!" Katie said, crossing her arms.

"What are you talking about?"

"I've tiptoed around you for months, afraid anything I say might set you off, and now *you're* the one who's sensitive? Seriously? Give me a break!"

"What's gotten into you, Katie?"

"Don't you dare turn this around, Jonas! I've tried talking to you for as long as I can remember and all you do is shut me out. You've got so many relationship issues that you can't open up to me about anything.

"Listen to us! We even fight like a married couple! Something has changed, and for the longest time, I've blamed myself, but you know what? I've realized the problem is not me.

"It's getting harder and harder to read you, and I barely know you anymore. You want to tell me what's going on, or are you going to keep pretending that 'everything is fine'?" She held up fingers mockingly quoting him.

"Would that I could," Jonas replied. His thoughts seemed to be elsewhere.

"What does that mean? Never mind, I know what it means—more games." She turned her face to the window. "I'm done!"

Another twenty-five minutes passed with neither speaking a word. Suddenly, his deep voice shattered the silence. "There's something I need to tell you. It ain't easy so

I'm just gonna' say it plain."

"I told you forget it, I don't care anymore."

"Jeez. How do I even tell you this?" His right hand tightened around the wheel. "I'm dying."

Katie quietly gazed in the direction of horses grazing nearby.

"Did you hear what I just said?" Jonas turned to her.

"I know."

He briefly glanced at her, in puzzled amazement. "What do you mean, *you know*? How could you possibly know?"

I think I've known for a long time." She fidgeted uncomfortably with the backpack on her lap. "It's hard to describe but ever since we left Oregon, I've felt an ever present pain whenever you're near me. Then, seemingly overnight, you lost a lot of your energy and always looked tired—much worse than before. Then that day at the diner, when Dorian asked you if I knew—for the first time, it all made sense.

"After all these years together, how could you keep something like this from me? How could you not tell me?" she asked with tears in her eyes. The colliding spectrum of emotions washing over her spanned from empathy for his fear and loneliness to a genuine sense of anger and betrayal that she'd been kept in the dark about his health.

He carefully considered his next words, but after doing so, still didn't know what to say. "You shouldn't feel bad. I never told anyone."

"I'm not just anyone. At least I didn't think I was." Katie again turned her face to the window.

"I'm sorry, little girl, you gotta' believe me, because over and over again, I tried to. I just couldn't find the way to tell you."

"How long do you have?" she asked, too hurt to look at him.

"Days? Weeks? Months? According to the doctor that diagnosed me before I journeyed to Africa, my shelf life should have expired years ago, so it's safe to say only God knows."

Chapter 20
Jackson, Mississippi: June 27

"How long has it been since you've been home?"

"Twenty-three years," he replied, guilt heavy in his tone.

Katie's brows rose. "Wow."

"Yeah."

Katie glanced at Chance lying calmly on the RV's sofa. "Can we take him inside the house?" The dog lifted his head and stared at her, as though he knew she was talking about him.

Jonas shook his head. "No, no. Chance will have to sleep in the RV. Momma's far more afraid of dogs than I'll ever be. If she saw him loose, she'd probably stroke out on the spot."

"I just feel bad about leaving him cooped up out here." Katie scratched under the Akita's muscular neck. "What about the barn? Maybe he could sleep out there."

"He'll be fine here. I don't necessarily want to have him runnin' around free."

"I don't understand what it is with black people and dogs."

"And you know so much about black people, right?"

"What's that supposed to mean?" Katie asked.

"When I was a kid, the police around here used dogs to keep folks in line. So you'll have to excuse me. For some of us, those memories die hard. Maybe, when you've lived a little, you can ask me about such things."

"Sorry. I didn't mean anything by it."

"Forget it. Just bad memories is all."

They emerged from the mobile home and looked around the small farm. The property was in disrepair and

141

unkempt. To his surprise, the chicken coops and pig pens were all empty.

"You grew up here?"

"Yeah, not much to look at, is it?"

"No. That isn't what I meant," she said awkwardly, trying not to take it personally, she'd been misapprehended twice in only a matter of minutes.

"This was home and believe it or not, for black folks in these parts, we had it pretty good."

"I think it's beautiful," Katie replied.

Jonas eyed the once bright canary yellow barn he painted in his teens, now faded to a dingy looking opaque. One of the oversized doors was missing several planks. The glass was broken out of two of the large windows. Along the edge of the overgrown dirty path to their right, cattails grew nearly chin high from the marshy edges of the moss covered pond he fished a thousand times as a boy.

A blue dragonfly the size of a hand flew past them in the direction of the pond. He caught a whiff of something indistinct that poignantly reminded him of the days he ran in these woods. Katie watched silently as he ambled closer to the water, where he bent and picked up a flat rock. He hurled the stone, skipping it seven times before it dipped into the center.

"Still got it." He smiled.

When Jonas returned to the top of the path, Katie followed him around the side of his mother's home. The once bright white siding—now a dingy shade of grey, hung in several places and was only one good storm from going the same way as the two shutters missing from the top window. Nearly every one of the post and beams of the brown fence surrounding the perimeter of the property were splintered or warped and desperately needing mending or outright replacement. Waist-high dandelions lined the wall and ivy bulged from the lattice underneath the front porch, which had a hole large enough for a child to fit through.

"Where's the holy water?" Katie asked as a thought popped into her mind.

Staring at the two and a half foot high weeds that had overrun the grounds, he felt guilty he hadn't been around.

"Here." He absently pulled the vial from his front pocket, and she held it close to her face, peering through the glass. No sparklies.

With the trepidation of a twenty-three year absence from home, Jonas took the toughest ten steps of his life. One banister leading up the paint-chipped riser, ravaged by termites, clung perilously to the side of the staircase. Resting atop the weather beaten porch: a pair of tattered wicker chairs. A white doily covered the surface of a faded hickory table his daddy built for his mother long ago. They stopped outside the door and Jonas raised his fist to knock. He paused, then reached for the knob.

"Anyone home?" With no response, he stepped into the house. "Hello."

Katie glanced around the room. "Maybe she's out."

Clear vinyl covered the majority of the floral print upholstered furniture cluttering the room. On the near wall, a large mirror hung above an antique piano lined with old photos.

Several seconds passed.

"Who's there?" a faint female voice replied.

Moments later, a delicate black woman emerged from the kitchen, dry dishtowel in her hand. For several moments, the old woman squinted at them.

Her facial expression held an acrimonious frown.

"Momma, it's me."

She came forward tentatively. "I thought...all these years...bless my stars. I thought you were dead!" Tears filled her eyes. The petite thinly-framed woman stopped in the middle of the room. "I can't believe this, my baby finally come home."

"Believe it. I'm home." He went to her, wrapping his long powerful arms around his delicate mother.

"I'm sorry, Momma." He rubbed her small back. "I'm so sorry."

The woman cried into his chest as Jonas held her in quiet embrace. The tender moment brought tears to Katie's eyes too. Being here, watching the long overdue reunion, made her feel like a voyeur whose prying eyes violated the sanctity of their moment. If she could transport herself to another place, she would have without hesitation.

"Momma, this is my friend Katie."

"Katie, it's good to meet you," she said.

"Thank you, ma'am, it's a pleasure to meet you too." Katie smiled, trying to cover the sting she felt of being introduced as anything less than family.

"How did you come by being friends?" His mother wiped the tears from her face.

Jonas sighed. "That is a very, very long story."

"Little girl, look at you!" She eyed Katie up and down. "Far as I can tell, you haven't eaten in weeks."

His mother turned to face Jonas, shaking her head disapprovingly.

"She's been eating fine, Momma."

"Nonsense, look at her." The woman gestured with her hand. "She's all skin and bones! Girl, come on in this kitchen and get you something to eat. I can't believe my baby boy is starvin' you like this. That just don't make no sense."

They both laughed at the playful reprimand.

"Momma thinks if a person's not overweight, they simply ain't eatin' right. And speaking of which, I smell something."

They followed Ms. Montgomery as she moseyed to the kitchen, her frailty all the more apparent. Katie motioned to Jonas to help his struggling mother but he did not understand what she was trying to tell him.

"Is that what I think it is?" he asked.

"Depends on what you think it is," his mother replied.

"Gumbo!" Jonas said with excitement.

"Yes indeed, an' raisin bread pudding."

"Oh, now that ain't right." Jonas smiled as he removed the lid and leaned over the slow boiling pot for a whiff. "Smells even better than I remember—when's supper?"

"Well, I got bad news for you because I just put on the pot a little bit ago. You know my slow pot gumbo won't be ready until tomorrow."

He stuck out his bottom lip in a playful pout.

"I'll whip up something for you, it'll just take a minute." She opened the cabinet.

"I can get it, Momma." Jonas told her.

"Boy, stop that. You know it won't take me but a second to throw something together."

He was about to protest further when she cut him a stern look that only a mother could give.

"All right then," he replied.

145

She set her dish towel on the counter, opened the fridge and dug around. "The cupboard's fairly bare because I haven't been to the market this week. I put most of what I had left in the gumbo. I figured I'd eat off it the whole week, and not have to go to the market until Saturday. If I'd known I'd be expecting company, I would have gone out already."

"You know what I've been missin'?"

"Funny. I always wondered if you'd ever outgrown 'em," she said.

"Never," he smiled, crossing to the cabinet. He took down two small plates and set them on the counter. His mother shook her head as she reached into the refrigerator door and pulled out a spotted, cold banana and a half loaf of buttermilk bread. The jar of crunchy peanut butter she retrieved from an otherwise bare pantry.

"May I help you with anything?" Katie asked.

"You can have a seat, you're a guest." His mother shooed her off, pointing to the small kitchen table by the window.

"Growing up, Jonas had a peanut butter and banana sandwich just about every day. Judging by the look on your face, I'd guess you'd rather have yours with jam instead?" She held up the large, nearly empty jar.

"Yes, ma'am, that's sounds great." Katie stifled a smile when Ms. Montgomery spread an insanely thick amount of peanut butter before plopping a large spoon of strawberry preserve in the middle of the sliced bread.

"Thank you," Katie said when his mother tottered to the table with the sandwiches and sat down to join them.

"So, you ain't raisin' hogs anymore?" Jonas poured three mason jars full of iced tea.

146

"Heavens no, I don't get around too well these days. My legs just ain't what they used to be. Can you even imagine me chasin' hogs around the yard at my age?"

A twinge of sadness peered from behind his smile. "How have you gotten by?"

"Boy, I'm not studying you. Stop fussin' about me."

"Seriously, Momma, how are you makin' do?"

"Food stamps, but before you get all worked up, don't forget the farm is paid off. It's not like I got babies to feed. The state don't give me much, but it's enough."

"Anything I can do to help?" he asked.

"Like what? I already told you I'm just fine. I've managed all these years, ain't no need in worry'n about me now."

Wracked with guilt, he fidgeted, even though he knew it was not an intended barb.

"Katie. Would you give us a minute?" he said in a soft voice. Katie sipped her tea nonchalantly, even as she was mentally prodding him.

Jonas, wait a sec. We need to test her.

His mother reached for the small pad on the table and thoughtfully scrawled a list of groceries she needed.

"The banana sandwich—only Momma could have known that." He mouthed.

That's all you've got?

Jonas frowned. He was annoyed by her thoughts, and it showed on his face.

"Did you notice the mirror above the piano? I saw her reflection—it's Momma. You saw the water, we both did! It was good. What's bugging you, Katie?" he said inaudibly.

You're right. I guess I'm all nerves—just trying to be

147

sure.

"Yes, of course," Katie said and excused herself from the table. She left the kitchen and walked towards a door in the hall.

"What are you looking for, dear?" his mother asked as Katie touched the knob. "That's the basement and there's a lot of junk down there. You're bound to trip on something and hurt yourself."

"I'm sorry. I was looking for the bathroom. I'd like to freshen up a bit, if that would be okay."

"Of course, it would. You'll find it farther down on the left."

"Thank you." Katie smiled.

Jonas waited until she had departed. He gazed across the table at his mother with a long, cheerless face. "Mom, I'm sorry about all of that stuff before with Daddy..."

"It's history, let it be," the woman replied.

"I understand but it has to be said."

"It wasn't your fault and what's done is done. I don't want to talk about that no more—" The woman abruptly broke off, looking toward Katie. "Little lady."

"Yes, ma'am?" she replied.

"You can stay in the room there at the end of the hall. Jonas will stay in his old room."

"That's not necessary, Momma. We have the RV outside. That's where we'll sleep."

"Sleep together in the car? You'll do no such thing, Jonas. It's not proper." She crossed her arms in disapproval.

"Yes, ma'am," he said in resignation.

***

Katie sprawled across the bed on her stomach as she

148

flipped through a magazine. She wanted sleep but even so late in the night, the poor ventilation in the house kept the room stagnant and hot. At wits end, she rolled off the bed and crossed the hardwood floor. She tried to open the window with the heels of her hands, but it would not budge.

"Oh come on! I'm dying in here." Finally, the seal weakened and the stubborn window gave, partially opening. She pressed her cheek against the screen, finding relief from the stale air by the unseasonably cool Mississippi breeze. Beyond her window, wind chimes clanged above the small back porch. The smell of gumbo drifted from outside the kitchen.

Nice woman, she thought, and figured things must have been really bad at one point for Jonas to walk away. She didn't know the details and was not about to judge him too harshly, but the better she got to know Mrs. Montgomery, the harder it was to swallow. The poor lady had been out here alone, all these years, with no one to look out for her. She didn't even have any neighbors close by.

Katie switched off the light before lying down. Jonas had checked on Chance and put him down for the night in the RV.

She turned onto her side and stared out the window. Thick clouds fully obscured the light of the moon. She had forgotten how quiet and dark it became in the country. No one would ever mistake Mississippi for Oregon, but the isolation of her farm felt far more secluded than the mountain range of Jonas's ranch. Here, far from the city lights of Jackson, the stygian black sky closed in like a magical darkness from a sinister fairy tale.

Katie seldom protested where they stayed, not that it

would have done much good. She had tried on numerous occasions to argue the benefits of city life and blending into the sea of unknown faces. That it was easier living amidst the hustle of people more concerned with getting where they had to be than bothering with who lived down the hall.

Besides, she argued, if ever the need for emergency services arose in the boonies, they were basically out of luck. Jonas stubbornly preferred rural areas for all the obvious reasons. Not the least of which the seclusion gave them a place to train far from the prying eyes of nosey neighbors.

Fewer people, he reasoned, meant less likelihood of some random citizen recognizing them and calling the cops. Those were all good reasons, but she didn't care. She was afraid of the solitude and not too ashamed to admit it.

Katie put her hands under her face. As she lay there, on the other side of the trees outside her bedroom window, a light came on in the barn. She stared at the barn's broken windows, hypnotically transfixed on the flickering shadow of an oscillating light within. Over what sounded like steel grinding on stone, she heard whistling.

What in the world is she doing out there this time of night? Katie was immediately bothered by the old lady being out alone, but tried to push the concern to the side. Ms. Montgomery made it clear she didn't need help doing the chores she's done for years on her own. Katie closed her eyes, but her conscience spoke up. *I should see if she needs help anyway.*

"Uggh!" She rolled to the side of the bed. When lacing her boots, a familiar tune crept through the open window—Dorian's song in the diner. Her blood turned cold. Ms. Montgomery's voice carried the melody:

"Oranges and lemons, Say the bells of St. Clement's.

You owe me five farthings, Say the bells of St. Martin's.

When will you pay me? Say the bells of Old Bailey—"

Katie crouched to pass under the window as she moved around the foot of the bed.

"—When I grow rich, Say the bells of Shoreditch.

When will that be? Say the bells of Stepney.

I do not know, Says the great bell of Bow.

Here comes a candle to light you to bed,

And here comes a chopper to chop off your head!"

Katie opened the closet and retrieved her sword, slipping its sheath over her shoulder before picking up the Artifact. She looked around for a safe place to hide it. The girl climbed onto the radiator, pushed aside a ceiling panel, and placed the chest inside.

After carefully returning the panel to its place, she jumped down and reached under her pillow to grab her pistol. A moment later, she tiptoed down the hallway toward Jonas's room. She turned the doorknob and slipped inside.

"Something is wrong," she whispered with urgency. Then, her gaze fell to his unmoving arm, outside the blanket that covered him. She moved closer.

"Jonas?" Katie pulled the covers from his face. When he stirred, she breathed a sigh of relief. "Wake up! Something's going on."

He rubbed his eyes, muttering incoherently. The strong smell of whiskey rose from his breath.

"You're drunk? Come on. Get up—I think one of them is here!"

"What are you going on and on about now, lil' girl?" He sounded perturbed.

151

"There's a light on in the barn and I can't find your mother."

"So? Maybe she needed something out there."

"Oh, come on. You are drunk if you don't find anything odd about a ninety-ish year-old woman who doesn't get around well, going out to the barn by herself, and in the middle of the night, no less."

"Just wait a doggone minute, and stop your fussin'. I'll check on her." He patted around the blankets looking for something.

"There's more." Katie peered through the door. "My window was open and I heard her whistling. It was the same creepy rhyme Dorian sang that day in the diner."

"So what are you saying?" Jonas rose unsteadily to his feet.

"I'm saying we've got to find her and get out of here."

As he stood, her eyes fell over his white tank top and shorts. She had never seen his arms. He always wore long sleeves.

Sporadic sores covered his arms and torso—sores from self-inflicted fingernail marks where he had scratched so often. It seemed impossible she'd never noticed him picking at his skin.

Highly transparent bluish-green veins branched beneath his dry and cracked skin. The cancer, the years on the run, the drinking—all of which explained the solemnity of a face painted with the weariness of a long, hard life. If the cancer didn't catch up with him, the whiskey would, but these sores—these were something much worse. It was his gradual transformation taking place before her, and she had been too close to see it.

Jonas caught the look on her face and threw on his denim long sleeve shirt. He opened the nightstand drawer and removed his pistol, then concealed it under his shirt.

"Let's check it out," he said, clearly cross with her.

He opened the door and slid past Katie into the hall. She trailed behind him, pistol in hand. From the den, they peeked into the kitchen. The back door leading into the yard stood ajar. The dingy white curtains around the window flapped in the breeze coming through the open door. The pot of gumbo on the range continued its slow rolling boil. As they scanned the room, Jonas shot her a brief glance that revealed the grave concern he realized for his mother. Katie was right, something was off and now he felt it too.

He drew the pistol from his waistband.

The kitchen door slammed shut causing them both to aim that direction. A moment later a crash rang up from storm cellar beneath them. Katie moved to the hallway door Ms. Montgomery told her to steer clear of.

Jonas pointed at Katie, motioning for her to open it and move aside. He stood with his gun trained on the door. Katie turned the knob and swung it open. He slid closer to the dark entry at the top of the stairs and flipped the switch. The light flickered a brief second before the bulb shorted.

"Stay here," he said.

He pulled a flashlight from his pocket and warily proceeded down the dark stairs.

Katie covered him from the top until he turned out of sight.

Jonas felt claustrophobic in the dank cellar which reeked of mildew and rotted wood. From the floor to the ceiling, old bed frames, broken tools, a splintered work table, and several old appliances that hadn't worked in decades, filled the cobweb laden room. Jonas stepped over old fence posts, careful to avoid the jagged nails protruding from the planks. He continued forward through the small row of debris lining both sides of the basement.

In the back end of the cellar was a crawl space under the house—the room Jonas and his brother never wanted to go near as children.

He had never been afraid of the dark, but for reasons he could never explain, the basement always made him uncomfortable. Even now, after all these years, the very sight ahead brought back those feelings of unease. He panned the flashlight's beam across the room while he worked toward the rear, observing broken glass on the floor and on top of an old dresser underneath the window frame.

Jonas passed through a row of ceiling-high shelves, lined with cans of paint, mason jars, and his mother's old sewing machine. In his peripheral vision, he glimpsed movement on the other side of the half glass, half wooden door separating the basement from the crawl space. His attention honed on the smaller room when something clattered inside. A pair of red eyes peered from within.

The closed quarters of the cinderblock walls echoed deafening gunshots, obliterating the window and mason jars. An inhuman screech tore through the space as he continued to fire.

Seconds later, a wounded opossum scurried from the room past the ray of his flashlight. With hesitancy, Jonas pushed the door with his foot and entered the small room.

He shone his light around the dark space but saw nothing other than more junk and a large ceramic water jug that had fallen from the shelf and shattered on the floor.

The door at the top of the stairs slammed shut.

Katie pulled on the knob but the door would not move. Katie backed away, as she prepared to shoot out the knob. Hairs on the back of her neck tingled as if someone watched. Behind her, Ms. Montgomery had entered the kitchen through the back door. Katie turned to glance at the woman already halfway across the room.

"What's going on?" His mother drew nearer.

"Jonas is down there and the door slammed shut and locked but there's no lock on either side." Katie leaned against the door. "Are you okay down there?"

"I'm all right." Jonas's faint reply trickled from the depths of the basement.

"Where were you, Ms. Montgomery?" Katie turned to face her. The woman stood in the middle of the living room, holding a heavy three-foot lead pipe. "I was out in the barn tending to things."

"Tending to what exactly?" Katie adjusted her grip on the pistol to her side.

"Young lady, I don't much like your tone. I'd suggest you mind your p's and q's."

"Pardon my manners indeed, but you still didn't answer my question." Katie moved farther from the door. "I have the gut feeling you're not who you're pretending to be."

"I don't know what's gotten' into you, little miss, but I'm afraid you're mistaken," the elderly woman scoffed.

Katie needed proof to verify her intuition. With a stone poker face, she tested the old lady. "Where's your apron? Thought you said you never take it off?"

"When I finish cooking, I put it away. Don't be silly."

155

Wrong answer.

The frail black woman smiled, tapping the heavy pipe against her thigh. Though the façade of Jonas's mother remained, her soft voice was replaced by Dorian's. "Put that thing away. Even if you could hit me, you know by now your weapons have no real effect on me." Then, he held his hand over a tabletop fan and it launched at Katie's face. All she could do was throw her hands up.

The fan's whirling blades smacked into her gun; the sharp metal cutting her hand, sending the dislodged weapon sliding on the floor. Katie scanned for the pistol but didn't see it. In pain, she drew the katana strapped around her shoulders, and stood ready to defend herself.

When Dorian saw the thin stream of blood course down the girl's forearm, he was filled with an insatiable blood lust. "It's getting late, so let's finish it. I'm still very sore about how things ended the last time we were together. You burned my face and left so fast, I didn't have a chance to say a proper goodbye." The smile vanished from the petite woman's face, and in a flash—the small body sprang across the room, over the sofa, landing in front of Katie.

Katie slashed trying to hold off the wraith's attacks, but with paranormal elusiveness, he parried and with an unbridled assault, blitzed Katie with the heavy pipe.

Jonas heard the sound of clashing lead and steel filling the living room above him. He dashed through the refuse, sprinting to the top of the dark cellar stairs. He threw his shoulder into the storm reinforced door again and again, but could not get it to open.

Just on the other side, Katie blocked the malevolent concussions, but the much heavier lead pipe rattled her with every blow. She hit him with a rapid succession of punches before smashing him across the face with her elbow.

Black blood oozed from his nostril. Dorian wiped his face, stunned she hurt him. Whirling a front round kick, she caught him by surprise and connected with the side of his face. Her second attack—a reverse hook kick—missed when he ducked under her thrashing leg. He dove forward and seized Katie, hurling her against the wall.

She slid to the floor, disoriented. He came for her. Her hand lifted the blade as the pipe smashed on her right forearm. She screamed and her sword skidded across the hardwood floor. Without hesitation, the menacing phantasm of Jonas's mother advanced upon the weaponless girl.

"Where is the Artifact? I know it's close. You're going to give it to me, and then I'm going to do to your pretty little face what you've done to mine."

She backed away from him, sneaking a glance of her sword on the floor, no more than ten feet away.

"Think you can make it?" he taunted. "Go for it."

Closer to the kitchen, Jonas fired at the heavy lock then kicked the door. The middle of the thin barrier gave way and splintered wood flew into the living room. "Get away from her!" he shouted.

Dorian turned toward him. Katie edged her way nearer to the sword.

"Where's my mother?" Jonas pointed his gun at the visage of the woman.

"Sugar, it's me," Dorian said.

"Cut the crap. You ain't foolin' nobody with this charade."

"I don't know, Jonas, seems I've fooled you just fine."

157

The wraith laughed.

"I'm gonna' ask you one last time. Where is she?"

Dorian's face held a wicked smile. "She's closer than you think." His voice rose as if a child sitting on a mammoth secret.

Jonas scanned the room, careful to keep the man in his sight.

"What's the matter—you don't see her? Hmmm...maybe you should check the pot."

"You're a liar!" he screamed.

"Am I now? Go on and check it yourself."

Wracked with pain, Katie held her left arm. "Jonas, he's lying! Don't believe a word out of his stinking mouth."

Jonas scooted toward the kitchen, weapon still trained on Dorian. His eyes fixated on the boiling pot atop the white range. At that second, the sight and the smell of the churning gumbo nauseated him.

He could not breathe. Perspiration beaded his forehead and his heart pounded as he willed himself the last few steps to the stove.

A fit of maniacal laughter came over Dorian. "Isn't it the darndest thing, how most everyone loves sausage, but no one, and I really mean no one, wants to see how it's made."

"I'll kill you! I'll kill you!" With a crazed look in his eyes, Jonas turned and fired. Rounds pulverized walls and furniture. Katie dove between the coffee table and sofa. She scrambled along the floor trying to recover her sword.

After the gun emptied, Jonas hurled the useless weapon at Dorian, who raised his hand and the pistol flew past him. Jonas charged the wraith boss, throwing erratic punches his supernatural dexterity evaded. Dorian snatched his fist midair and squeezed. The sound of cracking bones sent the large man to the floor.

"You should be on your knees when you are in my presence," Dorian snarled, looming over him. He raised the pipe over Jonas's head. Through the open kitchen door, Katie saw a flash of white, then Chance sprang, blitzing the monster from his blind side. The unexpected impact of the hundred-plus pound dog knocked Dorian from his feet.

The wraith screamed as the dog bit onto his wrist and thrashed its large white head side to side. Dorian dropped the pipe and Chance went for his throat, clamping his powerful jaws in a death grip.

Dorian clawed at the Akita protected by its mane of thick fur. He punched its underbody until Chance yelped and recoiled. Dorian jumped up, hoisted the animal overhead, and hurled him across the room, crashing into the piano.

Katie grabbed the katana from the floor as Dorian dashed from the house, escaping into the night. She hurried to the front door and stepped outside, down the porch stairs. Chance limping, followed close behind.

Jonas returned to the kitchen, and full of fear, removed the lid of the pot. He put the ladle inside and stirred the mixture before raising the scoop.

With a loud sigh of relief, he dropped the spoon, which clanged against the metal range.

"Thank you," he said in exasperation.

Katie crept toward the barn, peering through the night shadows at the unbarred door ahead. It opened and slammed shut in the wind as she approached. There was a nightmarish familiarity to the entire situation that terrified her so much she

159

fought down the compulsion to flee. Katie slipped inside, and though hardly able to raise her sword from injuries to her right arm and hand, she readied herself for confrontation. Tucked against the back wall, the GTO from the diner was parked with lights off and engine silent.

She advanced toward the vehicle, imagining the moment its motor would roar to life and run her down. Drawing nearer, Katie scoped for movement inside but the car was empty. Dorian was nowhere to be seen. Her eyes went to a utility light attached to an extension cord, hanging from a rafter in the ceiling.

She edged through the shed, with Chance on her heels. When she saw a brown rubber tool bin ahead of her, her mind flashed to the childhood nightmare in Oregon: *A dream where she'd gone into to the barn just like this one to calm the animals during a storm. She'd hidden inside a very similar container, and tried—without success, to escape the wolf-like creatures that came inside and slaughtered her cattle. Then, moments later, one of the monsters had snatched her from the container...*

Chance began whimpering before Katie peered around the wall of the first stall. When she saw the gruesome scene before her; she almost retched. She scrambled outside and toward the house.

Jonas loped in her direction with a shotgun he found in the closet. Katie intercepted him ten yards outside the barn's door,

"Where is she?" he asked, still in stride.

"No. You can't go in there, Jonas. You can't." Tears streamed down her face.

"Get out of my way."

"No!" she bawled. "Please don't!"

She raised her arm in front of her to stop him.

"Get out of my way, now!" he yelled.

"I'm so sorry," she repeated several times, throwing her arms around him, clinging to him with what remained of her strength, refusing to let him pass.

His legs gave way and he leaned against her, sobbing.

Katie held him in silence until he stopped, and then she turned to face the barn.

"Burn it to the ground," she said resolutely.

Jonas gazed unspeaking at the barn, questioning how much longer they could do this. He was one mistake away from getting them both either arrested or killed. He was slipping, even in his oft drunken state, he knew it. His friends were either gone or dead, and now, so was the last of his kin.

The sole living member of his unit was in northern Georgia. He was reluctant to bring any of this down on his old friend, but he knew there was little choice. He needed someone he could count on.

That crazy redneck Richard Trask was all he had left.

Chapter 21

North Georgia, June 28

As they drove up the winding mountain road, Jonas had a knot in his stomach the size of a grapefruit. He played the moment in his head over and over again, but now that the time was here, his courage failed him. He brought the RV to a sudden stop. As he stared at the private drive, his mind flashed back.

He gazed at the picture of his unit above the mantle of the fireplace in his cabin. He hadn't looked directly at the eleven men in the frame in many years. His guilt forced him to keep the albatross in plain view to allow their silent ghosts to provoke him every time he passed them.

He leaned forward in his chair and extinguished the ashes of the cigarette butt. He picked up the remote and turned on the TV. He didn't bother to look at the screen posing only as background noise to drown the somber silence that filled the room. His blurred attention turned to the coffee table in front of him where lay five .44 Magnum rounds lined next to the Smith and Wesson revolver and a bottle of whiskey.

He topped off his glass and then took a long swig from the bottle. Wracked by a violent fit of coughing, he rose from his chair and stumbled into the bathroom, spitting a mouthful of blood into the sink. When he looked at himself in the mirror, blood was splattered around his mouth and trickling from his nose. He wiped the blood away, washed his face, then returned to his chair in the living room, where he continued his drinking, working the bottle throughout the evening, until it was almost empty.

His whole life had been nothing but one failure after

the next, and in the end had amounted to nothing of consequence. And he had grown tired of living out an insignificant existence.

Over the years, he had played out this very same ritual countless times, but on this—the sixth consecutive time this week, he plopped down in the usual chair, preparing to up the ante. He reached for the wooden handle of the revolver and attempted to steady his trembling hand as he loaded five shells into the chamber instead of one.

Standing on the razor's edge of mortality made it difficult to calm himself as he tried to insert the last one. He was more ready to die than ever before, and he found it ironic that the mere act of increasing the probability of that success had caused him an apparent wavering of nerves.

He returned the weapon to the table and took a long swallow from the bottle, pausing as the hard whiskey shot down his throat. The liquor didn't give him courage to do the unspeakable; it only silenced the tormenting demons that stole his peace so long ago that he couldn't remember ever having any.

When his shaking hand settled, he reached across the table and picked up the gun again. He stared at it, certain fate would at last deal a merciful hand and the curtain would fall on his miserable existence.

With a firm spin of the stainless steel cylinder, he flipped it shut, and without further hesitation, placed the barrel in his mouth, closed his eyes, and squeezed the trigger. There was only an audible click of the sole empty chamber and nothing else.

"My lucky day," he said in disgust and flung the weapon on the table, reaching for his whiskey.

A sudden, shearing, white hot pain tore through his head. He crashed forward onto the table, falling unconscious to the floor.

"Are you all right?" Katie asked after his long silence.

"I can't do it," he said.

"Yes you can, I'm here for you."

"Ain't we just a pair?" He shook his head. A pitiful smile was on his face.

"What do you mean?"

"I mean look at us." He stared at her arm, still in a sling from Dorian's club. "You're physically banged up, and I'm an emotional wreck."

"Ha, at least my injuries are healing." She looked at her arm with a smile. "In a day or so, I'll be able to grip a weapon again, but what are you going to do, old man?"

His smile left him, and with a deep sigh, he gazed to the house up the hill.

"I don't know, Katie Bear. I just don't know."

"Come on. If you don't try, you'll never know. We've come too far to leave it like this."

Jonas turned to her, shaking his head. He was about to shift the RV into gear when she spoke.

"Wait." Katie turned to him. "Before we head up, I do have to ask you one thing. What makes you sure he won't call the cops and turn us in?"

"Richard?" Jonas smiled. "I don't know much anything anymore but I'm not worried about that happening. He's as solid a person as I have ever known. And, let's say he'd be far less enthused with an appearance by the authorities than we would."

Katie smiled. "Okay. Let's go see your friend."

"All right then," he placed the vehicle into drive.

Jonas parked the RV behind a small fishing boat hitched to a pick-up truck in the driveway. They climbed from the RV and headed toward the house when he remembered Chance.

"I should crack the windows," he said, turning back. When he glanced to Katie, he saw her fearful stare aimed at the house. Immediately, he spun around. A man stood outside with a shotgun pointing toward them. Immediately Katie recognized him from one of the cabin's pictures as the man with Jonas in their moment of hilarity.

Jonas went toward him with his hands in the air. "Not much of a welcome for an old friend. I just came to see you," he said.

"You've seen me, now git." Richard replied in a combative tone.

Katie held steady, uncertain of what to do.

"We should go," she said with an increasing concern as Jonas continued his approach toward the provoked man and the business end of his shotgun.

Jonas ignored her. "Never heard from you. Kept hoping you'd call or write at some point," he said.

"Yeah—well sorry about that; I guess life just got in the way," Richard replied sarcastically.

Jonas stopped. With an uncomfortable smile, pointed back toward the boat. "I wondered if you still fished," he asked.

"Not half as much as I'd like to," Richard said without warmth.

Jonas took a deep breath, mulling over what he might

say next. "So waddya' catch up this way?"

"Enough small talk, what are you doin' out here, Montgomery?" Richard asked in a combative tone. A brown-haired woman came outside and joined him on the front porch.

"Got nowhere else to go," he replied.

Richard scoffed. "That's your problem, sergeant!"

"My life ain't exactly been a picnic since we came home from the war, and I just figured after so much time had passed, you might have forgiven me by now."

"Is that so?" He laughed.

"Richard, please, not like this," the woman said with a gentle voice.

"Laura, go on back in the house, this don't pertain to you." He glared at Jonas. "Let me tell you something for nothing, you got some nerve. All the time in the world won't bring them back, not a one of them. Let me ask you. Before you came out this way, did you head up to Richmond and ask Rebecca Jacobs if she forgave you? How about you head up to Brooklyn and ask Carla Romano if she'll forgive you. No? Well maybe everything will be just right if you stroll up north to Lansing and drop in on the widow Kratzky's place to see if she's over what you did, and last, but certainly not least there's Frank, Jonas. Remember Frank?"

Katie followed Richard's red hot stare to Jonas, and when her friend's broken-hearted gaze fell to the ground, in an instant, she made the connection on the final part of the story Jonas had never before told.

"Maybe Mom—God rest her soul, finally has the peace in the grave that she could never find in this life, after having to bury her baby. A boy died far too young, fighting a man's war. He looked up to you and me so much, he followed us into the Army in the first place. All you had to do was keep watch, but you couldn't do it, could you? No. You fell asleep and let him run off into a Viet Cong ambush. So it stands now, my brother, and all of our friends—every last one of them are dead. And me? Well hell, I'm the lucky one." He raised his left pant leg to reveal a prosthetic limb. "And yet here you stand, fit as a brand new fiddle, so forgive me if I'm not overly sympathetic to your, 'woe is me.'"

"You made your point, lieutenant." Everything about the man's tone and posture obliged Jonas to disregard decades of their brother-like friendship and address him formally.

"You sure, Montgomery? Thought you'd drop in after what, forty-three years and we'd swap cooking recipes? You're a real piece of work, mister. You may have forgotten what happened that night but I never will. Skin it any way you want, but you abandoned your post and our boys paid a very dear price. There's blood on your hands; it's that simple and plain. This man's army weighed you and found you wanting."

"There's not a minute that passes that I don't regret the things I've done. Lord knows I made plenty of mistakes back then, but that ain't the man who I am today." Jonas replied.

"Isn't that convenient?" Richard scoffed again.

"Look, I didn't come out here to stir things up. Just needed to pass along that Momma's dead and what's more, I'm dying too. I ain't got much time left, so I just came to set things right."

"Well. I'm sorry to hear that. Your mother was a good woman." Richard fingered the brim of his ball cap as a show of respect. Then, without another word, he walked into the house and shut the door behind him.

167

Jonas gazed into the hot June sky. There was no hiding the pain the words inflicted on him. He opened the RV door and got in. "Just give me a minute." He tried to compose himself.

Sympathy filled her as she stared into his haggard, weary face. In that moment of sadness, for the first time, she had a glimpse behind the tough veneer of the hardened protector she had never been able to please. She saw the child he once was. Seeing Jonas so vulnerable reminded her how much she loved him. Consumed by his emptiness and brokenness, she reached over and touched his shoulder.

"It's okay," she said with a soft voice.

He turned the key, starting the vehicle's engine.

The front door opened and Richard walked down the stairs toward them. He approached the driver's side of the vehicle, slapping the hood.

"Come on in the house and get somethin' to eat, you stupid old fool." His facial expression and tone sounded more like a command than an invitation.

Jonas continued to stare out the window, his face full of remorse, his thoughts continents away.

"Go on inside now, go on." He pointed to his house. "You came all this way. May as well come in out of the heat."

***

Tensions eased after Laura suggested everyone adjourn to the deck and enjoy what remained of a pleasant afternoon.

"Can I get you a drink?" Richard asked.

"Just one?" Jonas raised his eyebrow. "Can you make it a double?"

"Done—you still take whiskey?"

Jonas nodded.

Richard turned to Katie. "Young lady, I can offer you Diet Coke, milk, water, or iced tea."

"Cold water would be great, thank you."

"Laura?" he asked.

"Water will be just fine for me too, thank you," his wife replied.

Richard disappeared into the house. A few minutes later he returned with a small wooden serving tray, placing bottled water in front of Katie and his wife. He plopped down on the bench across from Jonas and poured whiskey over the ice.

"Montgomery, age is catching up with you. Not to say that you ever did, but I gotta' tell you, pal, you don't look so well." He smiled.

"I guess I'm still sober, Lieutenant, because from where I'm sitting, you ain't exactly no Brazilian beauty yourself," Jonas said without a smile.

"No need to get testy, my man, no harm intended. I just meant—"

"So, Mr. Trask, what is this place called?" Katie interjected.

She knew all too well that whenever the topic of Jonas's health or appearance was brought up, he always became defensive, and Richard seemed the type who quite enjoyed deliberately getting a rise out of a man.

"These are the Blue Ridge Mountains. The Cherokee knew this place as the Sahkana'ga—the Great Blue Hills of God. Not the heavy touristy parts way down yonder over there." He pointed in the distance. "I'm talking about up here, away from the craze of it all. What we have here is six thousand four hundred twenty-seven acres of pure

169

unadulterated, unregulated, otherwise uninhabited paradise. Far from the people, further still from the ever so invasive prying eyes of the man." He smiled.

Jonas took a swig, rolling his eyes. "To translate, when he says *the man*, he means the government."

"I get the people part, but what's the deal with the government?" Katie asked.

"What's the deal with the government? Did she just ask that? Is she from this planet?" Richard asked.

"Goodness, child. You've gone and done it now." Laura laughed, shaking her head side to side.

Jonas held up both of his hands. "Trask—No. No! With all propers due, can we please not get started on this? I'm not in the mood."

"What's the deal with the government?" Richard ignored him. "Youths today!"

"All right already," Jonas coaxed.

Katie shrugged. It seemed certain she had been excluded from a whale of a back story. "Did I step into something?" she asked.

"Yeah, you could say that. Talk about anything you want, but for all our sakes, never go there, okay? It's literal public knowledge that he and the authorities don't always see things eye to eye."

"I've been misrepresented by today's media and society," Richard replied.

"Yes, of course you have," he said.

"All right then, brother, but you'd better school the youngin' here, or I'm going to."

"Richard..." Jonas's voice inflected.

"Okay...I'm just saying." He shrugged with his hands in

the air, as if declaring his innocence.

"So, what you been up to you these many years?" Jonas asked.

"This, that, and the third, but ain't none of it any good," he replied.

"Well, I guess not much has changed."

"You know that's right!" Richard's thunderous laugh echoed through the range.

He leaned close to Jonas to whisper, "Man, you always had a way with the ladies, but this one's so young, she ain't but knee high to a pup yet." Richard laughed again and gave him a sharp slap to the ribs.

Jonas shook his head in disbelief. "Don't be a crass fool. I'm just looking after her."

"You're a saint."

"Far from it, she needed help and I happened to be in the right place at the right time."

"Funny how that happens where there's a cute female involved," Richard teased.

"Give it a rest, Trask." Jonas replied.

"All right, man," he said and quit razzing him. "Since you asked what I've been up to, come on, let me show you."

He got up from the bench and led them through the cabin past the kitchen. In his den, he pressed the wall and there was an audible click. The wall opened revealing a hidden stairway descending. Motion lights illuminated the stairs.

"After you." He grinned, extending his hand with invitation.

Chance followed them into a basement area much larger than the footprint of the cabin. At one corner of the room rested an enclave with a small leather loveseat and recliner. Behind the loveseat, a handmade stocked mini-bar. Three 40" TVs were mounted inside the walls. A large rack of shelves stored dozens of canned supplies, bottled water, several flashlights, camping supplies, and batteries.

Most of the remaining portion of the enormous basement served as a functional training area. Around the floor: a heavy bag, treadmill, weights, and a very lifelike training mannequin. Almost a third of the basement was a glass-enclosed soundproof shooting range, equipped with targets for archery as well as firearms.

"In the event of any kind of emergency, I can seal the basement off. Laura and I have enough down here to hold out for two years, if push comes to shove."

"Talk about too much time on your hands." Jonas smiled. "I gotta' say I absolutely love what you've done with the place."

"Better Homes and Garden...I'm a big fan." Richard grinned. Both men laughed.

"Friend, that ain't even the half of it." Richard walked to the distant side. "Come and see," he beamed.

He picked up a remote control and handed it to Jonas. "Push the green button."

Jonas aimed the remote at the wall-mounted screens. "What, the Redskins are so good now they warrant having three TVs?"

"Ha-ha," Richard smirked.

When he pushed the button, classical music filled the room, emanating from the speakers mounted around the basement.

"Give me that." He snatched the remote from Jonas's hand. "You color blind, old man? I said the *green* one!"

He pushed the button with the same result. "Darned technology. I'll need to fix that," he said with annoyance.

"Mr. Trask, if I may ask. Why do you have three TVs?"

"You can dispense with the *mister*. My friends call me Trask. If the darn thing works right, yep—there." He pushed another button before the monitors came on. They displayed three different views of his property, including the road leading up to his home.

"We've got a lot of acreage out there, but these cover the only possible means to get up here."

"Crazy hillbilly." Jonas laughed.

"Laugh all you want, but you just never know." He turned off the screens and motioned for them to follow him as he approached what appeared to be another ordinary wall.

He pressed a section on it and crossed his arms as they watched a hidden panel slide to the side. Inside, behind more glass, a weapons cache including an ammunition re-loader, several composite and compound bows, arrows and bolts, a dozen pistols, a shotgun, and several modified semi and fully automatic rifles. A case of several of grenades, hunting knives, and hand-sized canisters sat across a shelf in the back.

"I'm a believer in preparing for every contingency. You could say this is my 'just in case life throws an unexpected emergency at you—please break the glass.'"

Katie curiously eyed the array of items behind the panel. "What are those?" She pointed to several canisters of military grade pepper spray.

Richard answered. "Those are temporary irritants."

"—and these?" She pointed to small unlabeled canisters.

"Permanent irritants," he said.

"A boy and his toys." Katie shook her head in amused

173

amazement.

"Indeed." Jonas smiled. "So many wonderful toys."

***

Late evening, they lounged around the hand-built barbecue pit on Trask's deck. While Richard's beef brisket smoked, he played the bass, stopping time to time to recall stories about the men in their unit.

"Is that a guitar?" Katie asked.

"Blasphemy." Richard smiled. "Young lady, this is called a bass. Would you like to hold it?"

"Really?" she asked in surprise.

"Sure. Hold it right here just like this," he said laying it across her lap as she sat on the deck's bench facing them.

She fingered the strings.

"Go on, just anchor your thumb and walk your index and middle fingers."

Katie smiled, and then slowly strummed the same song Richard played.

"How did she do that?" Richard looked at Jonas with astonishment. "Montgomery couldn't have taught you, he don't know how to play the bass. Where'd you pick that up from?"

"One of her gifts is her incredible muscle memory. She learns at an amazing rate and can do nearly anything she sees someone else do."

Laura laughed, cupping her mouth in astonishment.

Richard shook his head in disbelief. "You're a different kind of cat, little lady."

"The kid's special," Jonas replied.

He nodded in agreement.

Jonas asked. "Anyway, you never did tell me, how did

you end up down here in Georgia?"

"Not too much to tell. After the war, I came home and tried the corporate world for a few years, working for a defense contractor up in Arlington. It didn't take much time before I grew tired of bureaucratic hypocrisy, soLaura and I bought this place and moved far away from the lies men tell."

"What about you, Montgomery? I hate to ask, but word on the street is you've had a real rough go of it," Richard said.

"Rosy." He threw back another shot of whiskey. "As you might imagine, seven years trapped in a six-by-eight cage gives far too much time on your hands. A man gets to thinking about the things he's done and all the choices he's made that brought him to this point.

"You get to second guessin' about darn near everything, all of which is pointless, of course, because no amount of second guessing was going to change one single solitary thing. At the end of the day, the reality is never about what would have happened. The only thing that matters is what did. Too much time on my hands left me, far too often, staring at myself, and I didn't like anything about what I saw.

"When I got out, I headed east and found myself in Virginia, where I met a Jordanian woman named Leila Refai. She took me for all I was, bad as well as good—what little there was of it. I had a lot of bitterness and anger I carried all those years, and true to form, I let it get the best of me.

"And with the misfortune of a man twice snake bitten, I'd guess you could say I blew the only good thing that ever happened to me. Anyway, I knew I needed a change of scenery and decided to put as much distance between us as possible, so I bounced around quite a bit, before setting up in Oregon a few years ago.

175

"Not long after I got there, I met a kind old white man who told me he could use some hands. He said he owned a ranch and was looking for someone to help him mind and manage the laborers he employed. As it turned out, I grew up on a small farm, so it was a perfect fit for a man with a record and a difficult time finding employment.

"Duvall never asked about my past. Just gave me a second chance when I needed one. I had little more than the lint in my pocket and he took me in and let me live there with him. He was a good man—no doubt far better to me than I deserved.

"Spring the following year, he was in the fields when he died of a heart attack. Much to my surprise he left the entire ranch to me. I maintained the daily responsibilities but I took his death hard and began sinking further and further into self-pity and a whole set of new lows."

Jonas did not mention his attempts on his life.

"I was troubled and restless with recurring dreams of a man in Africa. For reasons I cannot explain, I felt a strong urging to go there and find him, so before long, I was off again. I traveled the continent for almost three and a half years, searching for this individual whom I had never met, whose name I did not know, and other than in my dreams, had never seen. All I did know was I would locate him in a church.

"I found myself in the Democratic Republic of the Congo, where I witnessed unspeakable horrors—atrocities to hundreds of people. There is nothing in America, even the worst of our city streets, or the darkest prisons, that comes close to the godlessness and depravity I saw.

"Time and time again, I saw the wholesale torture and rape of entire villages in the Congo: women, girls, even very young boys. So rampant was genocide, sexual assaults, starvation, and psychological intimidation over the people by tribal warlords, often even the authorities couldn't be trusted. I had several close calls with being captured and killed myself, if not for villagers that hid me, even at the risk of losing their own lives.

"I wandered through the continent, drifting through countless churches, finding more frustrating dead ends and unanswered questions. Many were dark and desolate, others had either been vandalized and looted, or destroyed and in ruin.

"Some months later, at the end of myself, I staggered into a tiny village in the Sierra Leone. When I arrived, the last rays of the sun retreated giving way to twilight. The stares and indistinct whispers of the locals were unsettling as I, an obvious stranger, wandered up the dusty road leading into the town. On the distant end of the village, I found a structure indistinct from any of the other homes near it.

"When I knocked, the door creaked and opened. I peered inside and saw several rows of empty pews on both sides of an aisle. Half way down the right side I saw an older black man unhurriedly sweeping between the rows. Behind the man, mounted on the wall, was a small, unspectacular wooden cross.

"Still sweeping, the man said to me, 'I've been expecting you, Jonas.' There was a confidence that made me even more uncomfortable than the fact he knew my name.

"I glanced around the dim room, half expecting to be ambushed by someone lurking behind pews. I glanced over my shoulder to see a half dozen or so people gathered in the streets watching me. A small boy, no more than five or six, had come closer and stood just outside. Unsettled by the gazes of the child and the other onlookers, I came in all the way, closing the door behind me.

'Who are you? How did you know I would come?'

'None of that matters as much as the very fact that you're here. Even so, you would not believe me even if I told you.'

'Try me.'

'What has made you come so far, Mr. Montgomery? What is it you seek out here, so far from your home in Oregon?'

'Fool. You don't know me.'

'For a thousand years dark forces have relentlessly scouted the realms in search of one very special object. And this is what has also brought you to my door.'

'I don't know what you're talking about.' I said, growing very impatient.

'Make ready for the Winnowing.'

'The what?'

"The frail man stopped sweeping, seeming to use the broom to hold himself up. When he stared at me, even in the low light, his piercing gaze burned.

'The storm is coming and soon there will be no light. Take heed and walk in it before the darkness falls and overtakes you.'

"Though I didn't understand what he meant, the man's strong conviction unsettled me.

"'Mr. Whoever-you-are, I ain't slept in weeks and I've been all over this continent in and out of every church I could find. All of them empty, burned to the ground, or in ruin— followin' figments of whatever last sense I got left. If I had any mind at all, I would have gone back home a long time ago, so I can promise you, I'll beat your tail before I listen to one second more of this foolishness. For the last time, who are you and how do you know me?'

'You cannot comprehend what you are unwilling to see—'

"Enraged I sprang forward and grabbed the man's collar and began shaking him.

'No more of your riddles, holy man!' I told him, through gnashed teeth. I pushed him backwards, still holding his collar as I prepared to hit him. As the wisp of a man stumbled backward, off balance, the broom fell from his hands and he nearly fell over the pew behind him. The man, no match for my strength flinched, closing his eyes, in preparation of the blow. He began speaking in a language I presumed was African, then he lunged forward and grasped my head in his hands.

"When he grabbed me, I could not see, enveloped by darkness, pregnant with fear. An excruciating jolt of electricity surged from his hands, passing through my body. I flailed trying to escape his grasp but the man, overpowering me, held fast to my head, and walked me backwards until I sat on a pew.

'My eyes!' I screamed. 'What have you done to me?'

'In the days to come, the world will be cast into darkness and seldom will the light of the sun be seen.'

"For what felt like an eternity to me—I had horrible visions of dark clouds falling upon the earth like a veil. Dreadful fiends from another world slipped in, moving amongst the shadows, as they made prey of our race.

"On the streets below, riots and looting broke out

179

worldwide, whole cities and countless people burned in the ensuing fires and chaos.

"I remained struck by the darkness, as the man continued to speak; his voice came from everywhere around me at once.

'The coming days will be not unlike the blindness you feel now. In a short time, your condition will pass, however the plague and night that will soon fall across the land will blot out the very sun.'

"In my vision, the holy man opened his hand and gave me two clear crystal vials.

'Take these, but do not drink them.'

'What is this?' I asked.

'Holy water,' he said. 'When the time of darkness is upon you, it will give you the clarity and discernment to illuminate the delusion.'

"He removed his hands and I slumped in the pew behind me, exhausted by the weight of what the man had shown me. Still weak and unable to see, I listened to his fading footfalls as he walked away.

'Out of the mist of the shadows, you will find a child. She is our last hope to turn back the night. Go now—even as I speak, peril bears down on you.'

"Then the door creaked, slammed shut, and the room was silent.

"I rested on the seat until a short time later when my strength and vision, albeit blurry, slowly returned. As I gathered my senses, my eyes adjusted to the room. I looked around the church for the man but he was nowhere. When I attempted to stand, my hands found something soft on the pew beside me. I picked it up and unfolded the scarlet velvet

180

cloth, revealing the same two crystal vials of water I had seen in the vision. I quickly wrapped and placed them in my pack. I edged to the door and peeked outside. The night sky buzzed with the sounds of locusts and other insect and animal sounds I was not used to hearing back in the states.

"No light shone from the dozen or so homes that surrounded the church, and the village was as empty as a ghost town. As I went door to door, my stomach knotted. Where could the people have gone in the short time I had been inside? Had I imagined everything? The cacophony of creature sounds became eerily silent. I scanned the night sky and the mysterious man's final warning returned to me...

Go now—even as I speak, peril bears down on you.

"His words reverberated through my mind and my blood ran cold. My pulse quickened as I continued to scan the skyline for anything out of the ordinary. I'll tell you this for nothing...at that moment, it was what I didn't see that concerned me most. I considered my mind was playing tricks on me, and I might have doubted everything I had seen were it not for the crystal vials in my pack.

"All of the sudden, the most incredible sense of foreboding fell over me, so I fled on foot in the opposite direction from which I had come."

When Jonas finished speaking, he placed the small, round vial on the picnic table in front of him. Laura watched in spellbound silence as the bottle wobbled coming to a standstill.

"We've been on the run pretty much ever since," he said with eyes cast upon the ground.

Laura gasped, peering fixedly at the crystal bottle. "My word, that's it?"

181

He raised his eyebrows in silent confirmation.

"What happened to the other one?" Laura asked

"It was shattered during a run-in with a wraith."

Richard took a long puff from his cigar, swishing whiskey around the bottom of his tumbler, seeming to mull over everything Jonas said.

"So, if I were to believe you are of right mind, and these vampires do exist, how would you kill them? Let me guess— tippy toe up on them while they're in their coffin and put the wood to them right? A bit archaic, wouldn't you say?" He laughed dubiously.

"Trask, believe what you want, but trust me on this: the wraiths are anything but vampires, and they're absolutely real. Forget everything you remember from the childish vampire stories we grew up with. For starters, they project different forms—at will. To make matters worse, the stronger ones even have other special powers I ain't never seen in no movie.

"There are three different kinds of wraiths. The first two, teenagers took to callin' Creepers and Dead Enders. The Creepers are wraiths that feed on the vitality of humans. The Dead Enders was just regular folk that were bitten repeatedly by the Creepers, then the darkness took hold of them. Once bitten, they wander about. I guess they say that because the victim's life is at a dead end, since there's no cure to the virus."

"That's awful," Laura muttered, looking away. Katie, who had been standing behind her, touched her shoulder.

Jonas nodded. "The third kind of wraith, Agents, are superior to the others in every imaginable way. They're cunning, diabolically ruthless beings that will use any tactic to exploit your weakness. They're experts in fighting and can appear as anyone they choose.

182

"They don't seem to be affected by any of the things you'd suppose. Also untrue is that myth about having to be invited in a home. Trust me, this bunch won't be waiting for any invitation to go anywhere. You can forget repelling them with crucifixes or garlic, needin' to sleep in coffins, or any silliness of that sort.

"The only one that is true: they share an intense hatred of the sun. Only the stronger ones can function in the daylight, and even those wraiths can face exposure for a short while before being destroyed. You need to know that even in their weakened state, it would be a serious mistake to take them lightly."

Richard smiled, still not convinced. "So, Mr. Positivity, I'm still waiting on the part where you illuminate us on how they can be killed. Every forsaken thing's got an Achilles heel."

"Yeah, if there is a positive, that's it. The wolf-like Gwigs—Gwyllgi they employ, and the common wraiths—the Creepers and the Dead Enders—can all be killed by normal weapons. Wraith Agents, on the other hand, are slowed by those means but killing them requires far more primitive methods: a stake to the heart, incineration, decapitation and the like. I'm sure you get what I'm sayin'."

"Oh, that's the positive, huh?" Richard laughed, raising his shot glass. "Well, then, I'm sure we're all perfectly safe."

Jonas shrugged and raised his too.

"Lord, help us," Laura said solemnly.

Chapter 22

Trask was everything Jonas had described in wasting no time getting her back to formal training. He woke her up early the next day and they got straight to it.

Jonas had prepped him the night before on what she had already learned: handling basic fire arms, survival training, and military hand-to-hand combat, including Jiu-jitsu and knife fighting, and what had been his military specialty, communications.

Richard had similar field training and expertise, however he possessed a much broader range of experience with various weapons. As an expert in munitions and explosives, he taught Katie creation and detection of various kinds of booby traps and improvised explosive devices. They prepared for various scenarios including possible encounters from what Jonas called "Friendlies"—humans who might get in the way but he designated as non-lethal threats. And on the other hand, human agents, very dangerous trained assassins, intending to capture Katie and kill anyone who stood in their way. Jonas saw a significant distinction between the two groups, but Richard made his opinion emphatically clear. In his mind, if push came to shove, both groups were one and the same.

The majority of their instruction, however, focused on surviving encounters with the most clear and present of all dangers: the Gwyllgi and Wraith Agents.

As with all aspects of her training, due to her acute muscle memory and eidetic memory, Katie quickly excelled. In a brief matter of weeks, she completed every objective they gave and learned every skill it had taken them years in the military to acquire.

Journal Entry: July 16

It's been three weeks since we arrived. We've trained daily and done little else. In the little TV I have time to watch, I've witnessed the black poison unfold its way throughout our world, sucking the very life from it and all of us. With the spreading rioting and chaos, it would be easy to allow my own fears and self-doubts to consume me. Yet somehow, in light of Jonas's admission about dying, these past few weeks in particular, I have made the most in my efforts to recognize every moment of nature's beauty and enjoy the sun.

At night, when I soak my aching muscles in the tub, I let my mind take me away to the serenity and refuge of my garden. Every time I remember my only means of escape, it is more perfect than before; the perfection and peace I once knew from what felt like many life times past. It was a time when the world, at least to me, had no problems. If there were any—they were not the thoughts of the carefree children that ran and hid playfully in the hedges; they were the problems of tomorrow, for which we had no knowledge of, nor concern for. Tomorrow was left to worry for itself. Now, after all we've been through, I'm just very thankful to be alive. I'm trying to take every day as it comes because I know tomorrow is not guaranteed.

Chapter 23

August 1

"Ms. Laura?" Katie called through the kitchen.

"I'm back here, dear," Laura replied from her bedroom.

"Hey, do you mind if I washed a few things this morning?" Katie held her dirty sweats as she walked through the bedroom door.

"Absolutely, all yours," she replied.

She saw Laura's folded clothes piled into an oversized briefcase. When Katie entered the room, the woman slipped her sweater inside and snapped it shut.

"There," Laura said.

"How are you? Is everything okay?"

"Child, I thank the Lord that he woke me up, clothed me, and put me in my right mind."

"Yes, I guess that's definitely something to be thankful for," Katie replied. "Where are you going?"

Laura pressed against the hardcover suitcase several times until it latched.

"Mimi is not well, so I'm going to go stay with her until she recovers," she said, speaking of her mother. She pulled the hardcover suitcase down the hall into the middle of the kitchen.

Jonas sat at the morning room table, sipping coffee as he read the newspaper, the ever present bottle of whiskey next to his mug. He heard the entire conversation but did not comment. His own curious gaze met Katie's nervous stare. These days, the mere mention of illness of any kind, immediately grabbed everyone's attention. Richard had not said anything about it.

"Sick? What's wrong with your mother?" Katie asked.

186

"No," Laura said, picking up the tense vibe between Katie and Jonas. "Not the flu, I'm happy to say, it's nothing like that. Mimi already had a bad hip and a few days ago she fell down the stairs and reinjured herself. She's going to be laid up for a while so I'm flying up to Colorado to look after her while she mends."

"That's a relief. What I mean—"

"I know what you meant, dear." Laura smiled. "If she recovers on schedule, I should expect to be back in a month or two."

"Isn't there anyone else that can help out?"

"Dad passed years ago and I have no siblings, so no. I was planning on heading up to check in on her anyway. Falls and the like are things not so unexpected at her age."

"Is there anything I can do to help you, Ms. Laura?"

Just then, Richard came through the front door. "Everything's packed in the car. Ready to go whenever you are." He grabbed the last suitcase.

"Okay, just a minute." His wife glanced at him, before taking Katie's hand. "Yes, there is something you can do."

"Name it," she said.

"Please take good care of Dick and Jonas, and do your best to keep them out of trouble, will you? Those two are lost without a woman's touch."

"Yes, ma'am, I promise I'll do my best." Katie smiled.

"Wonderful. Thank you, dear. I will see you soon." She hugged her.

"Be careful, Mrs. Trask."

"Likewise, Katie." She waved and closed the front door.

***

Journal Entry: August 20

I can't help worrying about Ms. Laura, but she calls daily and assures us it's not bad out there yet. Things are going slower for her mother than she'd hoped but she should be back by the middle of September.

The sky continues to darken, and outbreaks of the plague continue. It is no surprise people in outbreak areas have begun to panic. The rioting and looting in other parts of the world has grown much worse. It's very hard, but I know I have to continue to be watchful so the trouble doesn't sneak up on us and catch us unaware.

My own abilities grow but more wraiths will come. They will pursue me to the corners of the earth until the logical conclusion...my death.

Forever, I will be the hunted.

Chapter 24

September 19

Chance's ears perked up. He lifted his head and whined. He'd been sleeping at Jonas's feet, but when the man did not awaken, he jumped off the bed and trotted down the hall. A full thirty seconds before cabin's perimeter alarm went off, Chance knew they had company, and when the unusual low-pitched, intermittent sequence of beeps resounded through the halls of cabin, Richard, Katie, and Jonas knew too.

Richard was in the family room watching his large screen computer monitor and the alternating angles of cameras mounted in various places around the grounds. Two of the screens on the northeastern end of his four-hundred seventy acre property zoomed in on two dark sedans coming to an abrupt stop a half mile away. He watched as the men exited the vehicles and armed themselves from the trunks. Within moments, Jonas and Katie joined him in the room.

"What is it?" Jonas asked.

"Friends of yours, I presume?" Richard watched the screen with crossed arms.

"Either that or the IRS finally caught up with you for all those back taxes," Jonas replied.

"What's your guess then, humans or wraiths?"

"Wraith agents." Jonas glanced at the shimmering lights twinkling inside the vial. Upon a closer glance of the monitor, he saw Dorian among them.

"Well, if they have half a brain between them, I'm not expecting them to drive right up to my front door. They'll park a ways down the hill and trail on foot, figuring to get the drop on us."

"You seem remarkably calm, Mr. Trask," Katie said.

Richard scanned the cameras. "Wraith agent, Intelligence agent, IRS agent—I've been preparing for the arrival of unwelcomed agents for many years.

"One way or another, eventually they'd come and try to take something that don't rightfully belong to them. As far as I am concerned, one agent scumbag is just as good as the next.

"In either case, I've got some party favors out there to keep the lot of them entertained. In the meantime, I suggest you grab your things and follow me. We've got, at most, six minutes to get gone."

Katie and Jonas hurried through the cabin to get their things. Most of their gear had been staged, in case they would one day need to make an urgent exit on a moment's notice.

"Stay low and out of sight." Richard cupped Chance's snout. "That goes for you too, pup."

He led the way as they passed beneath the window-filled cabin and slipped down the basement stairs. Richard turned on the monitors to take one final peak. The lights flickered and all power to the house failed.

"I forgot to tell you, many wraiths emit an electrical disturbance whenever they're near that knocks down all power in the area."

"You should know me well enough to know I have everything on a backup. It'll kick on any second now."

"Their EMPs knock down backup power as well," Jonas added.

"All of these minor details might have been useful a few months ago when we began planning for this day." The beam of Richard's flashlight illuminated his frown.

"Think we can still get to your weapons cache?" Katie asked.

He kneeled and removed a small panel next to the weapons case. Just inside the panel, there was a small crank.

"Even the best laid Plan B has a Plan B. I can open the panel manually, but it will burn more time we don't have." Richard cranked the handle until the door glided open, revealing the glass-enclosed weapons wall. He holstered a Walther PPK pistol and handed Jonas his weapon of choice— an updated model of his own Colt .45. Richard turned and presented Katie with a semi-automatic P229 Sig Sauer .357.

"Maximum stopping power, think you can handle that, young lady? I got a bug zapper if you can't." He pointed to a smaller 9mm Glock.

"I'm good." She peered at the tritium night sights and checked her weapon to confirm it was loaded.

Richard removed the M16 with grenade launcher and placed four grenades in a special backpack, then started to close the door.

"Heck, what am I saving them for?" He reached in and took the other four, two of each kind, and placed them in his pack. "Get whatever you need, but don't take more than you can carry."

Katie grabbed a military knife, two throwing knives, which she tucked in her boots, a Mini-mag flashlight, a canister of pepper spray, and four extra boxes of ammo. Jonas collected three boxes of ammo and two grenades.

Richard glanced at his watch. "Three minutes—we gotta' get."

He trotted across the room and moved the panel that hid the escape exit behind the wall. He turned on his flashlight and after Jonas, Katie, and Chance were inside, replaced the wall's section concealing the exit, closed the door and dropped a steel latch reinforcing it from the outside. An audible click confirmed the anti-personnel device he wired to all of the cabin's windows and doors armed itself.

"Let's go!" He led them through the dark tunnel.

A hundred and fifty yards later they emerged from the carefully preserved Civil War mine that ran underneath Richard's home. Gradually, the slope of the narrow passageway ascended to the surface. They smelled the outside air as a breeze whooshed down the shaft from the opening. Richard slowed in front and held up his fist notifying them to stop. Silently he walked forward before peering around the corner. When he motioned, the three of them trotted to where he stood against the wall.

"See that?" he whispered, pointing to a concealed structure fifty yards away, almost invisible in the predawn darkness. Katie had been living with Richard for months and even in the light of day she never noticed it.

"I've got a vehicle inside, but we need to get there without being seen. You ready?"

Katie and Jonas both nodded.

"Slow is smooth—smooth is fast," Richard said.

They sprinted from the mouth of the concealed mine shaft, then a thunderous explosion erupted behind them. Sulfurous flames and searing white heat raced through the mine, knocking them off their feet as the entire house went up in a fireball. The flame and intense heat singed the edges of Chance's fur, covering his white coat in soot.

"Come on!" Katie yelled, lifting Richard from the ground while Jonas and the dog sprinted for the shed. Jonas covered Katie and Richard until they made it to the structure. They pulled open the door and jumped into the Explorer.

"Hold on!" Richard gunned the engine and blew out of the shed, his eyes locked straightforward as they navigated the narrow auxiliary road leading down the backside of the pass.

A startling crash on the roof broke his concentration making him lose control. Jonas fired three shots that tore through the top of the cab. Suddenly, a hand smashed through the windshield and seized Richard by the throat. A second later, the creature's head came into view. Dead black eyes stared back at him as the wraith, securing itself onto the luggage rack, began dragging him through the shattered windshield.

Richard fought against its strength, bracing against the wheel as he raised his pistol and started shooting. The first blast missed the creature but another hit its face at point blank range. The fiend exploded into a hot cloud. Choking and blinding ash swept through the confines of the small cabin, burning their eyes and nostrils.

Richard lost control of the vehicle, and they careened down the steep embankment, crashing into the trunk of a massive tree on the forest floor.

The rough crash jostled Chance around in the back seat, but he was uninjured.

Richard killed his lights. "Everybody all right?"

"I'm all right." Jonas replied, suffering a minor concussion.

Katie was slow to respond. "Yeah...I'm fine."

"Well, good, now that we've got that settled, be extra careful when you get out. This entire ridge is rigged with anti-personnel devices and we're right smack dab in the middle of a minefield. So when I get loose, you'll have to walk a direct line behind me and do exactly as I say."

"Mines? You've got to be putting me on," Jonas said in exasperation.

"You know I'm not." Richard climbed out of the SUV. He gathered his things and reached for Katie's hand. "You ready?"

Richard never saw the wraith. His instincts kicked in and with his hip, threw it fifteen feet away. With a rough bounce, the creature landed on a bounding mine. It died instantly when the mine's explosion lit the night sky. In the fire's light, Richard saw the silhouette of four more coming from the ridge.

Richard turned and started toward the deeper brush.

"Where are you going?" Jonas asked. "We're dead if we go out there in the dark!"

"Same outcome if we don't," Richard replied. "Stay close to me, there's a cave on the other side of the pass were we can get better cover."

Katie followed him with Jonas behind her and Chance in the rear. They moved through the dense forest and had advanced a few hundred yards when Richard slowed.

"Watch yourself." He pointed down, leading them around a perfectly concealed pit. Inside the pit, underneath a small pile of fallen leaves, three-foot long pointed stakes protruded from the ground.

They had not gone far when he warned again. "Careful." He pointed to another trap. This one activated by a tripwire connected to a large spiked gate suspended high in the treetop. It would swing through the trees, impaling the unlucky recipient at the end of one of the four rows of needle sharp spikes.

In a disorienting instant, the owls they'd heard and the

insect calls that filled the woods ceased their sounds. In the conspicuous hush that surrounded them, Jonas knew they were the ones walking into the middle of trap. It was the same foreboding quiet he'd heard that night in Africa and their ranger unit heard moments before the ambush in Vietnam.

"Trask," Jonas whispered.

Richard and Katie stopped walking in their tracks.

"What it is?" Richard asked.

"It's too quiet," Jonas said.

He nodded in agreement and motioned for them to crouch. He peered around the shadows but in the twilight saw no movement.

With nervousness setting in and perspiration soaking through clothes, they scanned the soupy fog, unsure whether they should continue in the direction they were headed, or detour from the path and move deeper into the brush.

The silence shattered when Chance growled and began barking out of control.

"Shhh!" Katie tried to calm him, but in the early morning still, his agitation continued to rise. Their eyes searched the darkness for whatever riled him. Richard's annoyance with him grew for giving away their position.

"Take cover!" she yelled. "They've taken to the trees!" Through her gifted eyesight, she caught movement and raised her gun and fired at a wraith the men could not see.

A creature crouched like a gargoyle in the thick foliage of a treetop and though Richard had no way of knowing it, he was in the cross hairs of the creature's rifle scope. Fractions of a second before it could cut him down, Katie targeted the only part of him exposed.

Her first shot hit the wraith's shoulder, and when it

195

lurched from the impact of her .357, she hammered it with two more shots in its chest. The fiend fell head first from the tree and exploded into a cloud of ash.

A second returned fire; several bullets whizzed close enough for her to hear them. Another ricocheted off the ground, inches from her feet.

Jonas raised his pistol but a sudden, searing pain tore through his left arm. He was hit, but steadied his aim and fired, finding flesh when his shots nailed the creature in the neck. It clutched its throat and crashed headlong from the canopy above.

He targeted another in the trees to his left. Two more thunderous rounds smacked its torso. The wraith screamed in angry protest before dying.

Richard unleashed his own brand of hell. He fanned the semi-automatic rifle from wraith to wraith in the trees above them. The rapid sequence of powerful rounds riddled the creatures with holes. Then, with the same suddenness that the forest had come to life, the night returned to the mausoleum-like still. The only sound was that of Chance's heavy panting.

For almost a full minute, they stood back to back, protecting each other's flanks—each of their weapons pointing into the night. There were others but with visibility growing worse by the hour, wraiths could have been feet away and it would have been difficult to see them.

They waited for another attack, but when it did not come, they used caution and continued down the narrow trail through the woods. They treaded past the last trap and continued until reaching a small clearing. Moments later, another creature sneaking in behind them screeched in misery when it walked into the trap.

"Keep moving!" He quickened his pace.

In the early twilight, they crept through the thick early morning fog and climbed down from a ridge before crossing a shallow stream outside the mouth of a cave.

"What now?" Katie asked Richard with a low voice.

"Beyond the cave, you'll come across a distinct stone marking a narrow path near the river's edge. Follow it northwest until your boots hit pavement. If you're in good shape, it'll take you little more than half an hour to get the stone and another twenty minutes to the highway."

Jonas shook his head in protest. "Trask, come with us. You don't know what you're up against."

"If it ain't worst odds than the thirteen thousand Viet Cong that overran us that night at Khe San, then I don't want to hear it."

"Would you believe me if I told you it is?" Jonas looked at his friend with grave concern.

Katie rubbed along the side of Richard's arm. "Mr. Trask, I agree with him, we should stay together."

He glanced at Katie as if he was contemplating what to do next. Then, after loading another clip into the M16, he replied: "Jonas, I don't got time to argue. Get them out of here."

***

"Where's the rest of your party, old boy? I only smell the fear of one. Seems to me, you're a little light." Dorian's haunting voice echoed through the fog obscured canyon.

"Funny. I was going to say the very same to you." Richard's voice returned to him from inside the mouth of the cave. From where he lay positioned behind large rocks, he saw the wraith standing on the nearby ridge less than forty yards

197

away but had no clear line of sight for a shot.

"I've got to hand it to you. That was quite a number you did on my boys back there," Dorian said. "They were simpletons—not the brightest among my race, but I'm impressed nonetheless. Truth is, I've been here for centuries and haven't seen a display like that since the wars. All the same, you need to know that I won't go so easily."

"I'll take it under advisement," Richard scoffed. "And now that you've done all that talking, I have a warning of my own. If you're as wise as you seem to think you are, you'll head out of here while you still can. With that said—if you're dead set on keeping that appointment with death today, I've got a place out behind my shed where the ground is soft."

Richard gazed at Dorian in the mist, waiting his opportunity. When the agent moved, he would be ready to take him out. He lost sight of the wraith, and suddenly Dorian was outside the cave's entrance. The man squinted, unwilling to believe his eyes. It took them fifteen minutes to descend the ridge and cross the stream. Dorian did it in seconds.

"Old timer, you'll be the only one getting buried today. I am immortal."

"My buddy told me that about you, and apparently he's of the same opinion, but as far as I'm concerned that remains to be seen."

Dorian approached the cave, slipping inside without Richard seeing him. He enjoyed the game. Other than Katie's and Jonas's persistent elusiveness, few had tested him the way this man had, and he would not walk into another one of his cleverly devised schemes.

Richard climbed several large rocks and took a position several yards above the ground. From his new vantage point, wedged in among the rocks, he had a bird's eye view of the area inside the cave's entrance and waited for Dorian to come into sight.

Several long minutes passed, but he never saw him approaching.

He maintained his position, but after five minutes went by, he knew the wraith had figured he was walking into an open line of fire and was lying in wait, likely until reinforcements arrived.

Though Richard could not see him, he knew the general area where the agent had to be crouching. An idea flashed through his mind, a very risky one—foolish in fact. He set the rifle on the ground and removed a phosphorous grenade from his pack and pulled the pin. He got onto his knee, still concealed behind a large stone, and was about to unleash the grenade, when he heard the sound of his wife's voice.

"Dick? It's Laura," she called to him from below.

"Laura?" he responded, raising his head to catch a glimpse of her.

"Please come out, everything's okay, now."

Since she went to Colorado, he'd spoken to her often but forced himself not to dwell on how much he missed her. Hearing her now made his heart ache to be with her. Seconds elapsed with the live grenade in his hand.

Richard snapped out of the spellbound trance and hurled the explosive, arching high in the air over the large stone in front of him. It bounced on the rocks, and landed a few feet from Dorian. A reddish flash and dense white smoke filled the cavern below. At point blank range, the wraith was pelted by particles burning at 5,000 degrees Fahrenheit. He unleashed an ear-piercing shriek that Richard, temporarily

199

deafened by the percussion of the grenade, could not hear.

Dorian flailed on the cave's floor, trying to extinguish the phosphorous burning through his skin and boring deep into his face and body.

Richard jumped from the rocky nest avoiding the billowy plume of smoke rising toward the heights of the large cavern. He shielded his face as he retreated from the vapors; but he never took his eye or the muzzle of the rifle away from the area he had last seen the wraith.

Dorian sprang upon him from one of the rocks up and to his left. Richard flashed the rifle to that side in time to get off two shots. Both rounds hit the wraith in mid-air and he fell to the ground at his feet.

"It burns. It burns so bad, Dick! What have you done to me?" The image of his wife wailed in torment.

"Get out of my head demon, you ain't my Laura!"

In an instant, the human guise fell. There before him, lay the wraith, neither in its projection of Laura, nor in the handsome likeness of Dorian, which it had assumed for over a century.

Instead, what remained was its true wraith form, grossly disfigured from phosphorous that liquefied his skin and muscular tissue.

The toxic fumes from the phosphorous grenade filled Richard's lungs, made them feel like they were melting inside his chest. He tore off his jacket and tossed it on the ground in case the particles from the burning compound had landed on him. He still coughed when he patted his pant leg and drew a cigar from his pocket. When he saw it was intact, a childish smile brimming with satisfaction broke across his face. Looking at the wraith with disinterest, he lit the stogie and took a long puff.

"My man, I simply gotta' know. Is that mess from my grenade or do all wraiths come out of the package looking like that?" Richard said in a very loud voice.

"Enjoy your short-lived victory while it lasts. Many others will come after me—we are as countless as the stars in the sky," Dorian replied with labored, shallow breaths.

Richard couldn't hear anything Dorian said but read his lips and smiled. "For some strange reason, you keep under-estimatin' me, pal. If I was a bettin' man—which I happen to be, I'd happily wager I got more than enough guns and ammo for you and all your friends. So, when you get back to Hell or wherever you came from, you better let em' know." Richard squeezed the trigger and fired a dozen rounds into him.

The exhausted man turned from the wraith's lifeless corpse and left the cave to catch up with his friends.

Jonas and Katie exited the woods, standing alongside the highway. She glimpsed his way.

"We have to go back," she said.

"He's gone—we've got to keep moving," Jonas replied. She turned a cold, disappointed gaze toward him and spun to retrace her steps back to the river outside the rear entrance of the cavern.

When he realized she was going no matter what, Jonas grabbed her by the arm. "We've gone over this. If anything happened to us, you're supposed to high tail it out of the area."

"Is that how the Army field manual reads? What page, because I missed it? Is it the one that details when one of us goes down, the others pretend it didn't happen?"

"No, Katie. The one that says nothin' can jeopardize the

mission."

"What freaking mission, Jonas? Leaving him out there to die is wrong!"

"Protect the box and whatever's inside, keep you alive. Beyond that, nothing else matters."

Chance's body stiffened, and he bellowed a throaty growl. Their eyes followed his gaze into the forest with the expectation of another attack.

Jonas was out of ammunition and Katie was well into to her final clip. If there was another defense to be made, they would have to make it with military knives and her sword. But when the Akita's aggressive posture switched to a wagging tail, they glanced at each other with uncertainty. The dog tore off down the trail.

"Chance!" Katie followed as Jonas ran after him. They hurried through a light trail until close to the river. Richard limped into a clearing along the path below.

"Trask!" Jonas shouted several times, and dashed ahead. His voice filled with such urgency it put her on edge. When she rounded the bend—through an opening in the trees, she saw Dorian severely injured, coming up behind him.

"Richard!" she screamed, but still deaf from the explosion, he could not hear them.

Jonas eyed the trail then leapt from the side of the steep embankment, skidding as gravity propelled him toward the ground. He took a bad step and twisted his knee, taking a rough tumble down the side. Dorian drew closer to Richard who was completely unaware of the wraith's presence.

Katie raised her pistol, and took aim. Jonas lay on the ground holding his knee in pain. "If you got the shot, take it!"

As she stared through the tiny dots at the moving target directly behind Trask in her line of sight, Richard swayed side to side, jerking in and out of her weapon's sights.

If she mis-timed his jagged movements, in all likelihood, she'd hit him.

"Trust your aim!" Jonas screamed as though reading her mind. He watched as Dorian closed in on his friend.

Her heart pounded in her chest and sweat beaded across her brow.

"Take him out, now!" Desperation filled his voice.

When Richard's eyes rose and saw Chance sprinting toward him, he knew there was trouble and drew his military knife from the sheath, turning to meet the attack.

Katie exhaled and pulled against the trigger's tension. From her hesitation, Dorian plunged his fangs into the side of Richard's neck. The man screamed and the knife dropped from his hand.

Chance seized Dorian, sinking his huge canines into his arm, dragging him away from the defenseless man. After a vicious struggle with the dog, the wraith broke free and lunged for the man, set on killing him. Richard staggered to his feet, dazed from the onslaught, and ran for his knife lying at the edge of the water.

As he reached for the weapon, Dorian grabbed him. Katie wheeled into the clearing, set her feet and this time without hesitation—fired. All four of the Magnum rounds hit Dorian in the chest. He reeled backwards, over the side of the bank.

The wraith floated face down, near the shore. She stepped toward the rushing water, then froze. Her heart flipped, breathing hitched.

In her mind she saw dark, roiling water grabbing her body wearing a white garment and forcing her under. Her legs scraped against rocks and speared twigs. Lungs filled with water, stealing her breath. Going to die, going to-

"You all right, man?" Jonas hollered.

Katie snapped to the present. She eyed Dorian lying motionless, body swept downstream. He was not dead.

On the bank, Richard slumped to the ground and Chance padded over to him and licked his soot-stained face. Katie went to Jonas and helped him get to their friend and the dog.

"I'm straight." Richard cupped his neck. "Hurts like hell, but luckily, he missed my jugular."

"I should have taken the shot." Katie blamed herself for his bite and what her indecision led to. No one needed to say what the three of them already knew: any wraith bite, no matter how small, left most victims marked. The wraiths would forever smell Trask, and now he was guaranteed the same tumultuous lifestyle they had endured for twelve years—one always on the run.

"Don't do that to yourself." Richard shook his head in disagreement. "This is on me. If I hadn't been so arrogant, I would've finished him in the cave."

Katie glanced toward Jonas and caught a frustrated look on his face. Though he did not speak, he blamed her.

Richard stood on the riverbank, rinsing his neck until the bleeding stopped and treated the bite with the first aid kit in his pack. Afterwards, he dressed Jonas's sprained knee, and they hiked the tedious climb up the trail and the four-mile walk along the rural mountain road. Almost two hours later, they arrived at a small service station and bus stop.

***

"Where will you go?" Katie asked.

"I'll head out to Boulder and catch up with Laura and her mother. We'll shelter out there until all of this plague stuff blows over."

"They'll come for you, Lieutenant." Jonas said with a somber face.

"Then let them come. I still got plenty of fight in me, and I'll be ready, don't you worry."

"I'm sorry for everything." Katie's eyes sunk to the asphalt.

Richard lifted her chin and looked her straight in the face. "I told you, don't be. And as for the house, in all honesty, Laura was never fond of it in the first place. Wherever we settle, we'll start over again. Maybe this time, she'll even get that sunroom she's always been asking for." He smiled. "What about you two?"

"The clerk said another bus north will be here in an hour or so. We'll head up to Virginia," Jonas replied. "I'm gonna' find Leila and see if I can make amends."

Richard nodded in approval and hugged Katie. "It was my pleasure to meet you, Katie. You are a remarkable young woman."

She tried to smile but could not. "Thank you, Mr. Trask. Take care of yourself. Tell Laura I miss her and give her my thanks for taking us in."

"Copy that." Richard turned to Jonas. He stared at him for a long moment before extending his hand. "It was good to see you, Montgomery."

"Vaya con Dios, brother, it was good to see you, too," Jonas said in an emotional tone as he shook his friend's hand.

205

They gave each other a firm embrace.

He glanced at Katie and Jonas one final time, tipping his ball cap, and then boarded the coach.

Jonas gazed on as the bus pulled away. But before it even moved beyond eyesight, Katie turned about. Her attention swept the tree line and stretch of highway behind them. She was relieved Trask found safety, for now, but they were vulnerable and exposed here.

The isolated fill up station rested in the midst of upland woods spanning as far as she could see. She believed Dorian lurked out there somewhere—probably watching at that very moment, injured and full of fury. Soon the vengeful wraith would come for them again.

Chapter 25

Staunton, Virginia

Katie and Jonas rode the bus to its final stop in another rural location. The next charter would not depart until morning so upon the suggestion of the driver, they sought out cheap lodging nearby.

They walked into the motel lobby and were met by the curious stare of the thin, balding man sitting at the front desk. He was watching an old black and white show on the TV.

"We need a room. I assume you've got a vacancy." Jonas leaned against the counter to take the weight off his throbbing knee.

"Sure do. That'll be twenty dollars if you stay all night and twenty dollars iffin' you don't." The man's beady eyes passed back and forth between them.

"It ain't what you think." Jonas felt obligated to reply.

"Never is," the man replied.

Jonas handed him thirty dollars. "We were not here."

The man slid the key across the counter and they crossed the parking lot for their room.

As force of habit, he entered first, hobbling to check the bathroom and closet. All cleared, he removed his firearm, set it on the table, and concealed it with his jacket. Rifling through the duffle bag, he grabbed the whiskey and settled at the dinette between the bed and window. After propping his sore leg across the adjacent chair for relief, the man took a long, thirsty drink.

Katie watched him guzzle the liquor as though it were water. He didn't need to look her way to realize she was staring at him. Jonas set the bottle on the table and wiped his mouth with the back of his hand.

"Something you want to say?" he asked in irritation.

"No." She turned away.

He picked up the remote control, turned on the TV, and began flipping through the channels until he found one with international coverage. They moved through feeds of various news reporters on location in China, North Korea, India, Syria, Iran, and the Democratic Republic of Congo. In the United States, there were similar outbreaks, though much smaller. In Los Angeles and Dallas, the problems were rioting and looting.

A reporter stood on the corner of a street in downtown Damascus. As he spoke, several military Humvees and large trucks roared past.

"If you're just joining us, I'm Dave Ross, an investigative reporter with the Associated Press news. Local affiliates here are reporting another small series of earthquakes and aftershocks that have rocked various parts of the world.

"We're on location in the Middle East, where eyewitness reports confirm that shortly following the most recent earthquake, more of the black smoke poured into the sky.

"In other countries throughout Asia and the Middle East—all regions hit by the strongest quakes, the smoke is so dense, it has blotted out much of the sun. In many cities within these regions, the psychological toll of the devastation is what witnesses have described the darkness as *suffocating* and something that they can literally *feel*.

"I have interviewed quite a number of people here in Damascus, many sharing accounts of people being savagely bitten by others.

"While it seems irrefutable that the creeping black cloud is a direct result of the earthquakes, the White House continues to deny any correlation exists between the clouds and plague outbreaks in those same cities.

"However, given the sequence of events, it seems implausible there is no association between them.

"In related news, throughout these locales, we have seen at least two bite victims in a catatonic-like state wandering the streets without destination or reason. Here in Damascus, the World Health Organization has already quarantined Al-Salihiyah, and with the assistance of U.N. Peacekeepers, are attempting to enforce containment of victims in Al-Zahra al-Jadeeda—an area already plagued by war."

The camera panned to show a female government official as he continued.

"With us now is the W.H.O. spokeswoman, Yvette Saunders. Ms. Saunders, in your own words, can you describe the situation here?"

"We are in the preliminary stages of our analysis, but at this time many of the symptoms are what we refer to as the Cotard's Syndrome. The victims imagine sores covering their body and pick at them incessantly, which in turn causes real sores.

"In extreme cases, a fraction of these individuals remain in an upright coma-like state, but I hasten to add these are the rarest of circumstances. Our quarantine is merely a precautionary measure for the Syrian citizens, and it would be very much appreciated if everyone would maintain calm at this time."

The sound of machine gun fire echoed in the distance.

"You indicated the medical term is *Cotard's Syndrome*," Dave said. "This is the same term the president of the United States used in his state of the Union address last February. I believe this is the same as what is referred to outside the medical community as the Walking Corpse Syndrome. Some call the epidemic the Black Flu, which seems more appropriate."

"I believe it is very reckless to put things in those terms," the woman snapped.

"Well, according to various eyewitness accounts, there are a number of consistent symptoms relating to the virus. If you'd like, I am happy to describe what I have seen and heard for myself," he replied.

"It seems in most cases the sickness plays out in three stages." Still glowering at him, she cleared her throat, carefully considering her words.

"Stage one symptoms have included individuals complaining about unseen sores or even worms crawling in and on their skin. Many cannot stop scratching or picking at their imaginary sores.

"The sickness, for most, causes their skin and gums to dry out, which often leads to a perpetual grinding and gnashing of teeth. We have also observed cases of moderate paranoia in several stage one subjects.

"Individuals suffering from stage two symptoms experience a heightened sense of nervousness and paranoia. With shaking hands, they are subject to profuse sweating and are often restless. Some of the more extreme of the stage two victims have also complained of hallucinations and when provoked, become highly agitated.

"Individuals with stage three symptoms, --which I hasten to add are very uncommon, have complained of extreme lethargy and fatigue. The eyes of the afflicted become gaunt and their skin becomes drier and emaciated. The onset of stage three brings severe disorientation and incoherence.

"Some find themselves milling about confused, lacking emotion and purpose, and are unresponsive to anyone, even loved ones."

"What is the origin of the disease?" Dave asked.

"As I stated before, our actions regarding this sickness are *precautionary,* so it would be very helpful if everyone would continue to remain calm."

"I'm sorry, Ms. Saunders. You didn't answer my question. Does the W.H.O. know the cause of this disease? Will you confirm reports that indicate the common symptoms of every victim are the presence of one or more bites from some unknown creature?"

"What? Are you seriously implying that monsters are the cause of this sickness? Do you have any idea how absurd those words sound?"

He smiled at her. "Monsters? Now that's an interesting choice of words. I said *creature*, because at this point, no one has any idea what has caused the bites and yet, you chose to characterize them as monsters."

"Do not attempt to bait me by putting words into my mouth, Mr. Ross."

"Ms. Saunders, a reliable source within the Centers for Disease Control has indicated when people are bitten—three times to be precise, similar to rabies and the infected, in turn, bite others and also infect them. Is it accurate to say this is how the virus is being transmitted?"

He moved the microphone closer to her.

"I would prefer not to comment on the opinions of undisclosed individuals from other organizations, but to answer your question—that is incorrect. Rabies is transmitted by a single bite," she replied.

"I am fairly certain you understood my meaning, Ms. Saunders. My source advises this 'Black Flu' has a communicability rate of 92% for anyone bitten three or more times, and there is currently no cure. Is that accurate?"

When one of the men standing behind her whispered to her, she cleared her throat.

"We're done here." She pushed the camera away, and climbed into a military vehicle with other men. "We will share further details when more information becomes available."

Dave followed behind the woman, still holding the microphone toward her as she slammed the door.

"People have the right to know the full truth, not just the portions the government deems," he yelled as the vehicle sped away.

The station continued their worldwide coverage of the disaster.

Katie wondered why Jonas had not changed the channel. The news report was shocking and she struggled to comprehend what she was seeing—the sickness and death of the quarantined areas, horrific and unstoppable. Katie found it surreal to see the world as it became unhinged. Most people were in one of three camps—afraid to leave their homes; rioting and anarchy; or one of the unfortunates already thrice bitten, roaming the streets like soulless zombies with no apparent purpose. A few minutes were all she could stomach before turning away from the screen.

Jonas fidgeted in the chair. He was restless, troubled by the news but said nothing, taking another shot of whiskey.

He wondered how long before the various governments

censored media outlets as they tried to stem what was sure to become widespread panic. The obvious reality was already far more desperate than the CDC had been willing to admit publicly.

"It's horrible. Please turn it off," Katie begged, averting her eyes from the news program.

"What? Uh, yeah—you're right." He fumbled for the remote and knocked it off the table. When he bent over in his chair to pick up the control, he noticed movement across the parking lot at the motel lobby.

Chance lifted his head from the floor and growled. Katie sprang from the corner of her bed and retrieved her weapon.

"Shhh!" Jonas chided him, standing from the chair. He came to his feet too fast and the effect of the alcohol caused him to sway. The man steadied himself between the wall and the back of the chair and peeked through the blinds.

The lobby light across the parking lot cut off. He peered at his watch. The time read 9:37 p.m.

"It's early yet, something ain't right," he muttered.

"What is it?" Katie asked

"Get the TV!"

She pressed the power button on the console, and the picture tube of the old TV turned to a bluish white dot in a slow fade to black. Jonas turned off the lights. The ghostly blue glow from the diminishing pinpoint of the tube cast spectral shadows across the room.

Had he seen something leave the office? The country darkness, sleep deprivation, and old Tennessee whiskey combined to make him wonder if his mind was playing tricks on him. He kept his eyes trained on the direction of the lobby as he reached under the jacket on the table and pulled out his

Colt.

"Can you see anything?" she asked, taking a position on the opposite side of the window.

"Give me a darn minute," he said. "I'm still not sure what I see yet. Fetch my bag over there, get the vial and tell me if you see anything."

Under the fading light of the ancient television, Katie crawled along the wall toward the bathroom and pulled out the black canvas bag next to the closet. She fished through his clothes until she felt the hard glass bottle. Three small bluish white lights gleamed in the midst of water.

"Three of them," she reported.

"Fantastic." He peered through the blinds. "Get ready. They're coming for us."

Chapter 26

Prepared to dig in and make a stand, Katie nodded, pulling the P229 .357 SIG from her pack and returned to her position on the backside of the mattress. She squared her weapon on top of the bed, taking aim at the motel room's door.

The creature hit the door with such explosive force that the top hinge dislodged and the back corner of the flimsy door bent inward.

A second collision hurled the door across the room into the mirror, shattering glass everywhere. The wolf-like Gwyllgi leapt into the room.

Jonas and Katie were about to shoot when Chance sprang forward and in the way. With a vicious snarl, the fearless dog pounced on the creature. It moved to the right, trying to get around him but Chance intercepted, and with his tremendous power, pinned the monster to the wall. Chance sank his huge teeth into its throat and clamped down, holding fast.

Jonas saw an opening and fired, hitting the wolf in the shoulder. It hesitated and then lunged past Chance. Katie's own cannon spit two 125-grain Magnum load hollow point rounds. The first shot hit in the chest, the second one in the head, delivering the fatal blow.

Two more wraith-hounds, larger than the first, crashed through the window. Jonas raised his weapon, stumbling backwards. On account of their astonishing dexterity, they were upon him.

The larger of the two bit into his left wrist and thrashed its head, yanking the man toward the floor. Chance snapped down on its hind leg, crunching bone, and Katie pumped two rounds into the Gwyllgi, killing it—but not before the third one also attacked Jonas. With primitive savagery, it plunged its teeth into his muscular black neck.

Jonas screamed in excruciating pain as he dropped his gun.

Katie shouted, "You're here for me, come and get me!"

The animal released its deathly bite upon the man and snarled at her. Its eyes revealed a cunning intellect, not at all the mindless killing machine she had always believed.

When the wolf turned and she had a safe angle, she fired three times, all three hitting the hellion in the center of its chest. The high velocity rounds tore gaping holes in the beast's torso and it fell lifeless.

Katie stepped over the remains, hopping over to Jonas, critically wounded. He slumped against the wall, cupping his injured neck. Jonas glanced around the room for anything to use as a bandage.

"Who am I kidding," he mumbled under his breath. He decided that even if he stopped the blood, it wouldn't matter given these were his second and third bites. The intense pain in his neck burned as if on fire. "I'd say housekeeping's gonna' be pretty pissed." He laughed, making his pain much worse.

"Hold still. Don't move." Katie ran to the bathroom and returned with a towel.

"Kiddo, seems my work here is done."

She knelt beside him and pressed the towel to his throat. "Don't talk like that. You're going to be fine. Hold this." She pulled a pillowcase from the bed, wrapping it around his neck to secure the towel in place.

"Katie, you know what you gotta' do."

"I don't know what you're saying," she lied.

"Yes you do, lil' girl."

"I'm not so little anymore." A sad smile crossed her face as she wiped away the hot tears welling in her eyes.

"True. We've been together for so long....ol' habits." Pain flared and he grimaced again.

"I know," she said.

"Katie, I need you to realize I couldn't be more proud of the woman you've become. You are the one that gave me hope when all I had was lost."

This time she sat by his side and put her head on his shoulder, not smiling. He winced as he put his arm around her.

"Don't you worry one bit—everything's going to be fine," he said, but for once, his usual platitude was not the least assuring to her.

Jonas felt a queasy disembodied sensation as the virus worked its way through his system and his life slipped away.

216

She watched him as he slipped his fingers into his front shirt pocket and pulled out a small picture. He stared at the photo and kissed it.

"I need a pen."

She handed him one from her pack. He flipped the picture over and jotted on the backside.

"Catch a ride to this address. Tell her you're a friend of mine and she'll look after you. I'd give you the phone number if I had it, but she changed that long ago. Sick of me calling I guess."

She looked at the striking Jordanian brunette in the picture. All these years she had never seen this picture he carried with him.

"She's beautiful. Is this your wife?"

"Ex-wife, but that's semantics. I never stopped loving that woman. Don't know what she ever saw in me, that's for sure. Smart and classy and tough as an alley cat; we loved as passionately as we fought. I reckon' some of the best days of my life I spent with her, heck—probably some of the worst ones, too."

A soft chuckle gave way to a warm, tender smile that Katie had never seen on him. As her friend lay there, taking his last breaths, his final reminisces of the woman he loved erased the frown lines and the years of a man that had grown weary of the travails of his troubled life.

"Leila is good people. You can trust her. You'll be needin' this, too." He winced as he pulled out a crinkled wad of dollar bills from of his pocket. He raised his hand to give it to her but his arm fell weakly to his side and crumpled bills fell beside him. He brushed the cash to her. "Take it."

"I don't want it," she replied, sounding like a rebellious

toddler.

"Take it," he repeated, much weaker this time.

Watching what had been such a strong man, now too frail to lift his blood-stained hand, was more than she could handle. And for the third time in as many minutes, profuse tears streamed down her forlorn porcelain face.

"What would you have me do, Jonas? Are you really asking this?" Her voice rose in teary frustration.

"We always knew there was a possibility of it coming to this. We've gone over it time and time again. Time to let go. Remember what I taught you. No mercy."

"No!" she said in anger. Her powerlessness made her furious.

"You know how this goes down, Katie; three bites—and then the darkness."

She shuddered, unnerved by the imagery of his fateful words.

"I don't need to remind you not to be around me when it happens."

"Let's wait and see what happens. Even you said sometimes the fever breaks—"

"Katie," he cut her off. "Stop this now. In your heart you know I'm right."

"We'll call a medic and get you to the hospital." She took out her phone. He put his hand over the cell before she could dial 911—the only call the service-less phone could make.

"We can't just give up..." She was silent when she saw his other hand. He was giving her his pistol.

Jonas looked her in the eyes. "Do it."

They'd both seen the same report and knew he had little

more than a prayer, with the "Black Flu" registering a communicability rate of 92% for anyone bitten three or more times.

Still, she had fierce loyalty to the man who saved her life countless times. She felt unspeakable guilt at the mere consideration of ending his special life in this sleazy, half star motel.

"I'm so very tired, Katie bear...very tired. You should finish it and head on out."

Standing a few feet in front of him, she raised the pistol, and aimed at him. Her hand trembled as she began to squeeze the trigger. She closed her eyes and imagined the peacefulness of her faraway place.

"I can't, Jonas. I can't do this!" Katie returned the gun to her backpack, along with the vial of holy water he had been carrying. A few minutes passed with more incoherent mumbling.

"I'm just gonna' rest a bit now, Mother."

"I won't leave you, Jonas," she said.

Jonas's body drooped as he nodded off. This time his head came to a rest on her lap; his gaze permanently transfixed on the ceiling as if lost in deep thought. His brown eyes dulled when the last vestige of light passed from him.

She hoped her dying friend would find peace in his final thoughts of the woman in the photo.

Katie sat on the floor, despondent, weary. They had been on the run for what seemed like a millennium, and then just like that, things came to an end.

Over the next few minutes, she watched over the man as the third stage of the virus rapidly consumed him, transforming him before her eyes. His face became gaunt, all the more prevalent the weariness he described. Even his dark skin could no longer hide the telltale red discoloration of the virus passing through, working its way to his heart like the poison of a viper.

Maybe he would be one of the lucky few to beat the transformation, and in no time, good old Jonas would return to his normal grumpy self.

She gazed at the red numbers on the LED digital clock. 12:16 a.m. Just shy of three hours since the attack. She assumed his fever would quickly run its course and break by dawn, and they could sneak out before first light. In truth, she had never witnessed the cycle from start to finish and had no idea what to expect. He was weak and the going would be slow, but they had time. If the cops hadn't come by now, they weren't coming.

"You've always watched over me, Jonas. This time, I'm watching over you, no matter how long as it takes."

She retrieved a pillow, placing it under his head to make him as comfortable as possible. With a sigh she sat on the floor against a distant wall where she could better keep an eye on both him and the gaping doorway. Holding the pistol in both hands, she began to sing. Before long, exhaustion overcame her and she drifted off.

She dreamt of a beautiful park -- the same garden her mind often led to during the afflictive days of her captivity. A path made with tiny cobblestones passed along a bench up ahead. Atop the seat, the Artifact lay. When her eyes locked onto the chest, she hurried forward to take it.

Sudden, frantic, desperate utterances tugged at the edge of her unconscious mind, wresting her from the deep sleep.

Katie ignored them, refusing to wake. She wanted to stay in her safe place, her magical escape.

Get out, get out, get out. The words came as a repeating whisper.

Get out. Get out. Get out. The dreamland shook, and the beautiful sky filled with black smoke, blocking the sun. She knew what was coming next.

GET OUT! GET OUT! GET OUT!

Katie awoke, shaken to consciousness by the nightmare that was all too real. Her eyes sprang open. She was ready to fight. Her attention was sharply drawn to Jonas. He had moved closer to her before again falling unconscious on the floor. Her eyes went to the clock's red display: 12:28 a.m.

An unmistakable compulsion to flee the motel pressed upon her. She felt the Artifact's power.

"Shall I leave him to die, alone in this wretched place?" Her angry scream filled the room. "I'm done with all of this! Do you hear me?"

As instantly as her explosive voice shattered the stillness, the empty silence returned. Resolved to the bleak reality of the situation, she crawled to and knelt beside Jonas. She touched his cheek. "It is I who has failed you." Tears streamed down her face. Katie wanted to stay with him but knew if he transformed, she really would be forced to kill him. Katie tugged on his necklace until the clasp of the blood-stained cross broke loose.

She shoved clothes, the necklace, and the holy water vial into her pack. "Come on, boy." She summoned Chance.

221

The Akita padded over to her, head hung low. His white fur matted in blood from his own wounds. He glanced at the man, and then came to her, nuzzling his snout in her palm and licked her hand.

She stared down at his large white face knowingly. "I understand."

Chance returned to him and lay down, resting his head across Jonas's chest.

"Good—very well then." Katie wept. It was only a modicum of solace that the dog would provide him the company she could not.

Jonas had spent years preparing her for the possibility of his sudden death, but saying it was one thing, facing it was another. And when the stark reality of the situation hit her, she came undone.

For the first time in fifteen years, she would move on without him, never to see him again. This man had laid down his life for her, having asked nothing in return. The depth of her pity was immeasurable; she was inconsolable and heartbroken beyond words.

Katie touched his hand and prayed silently for a few brief moments before rising to her feet. She stepped over the charred remains of the wolf by the door and left the room, emerging into the chill of the pre-dawn morning.

She walked down the dark gravel road into an uncertain future, leaving the motel, Chance, and Jonas far behind.

Chapter 27

Ashburn, Virginia: September 20

"Mind slowing down? We should be getting close," Katie said.

The woman in her early forties who picked her up a few miles outside the rural town of Staunton complied. She switched on her turn signal and gently decelerated as they exited the evening traffic. They turned onto an unmarked road and slowly drove a wooded, unpaved drive for what was a little less than a half mile but felt much longer.

"We'll pass a utility road and a barn before we get to the house on the right."

Sixty or so yards into the forest, set back in the clearing, they found the house. The blue minivan stopped in front of the black mailbox numbered 33781. The wings of the weathered wooden duck affixed to the side of the mailbox spun backwards in the brisk wind. Katie turned a caring glance at the young children sleeping in the back seat, envying their carefree existence.

"Thank you again, Mrs. Dansby," she said with a quiet voice as she opened her door.

"Are you sure about this?" the concerned mother asked.

"I'll be fine. Things are going to be better, I suppose." Katie stepped out of the van onto the dusty gravel and closed the door quietly to avoid waking them. She waved as the van turned around and drove away, then pulled her backpack over her shoulder. Filled with reluctance, she walked toward the house.

She had envisioned this moment a half dozen times over the past few hours, and no matter how many times she went over it in her head, there simply was no easy way to deliver the kind of news she had. Katie fought her dread as she climbed the blue painted stairs of the country porch. She hesitated once again before opening the screen and rapping on the inner door.

Chapter 28

"Who in the world?" Leila Refai mumbled when she heard the knock. Living in a rural area of Ashburn, Virginia, she was not accustomed to visitors, especially at this hour. She rose from her laptop and peered from the second floor window of her study, but when she didn't see any vehicles in front of her home, she reached into her desk drawer and pulled out a pistol. She put it behind the small of her back and pulled down her black sweater to conceal it.

With an increase of news stories about the looting and violence breaking out around the world as a result of the Black Flu, she refused to be complacent. She peered over the balcony through the two-story foyer and saw a tall Asian girl standing outside her front door.

She came down the stairs and peeked out the window. When she saw the girl was alone, she turned on the porch light and opened the door.

"Yes? May I help you?" Leila asked. When she noticed the blue sapphire ring on the girl's finger, her suspicion grew.

Katie stared at her for several long seconds, still searching for the right words. The woman, now wearing short hair, aged very little over the many years since the photo.

"Ms. Refai, my name is Katie Mitchell." Having no idea where to start her incredible story, Katie took a deep breath and told it to her from the beginning.

Leila listened in silence, cupping her mouth in despair,

as she recounted the attack at the isolated Stanton motel that had taken the life of the only father she ever knew.

When Katie finished, she took the woman's hand to comfort her. As soon as she touched her, Leila's transcendental empathy washed over her, filling her with the depths of both the love and the despair the woman felt for him. Katie embraced the woman that Jonas had never stopped loving, and together they bitterly wept.

Chapter 29
January 17

Leila walked into the house, put her tote in the closet, and hung up her jacket.

"Katie. I got dinner!" she shouted up the stairs before heading into the kitchen. She put the rented movies on the counter beside her keys and set the table. The woman called for her again. Katie's coat draped off the back of one of the chairs, and the old car Leila bought for her sat outside. Becoming concerned, she went upstairs and peeked inside Katie's room. When she saw the catastrophe throughout the room, she could not speak.

The sword was propped in the corner. Her desk and a table looked insufficient to hold all the equipment that covered them: A network switch Leila had never seen before, along with the computer and printer she'd insisted could not be fixed. Some repaired speakers and several of her old hard drives the girl dragged up from the basement and rebuilt. Two old monitors Katie had repurposed to serve as intrusion detection devices for spying the perimeter of the house. Her gun lay next to the computer's keyboard and mouse.

Stacks of pads filled with Katie's hand-drawn sketches piled up on the distant nightstand. Rows of books about everything from fiction to tech manuals, lined one of the walls, and an almost impossible mound of clothes were haphazardly strewn over most of the floor and bed. More of them hung from several open dresser drawers.

As her eyes moved across the disarray, she could only guess how the girl even knew the clean ones from the dirty. And there, somehow, oblivious to the calamity before her, Katie lay across the middle of her bed with ear buds in her ears. She'd fallen asleep, listening to music, with her face atop her journal.

"I got dinner." She stepped over a pile of clothes and into the room. When her eyes passed over the beautiful and mysterious chest Katie kept on the nightstand, Leila glanced at her to confirm she still slept. Upon seeing the girl had not stirred, she crossed the cluttered floor and touched the artifact. She'd never seen it up close before. Immediately Leila felt drawn to the object Katie showed so much protectiveness about. She ran her fingers alongside the beautiful box, wondering about the curious glyphs that covered the outside. Looking for a way to open it, she started to pick it up.

Katie bolted upright in the bed and the woman jumped. "Can I help you?" she asked.

"I—I ordered Chinese and picked up a couple of movies. Do you feel up for a ladies night in?"

"Thanks, but I'm not hungry." Katie returned the buds to her ears and continued writing.

"Food will be here in half an hour." Leila disregarded her, knowing she could still hear her. "Not to be a nag, but you mind picking up a bit before you come downstairs?"

***

Thirty minutes later, Katie sauntered into the kitchen, still listening to music. She schlepped to the refrigerator, grabbed a bottle of Coke, and sat down for dinner. Leila turned off the TV and joined Katie at the table, then poured a glass of merlot.

"So, how's the job hunt going?"

Katie passed her the box of lo mien.

"Fine," she said simply.

"That's it—fine?" Leila took a sip of wine and tried not to be aggravated by the ever present black cords dangling from the girl's ears.

"Could you take those out for just a few minutes?" she asked with a patient smile.

Katie sighed audibly, once again removing them. This time she slipped them into her sweatshirt pocket.

"I've been dying to talk to you all day. Tell me how your interviews went. Three of them, right?"

"No. One of the hiring managers canceled. He just said that something came up. As for the other two positions, it seemed obvious they were looking for somebody else."

"Sometimes it feels that way during the interview and then, when you least expect it, the offer comes. I wouldn't jump to the conclusion they didn't like you."

"No jump necessary. They didn't."

Leila touched her arm. "Oh, honey, I'm sorry. What don't you think went well?"

"At my first interview, the manager said they have a certain corporate image they need to maintain, whatever that means. The second company, two people interviewed me at the same time. I thought I hit it off with the woman but the man said, though I seemed fully capable, he didn't feel comfortable with my lack of experience."

"These were the IT jobs you showed me? Doing some kind of network security? I don't pretend to know the first thing about any of that stuff, but you seemed confident you could do the job, right?"

"I can do it. That guy hit me with every question he could think of and I answered them all. I bet I knew more about networks than he did, but when the interview ended, he

228

said the position was better suited for someone with a little more corporate experience."

"Well, don't let this discourage you, Katie. Interviewing for a job is not an easy thing, and even under the best of circumstances, it takes time. You're a bright, resourceful young woman and I'm confident something will break your way soon enough.

"Thanks, but I don't know. The social media drones on and on that the plague has companies all over the world concerned and waiting to see what happens."

"Well, I'm sure that's true to an extent, but it's still a bit sensational. Every few years, something happens around the world, and there is widespread panic about how near the end is. And just as fast, everyone forgets about it and moves on with their lives, as if nothing ever happened. Trust me—they'll find a cure and these fears will blow over soon enough. When they do, just watch how fast the businesses snap back. You'll see."

The look on the teen's face made it apparent how dispirited she felt. Katie had always felt tremendous respect for Leila and knew she meant well, but she also believed the tough, hard-edged woman tended to be naïve. Leila often spoke about the difficulties of growing up in Jordan, until leaving the country in her mid-twenties. But decades later, Leila's perspective had turned soft—borderline complacent— insulated by the lectern of her American classroom and whatever half-truths she was spoon-fed from the evening news. To her, it seemed the woman had forgotten the very different reality of the streets, particularly those abroad.

"Hey, don't be like that. You can do this," Leila said with a supportive smile. "Tonight, we can take a look through your resume together. I'll make some suggestions about how you can make it stronger. Even though you have the knowledge to do higher level technical things, maybe for now, you should start with something that's a bit more entry level—just until you get some experience under your name. Sound like a plan?"

Katie stared at her plate as she took a bite of the spring roll.

"Are you okay?" Leila touched her arm again.

"Yeah, I guess so. At first I was truly excited about a fresh start here but after nine interviews, two job fairs, and several dozen unanswered applications, I think I'm just beginning to accept what I knew all along. Corporate life isn't for someone like me. Besides, who wants to sit in a fishbowl all day anyway? And the entry level and service jobs around here are already taken, most of them by kids in high school."

"Well, what about friends or the gym we go to? That could be a great place to network for jobs and make new acquaintances. Who knows, as a bonus, you might even bump into a cute guy."

"You're kidding, right?" she asked with a flat tone.

"Why not? Don't pretend you haven't noticed Mr. Dimples, you know the one—tall, dark, and *yummy*. Goodness, if I were but ten years younger..." Leila tried to lighten her mood.

"Can we change the subject? Please?" she replied, with an angry red blush.

"Stop being defensive, Katie, I'm worried about you. You've been here for four months and other than training and working out, all you do is read, draw, write in your journal, or play on the computer—day and night. Basically, you have no life."

"You think I'm sitting around, playing games all day?" Katie shook her head with annoyance. "What can I say so we can move from this interrogation?"

"Oh come on now, don't be so thin skinned." Exchanges such as this one left the experienced professor—used to large lecture halls full of young adults, feeling much more than a generation separated the two of them. Not wanting to let the evening be ruined, Leila masked her frustration through a forced smile. She retrieved a white plastic shopping bag from under her chair and placed it on the table in front of her. Maybe the gift would reverse both their souring moods.

"What's that?" she asked.

"I bought you something. Go on, open it," the woman replied.

Katie reached inside and removed a black case with a clear plastic top.

Leila smiled. "I'm sure I'll live to regret it, but I got you a new phone. I've never understood why you keep that old thing, but now you can finally get rid of it."

Katie stared at the new device and thought of Jonas as a sorrowful pang tore through her empty insides.

"You can send emails, browse the internet, music, games, everything. It even has a—" Leila stopped after seeing her face. "What's the matter?"

"Nothing."

"I thought you'd be elated, especially given how much time you spend on the thing."

"I—thank you," was all Katie could bring herself to say.

"You're welcome but if you don't like it, I can return it. I just think since you'll be working soon, and people will need to reach you, it would be a good idea for you to have a phone that does what it's supposed to. Not to mention should you have an emergency."

"Thanks. It's great, really."

"So, have you taken a look at any of the books I brought home from the university? There are numerous drills that might help you develop your powers. Maybe try a pencil on the counter and see if you can roll it off the side," Leila said half joking.

Katie rolled her eyes. "You read too much fiction. It doesn't work like that."

"Tell me then. How does it work?" she asked in exasperation.

"It just happens, when I'm afraid or really ticked. The only power I seem to have any control over is my telepathy and even that's hit or miss lately. You act like I can just do stuff anytime I feel like it."

"Well, maybe not yet. But like everything else in life, perfection takes a great deal of practice and tremendous patience."

"Wonderful, a lecture—perfect after a long week," Katie grumbled under her breath.

"Okay, out with it. What's really bothering you? You've been—"

"I'm going to Hong Kong," she blurted.

"Excuse me?" Leila replied.

"I'm going to China in the spring. If you could loan me the money, I'll work it off when I return. If not, I'll sell the gun, and if I have to, my sword too. I hate to do it, but they're the only things I own that are worth anything."

"I don't understand. Why do you feel the need to do this? Go to China, I mean."

"I need to find my parents and fill this gigantic hole in my memory. I also need to understand why it feels like half the world is determined to capture or kill me when, as far as I know, I haven't done anything wrong."

"I'm sorry, Katie, but this is not a good time. Let's table this until next year. When I've saved up enough time off from work and I can go with you. We can even make a vacation out of it, if you'd like."

"Thank you, but this is something I have to do alone."

"That's absolutely out of the question! You're too young, and it's far too dangerous."

"*Too young*? I've been on my own since I was seven."

"All the same, I don't like the idea. I'm sorry but you can't go." Leila shook her head.

"I'm sorry too because I hoped you'd understand. But I'm not a child. With or without your blessing, I'm going."

"Katie, I know you've had a pretty crappy week, but this is absurd and you're letting emotions cloud your judgment. I won't be party to an unwise decision that could get you hurt, stranded in a foreign country, or worse. You're not going and that's final. If Jonas were here, he would tell you the very same thing." Leila shook with frustration as she placed the wine glass to her lips.

"Don't you dare speak about him!" Katie shouted. Instantly, the wine glass exploded in the woman's hand.

"Oh no! I'm so sorry!" Katie cried. She stood and picked up the shards of glass from the table, putting them on her plate. "I don't know what happened."
Leila stared straight ahead, unmoving and speechless. Her stunned face turned pale and full of horror. When Katie saw the fear she had caused, the plate fell from her hand.

"I'm sorry." Tearing up, she dashed to her room and slammed the door.

***

The following Monday afternoon, Leila sat in her favorite chair grading research papers when Katie came home from the gym.

"Hey there." She glimpsed at the girl when she came through the front door.

"Hello," Katie replied.

"I have time to practice some with you today, that is, if you're up to it."

"Sure, let me put my gear upstairs." It relieved Katie to see Leila recovered from Friday night's incident. Since the outburst, the silence around the house had grown awkward. Leila put on her coat and they went outside.

"How was your day? Did the interview go well?" she asked as they strolled toward the old shed in their back yard.

"Not so good, and I have some disappointing news to tell you."

Leila slowed, searching her face with concern. "What?"

"The manager said he would keep my application on file and if anything becomes available needing my skills, he'd let me know." Katie had a long look of disappointment.

"Oh, honey. I'm so sorry. I know how much you wanted this job." Leila reached out to hug and console her when an odd, silly grin broke across the girl's face.

"Why are you smiling?" she asked with a perplexed look.

"I'm just kidding. I got the Albion job!" Katie screamed with glee.

"What? You were putting me on?"

"Yup! Can you believe it? I start on Monday."

"That's wonderful!" Leila hugged her. "I'm so proud of you, Katie. See, I told you, you could do it!"

She beamed brightly. Leila smiled too.

"Tell me about it. Is it full time? What are your hours?"

"They're not positive about my shift yet. The monitoring center is open twenty-four hours a day, seven days a week. The open slot is 10 a.m. to 6 p.m., but shifts are based on seniority. He said his team gets priority and I would backfill the vacated slot. I'm sure they'll start me on the midnight shift since most people prefer days."

"Ouch!" Leila squinted. "Well, hopefully, you won't be stuck on the graveyard shift too long."

"I'm fine with it. You know me, I'm pretty alert at night. I'm just really pumped to work again."

"You'll have to let me know how I can support you." Leila hugged her again. "I'm so excited for you, Katie! This weekend, I'm taking you out to celebrate. Can I just tell you how proud of you I am right now?"

"Thank you. Me too." She grinned.

"But before we begin our drills, I just have to know."

"What?"

"The new job...any cute men?"

235

Katie stuck her lip out in a playful pout. "Not even one."
They both broke into laughter. She followed Leila into the
large shed. The woman moved some gardening supplies and
hoisted huge bag of birdseed out of the way so she could reach
the small cans of paint on the shelf. "Would you grab a few of
these?" Katie filled her arms and trailed her to the picnic table
underneath an enormous oak tree.

"What are we doing?"

Leila motioned. "Bring those over and set them down."
Katie did as instructed and watched her line them along the
edge.

"Now, stand next to that tree and face me. I want you to
focus on one of these cans and concentrate on knocking it
down."

Katie went over and turned. She took a deep breath and
tried to relax her mind as she stared across the yard at the
small, stacked paint tins.

"Shut out distracting thoughts. Narrow your attention
only on that can," Leila coached, but no matter how much the
woman tried to convince her that she could develop the
control of will and topple the canister, the girl did not believe.
And after an hour of futility and obvious frustration, she ended
the practice.

Chapter 30
Reston, Virginia. February 8

Jaime leaned over the flimsy partition separating her
from Luke Ramsey's desk. "I heard Dan's extended an offer to
someone, and they're supposed to start today."

"What? Last I knew he hadn't found anyone solid," he
replied.

"That's not what I heard. Word on the street, they planned on making an offer to somebody at Booz," Morgan, another technician, said. He always seemed to know the going's on that no one else did.

Jaime replied, "With only one interview left after this Booz guy, they were completely settled on him. Looking at the final candidate's resume and qualifications, it wasn't even close. She stole the job."

"Wait...*she?*" Morgan rubbed his hands together in anticipation.

"Is she any good?" Luke ignored him.

"Well, Dan and Susie interviewed her and both thought very highly of her. Now Dan is one thing, but you know Susie isn't impressed by anything."

"True," Luke agreed.

"Susie says she's green but a bit of a prodigy. I'm hoping she ramps up fast, because these extended shifts are wearing me out. My cat hasn't seen me for weeks," Jaime said.

"Spare us the feline details. All this chitter chatter and neither of you has answered the real question." Morgan palmed a rubber football before zinging it toward Luke. From his chair, at the last second, Luke reached out and snagged the errant pass.

"Which is?"

"Is she single?" Morgan smiled.

Jaime shook her head. "Do you ever give all that a rest?"

"Does opportunity ever sleep?" he replied. "Then neither do I."

Luke drew back his arm to return the pass, but stopped in mid-motion. He watched with piqued interest when his manager escorted a beautiful young woman into the enormous Global Network Operations Center.

"Nice outfit," Jaime said after following his gaze.

"What's up?" Morgan waited for the pass with outstretched hands. He turned to follow their gazes. After taking in an eye full of the girl, and his chair almost toppled, he said, "Hold up! Nobody said we brought in *talent*— I got dibs."

"And here we go," Jaime said.

Morgan's classless predictability always amused them. Playing it up, he grinned.

"Thank you, Dan." Morgan said, referring to their manager, out of earshot on the other side of the large room. "Dan, my man, since you gave me an early Christmas, I promise I'll never play online games during work hours ever again."

"Yeah, right," they both said at the same time.

Katie sat in Dan's office, filling out forms and talking.

The entire time she was inside the room, both Luke and Morgan passed frequent glances at her through the window. After a short while, Dan and Katie emerged from the office and he led her on a tour of operations.

When Luke saw them turn his way, he leaned back in his chair, attempting to look casual and cool.

"Everyone say hello to Katie Mitchell. She'll be joining our team," Dan said.

"Go—good to meet you, Katie," Luke stammered with a stupefied gaze.

"It's great to meet you. I'm Morgan, at your service." He held her shaking hand and gave her fingers a tactless kiss.

"Jaime." The woman waved, rolling her eyes at Morgan.

"Hi, everyone." Katie smiled, after taking her hand back.

"Love the brow." Morgan pointed to her face.

"Thanks," Katie touched the barbell piercing above her left eye, as if she had forgotten about it.

"So, where did you work before, Mitchell?" His elbows rested on the edge of his cube wall.

"Just a small start-up you've never heard of," she replied.

"Maybe I have. Is it local?" Jaime asked.

"No, I'm not from around here. Oregon," she said in an even, matter-of-fact tone.

"Oregon, that's interesting."

"Really? Why is that?" Katie asked.

"I just don't believe I've ever met anyone from Oregon. How did you ever end up all the way out here in Virginia?"

"Long boring story, not even worth your time." Katie dismissively waved.

"I'd like to hear it sometime." Jaime smiled.

Katie hoped that was the end of the woman's interrogation, but she wouldn't let her curiosity go.

"What kind of network security experience do you have?"

Luke shot Jaime a glance that she needed to lay off.

"I have extensive experience monitoring some smaller networks, but to be honest, nothing like what you have here. Don't worry though—I'm a very fast learner."

"If you don't mind, Miss Mitchell, I'll show you around the rest of the facility and get you over to HR," Dan said.

"Welcome to the team," Luke said after regaining most of his composure.

"Good to meet you all." With a warm smile, Katie followed Dan toward the sliding doors.

Chapter 31
February 26

The immense, state of the art, glass-enclosed Global Network Operations Center, with its raised floor and long rows of bell curved desks, reminded Katie of the bridge of a movie's spaceship. The GNOC, powered by next generation Cisco equipment, had been designed to accommodate a staff of 58 technicians.

Each workstation was outfitted with a panel of three attached monitors. At the front of the chamber, a mammoth wall of dozens of screens oversaw network threats, cybercrimes, and blackouts around the planet. Red points on a silhouette of the United States logged incidents of outages and service failures. Regional, national, and global news updates from NOAA, the Weather Channel, CNN, and the New York Stock Exchange ran non-stop.

With around-the-clock coverage of every aspect of the news, she had an inside view of the outside world, all at a glance. Thanks to Jonas's paranoia, she'd known networking specs for years. It was perfect. Her sharp, analytical mind and strong grasp of technology allowed her to bypass the mandatory two-month cross training. After shadowing Luke for a few days, her training wheels were removed and she was permitted to work alone.

Still, working in a NOC did not entirely fit what she'd always envisioned—and certainly not what she'd gathered from the interview, believing they'd have virtual non-stop responses to alarms during the shift. But when they weren't spending hours trying to get the right person on the phone for help with outages, there were long bouts of inactivity. Techs chatted with each other on instant messenger or social networks, played on their phones, or gossiped about other shifts—none of which Katie had interest in.

Tonight, with only one major incident, time dragged on. The news of the past week looped in CNN's coverage so many times, they'd all grown tone deaf to it: A minor earthquake in Egypt's capital, resulting in numerous injuries—though surprisingly, not a single casualty. On the center's largest screen, the news network continued to report the about the latest incident of black smoke, which could faintly be seen above a decimated Cairo street, looking like a bomb had fallen on it.

At the front of the room, Morgan sat next to Dominic, engrossed in a computer role-playing game, *Divinity, Original Sin*. A few rows behind them, on the opposite side of the room, Luke managed to block out the brash bantering of the two in their game. His eyes fixed on notes and a textbook, studying for another certification. She had no interest in games, and with little activity to monitor, even after four ineffectual espressos, boredom quickly led to Katie's drowsiness.

She looked at her backpack, and then glanced beyond the glass-enclosed windows—strictly a matter of caution since she knew everyone else departed the building hours earlier. Confident the three men in the room with her would not notice, Katie reached down for her backpack. She pulled out the artifact and placed it on the table in front of her. Fingering the glyphs as she had done countless times, she gave the object a long hard look and set her thoughts upon opening it, but nothing happened.

Over the past twelve years, whenever she relied on its capabilities, it manifested itself and came to her aid, particularly in the most dangerous and desperate situations. But ever since coming to live with Leila, it fell dormant—almost as though she'd lost the mental connection she had to it.

The long stretch of inability to summon any of her powers kindled a frustrated hunger, burning deep within. Never before had she wanted so much to pry open the enigmatic chest, once and for all, and discover what was inside.

She sipped from her mug, browsing blogs, news articles, and photos taken around the world of the plague, and the black smoke that filled the sky. Then one article caught her attention. A farmer in relatively nearby West Virginia shot an intruder in his doorway. When the local authorities arrived, the farmer claimed the person he shot curled into a smoldering ball of soot.

Naturally, unable to find anything more than the pile of ashes inside his home, they were skeptical of the man's account. Upon reading the full story, she doubted he had encountered an agent, more than likely, one of the much weaker dark creepers looking for a meal, hoping to make easy prey of the rancher living in seclusion.

She continued searching for references to the object -- her keywords: real magic, glyphs, artifact, relic, and chest. Looking through various symbols—anything that might give her a clue as to the nature of the apparatus, she skimmed through hundreds of results, all related to video games and fantasy books, but nothing tangible.

She realized the exercise was an absurdity, and what was she expecting anyway? A big classified that would advertise: "Missing, one powerful magic box?" After all, only curiosity made her search for its origins in the first place. She felt a kinship to it, it was drawn to her and she to it—like the artifact had always been intended for her.

What would she do if confronted by the rightful owner who wanted it back? What was she *prepared* to do if they came for it? No matter who or what blew through town, Katie was determined she would never allow it to be taken from her.

Just then, a wild thought crossed her mind. She pulled her old phone she still carried from her pocket and flipped through the screens until she found the text message she'd received in New Mexico several years earlier. It seemed so obvious, she couldn't figure out why she'd never considered it before now.

It took some time but with the company's sophisticated tracking software, she identified the IP address of the anonymous message. Spoofing a fake number, she got ready to place a call to that IP address through a dummy server that showed an originating phone number in Niagara, New York—safely hundreds of miles away.

"Hey. What are you up to?" Luke asked innocently. Katie had been so focused on setting up the call she didn't notice him get up from his desk. She barely managed to get the chest into her bag before he rounded into her aisle.

"I thought I detected an intrusion." She bit her lip.

"We didn't get any notification." He looked at the big board before glimpsing at one of the screens on her desk.

243

Right away, he knew something was off. Looking into his face, she decided not to carry on the ruse. She'd never been good at lying anyway.

"I need to level with you about something."

He crossed his arms. "Go for it."

"Seriously, Luke, I need to know I can trust you."

"Of course you can. What's going on?"

She glanced toward the front of the room to make sure Morgan and Dominic were not listening.

"Have a seat," she said.

He pulled the chair from Jaime's empty workstation and sat beside her.

"Ever since I was a kid some men have been after me. To be totally honest, I still really don't know why." She would not mention the box to him, and stopped far short of sharing the unbelievable aspects of the story, especially about the supernatural wraiths and the Gwyllgi.

"What do you mean they are *after you*?" He frowned. "What did you do?"

"I didn't do anything. I was only a kid. They've been hunting me like an animal for as long as I can remember. It started all the way back in Oregon and I've been on the move ever since. Years ago, I got this text." She showed him her phone. He stared at the screen with a bewildered look that reminded her of the same expression on Jonas's face when she'd initially shown it to him.

"After all these years, you've decided to try and figure out who sent it."

Katie raised her eyebrows in silent confirmation. She searched his face, having no idea what he might do or say next. If he alerted their manager, it would cost her the job.

"What are you waiting for? We've got a call to make." His smile brimmed with curiosity.

She turned her chair to face the computer and made the attempt. With every crackling ring of what sounded like an overseas call, tension knotted in her bowels. She wiped the perspiration from her clammy palms on her jeans. But after the call went unanswered, she waited for the away message to pick up.

She might obtain a name and see what more she could find about the identity of the mysterious person who warned her of danger an hour before Dorian wandered into the New Mexico diner.

With a little more work, she might even determine the phone's electronic identification number, allowing her to track its location real-time. The hollow ringing abruptly ceased. Several seconds passed and she figured the call dropped.

"Hello?" A male voice on the other end startled her. Quietly, she placed the cup on the desk.

"What's happening?" Luke mouthed, when he saw the petrified look on her face.

"Who's there?" The person on the other end asked.

The long space of silence left her reluctant to breathe with fear he would hear her. The call was a colossal mistake she already regretted. It dawned on her, though the text had warned of danger, that did not guarantee the message's sender was friendly. What if he had other ideas?

Jonas told her many times they could trust no one, and in a moment of temerity, she may have inadvertently given a clue of how to find her. Katie wanted to terminate the call but she froze. Her extremities tingled with a sudden loss of circulation as panic set in.

"Xiang Shi, *is that you?*"

The startled girl shot backwards in the wheeled chair and flung the hands-free set from her head like it burned her. Anxiety she'd not felt in years rippled through her. Whoever this man was, he'd used her real name—a name no one in the United States should have known.

Involuntarily, her eyes whisked back to her bag. She had no idea who held the phone on the other end but he obviously knew who she was. He was still looking for it—for her. The call ended, and the man was gone but the new life she had created for herself no longer felt safe.

Chapter 32

Over the next month at home, Katie and Leila repeated the same exercises every Wednesday and Saturday afternoon. The phone incident troubled Katie to the point she pressed to rediscover her powers, but she could not hold her concentration during the drills.

She made excuses and complained. Leila recognized something troubled the girl and kept her patience. She decided it might be time to break the monotony and introduce new activities, with hopes she could give Katie that single spark she needed to tap into her abilities.

Some of the supposed easier exercises consisted of sliding coins and rolling marbles off the top of the kitchen counter, to very difficult: extinguishing a candle's flame by focusing on it. After many weeks of little success, Katie hit rock bottom, consumed with frustration, and wanted to give up altogether.

"You just need to clear your thoughts. Don't think about cold or anything else, and force your will on the target. Pick any one of them and just be patient and it will come to you." Leila set up eight cans on top of each other like a shooting gallery at a roadside carnival.

As Katie stood gazing at the half empty paint cans, she already felt defeated. Her arms were crossed and her thoughts were someplace else.

"This isn't working. I told you it would never happen but you didn't listen. It's a total waste of time and its cold out here." In resignation, she turned and went back toward the house.

Leila screamed, "My goodness, you're such a quitter!"

"What?" she said in shock.

"Complain, complain, day and night. The fact is, Katie, you're *weak* and all you've ever managed to do is run from every problem that ever confronted you."

"Whatever! What would you know about any of it?" Katie yelled and turned to leave. Something hard struck her in the back of the head.

"Hey!" Katie screamed, turning to see what hit her. Leila scooped a handful of the large thorny acorns that littered the yard.

"Coward! Yes, I said it! Go ahead and run just like you always do!" she screamed louder and threw another nut. This one struck her in the middle of her forehead.

"You're crazy!" Katie shouted aghast, backing away from her. "What's wrong with you?" She considered the possibility that the woman was playing around, until she flung the entire handful of the projectiles.

As acorns were about to pepper Katie, they stopped in mid-flight, as if stuck on an invisible wall, and fell to the ground in front of her. Simultaneously, all eight of the small cans toppled from the picnic table.

"That a girl!" Leila exclaimed. Confused, Katie glared across the yard.

"Not much of a surprise that anger's still your strongest trigger. We'll continue to work on that, but I'm happy to say, I think after all this time, we're finally getting somewhere." Leila smiled.

Chapter 33
Dulles, Va. April 7

"Excuse me, party people. Duty calls," Morgan sophomorically announced, rising from their booth.

"Me too. Where is it?" Katie surveyed the crowded French-Asian fusion restaurant.

"Right this way, miss." Katie slid out and followed him. Jaime glanced over her shoulder until Katie disappeared around the corner. She turned to Luke and leaned closer to the table.

"*So...*" she raised her eyebrows with a knowing smirk.

"So, what?" he gave a bewildered face.

"So, you've been spending a lot of time with Mitchell."

"Yeah, just showing her the ropes. She wasn't kidding about being a fast learner. She's cool." He nodded.

"Don't give me that *cool* thing, Luke. I see how you look at her. You sure that's all there is to it?"

"You're imagining things, Jaime, and what's with the inquisition anyway?"

She gasped, with a huge disbelieving smile. He fidgeted with his straw.

"What is it now?" Jaime grabbed his phone from the table and glanced at the call records.

"Give me that!" He reached for it.

"Look at this: Monday night, outgoing call to Katie. Tuesday night, two more calls. Nothing Wednesday, but an inbound one from her Thursday night. Let's see, three calls from Morgan, then wait for it, surprise, tonight—another inbound call from Katie. No wonder you're always busy when I hit you up."

"Give me that! Ever heard of privacy?" Luke snatched the phone from her., his face a deep shade of rose.

"Privacy?" She laughed. "We've been close friends for almost ten years, so good luck with that. And as one of your closest BFFs, allow me to save you. Not only is the girl a bit on the young side for your tastes, Katie's definitely not your type."

"I wasn't aware I needed saving but thank you, and let it be known I have never had a type."

"Convince yourself of that, lover."

His face turned from the blush to a solemn frown. His attempts to disguise either of the two expressions failed.

"See? It doesn't happen very often but it's pretty evident when you're interested in someone. Looks like this time you've got it really bad. Women just know these things. You could almost say it's our Spidey sense."

"Let it go, web-slinger. I don't have any idea what you're talking about," he lied.

"I'm talking about that thing you do with your nose— yeah that one." She reached for his face.

He swatted her hand. "You've got real issues. Time to see a professional."

"Yeah, well, that's not exactly news now, is it?"

"Anyway, what makes you say that?" He couldn't resist.

"Say what?" With coy confusion, she bit into her last sushi roll.

"That Katie's not my type. I'm curious why you say that, or how you would even know, for that matter."

"See, I knew it!" She squealed with such excitement.

"Don't be juvenile, Jaime." He realized too late she'd baited him.

"Look at you. Could it be more obvious? The ever unflappable Luke is on the defensive." She dabbed the corner of her mouth with her napkin. "Don't get me wrong, she's a sweet kid, but with that angelic face, I'd bet she still gets ID'd at the movies, while your speed is more like bars and bands."

"*Again*, we're only hanging out. Try as much as you want to make it more. She's different and, to be honest, it's a nice change. By the way, she's much more mature than you'd believe."

"I'll bet." Her devilish smirk lingered.

"Don't." He shook his head, wishing she would spin off on another wild tangent, as she was oft prone to do.

"I swear, sometimes it's just too easy." She finished her drink. When Katie and Morgan returned, she saw the guilty look on Luke's face, and glanced between them with smiling suspicion.

"And why do I feel I walked in on the tail end of an inside joke?"

"Not at all." Luke played it off. "We were thinking about ordering dessert. You in?"

Katie slid back into the booth next to Jaime. "Dessert? No, no, I'll pass."

"Come on, live a little, it's on me," Morgan said when he sat. He slid the menu in front of her, pointing to a picture of a crème covered Grand Marnier soufflé on the inside flap.

"I'm sure it's every bit as delicious as it looks, but after all that Sushi, I'm busting opening all my seams. Can I get a rain check, Morgan?" She smiled.

"You better believe I'll hold you to it, Mitchell." He shook his finger at her. A woman at a nearby table began coughing, and a conspicuous hush fell across the restaurant. When the fit of rough coughing stopped, she looked around, aware that most of the people around her stared.

"I'm fine." The woman held up her hand. After a few uneasy moments, patrons returned to their meals.

"Katie, have you been following the plague?" Jaime glanced at the woman again.

"I try not to." Katie chewed a mouthful of ice.

Morgan seemed stunned by this. "Wow, I don't know how you manage that one. Did you see what just happened? And it's like that no matter where you go, everyone's paranoid."

"I try to stay busy and keep my mind on other things, like my trip," Katie said referring to her upcoming travel to China. All she'd told them was she planned to visit a close aunt getting up there in age. It had been enough info for Morgan and Jaime, only Luke wanted more details about exactly where, and when Katie would return. He'd even insisted on taking her to the airport, which finally, she'd agreed. "Besides, worrying about all that stuff won't make it go away, will it?"

"Of course not, but I can't help wondering how long before Wraiths and Creepers are roaming through *our* backyards looking for a snack."

"One too many movies, *way* too many role-playing games for this one." Jaime laughed, gesturing to him with her thumb.

"Whatever. My ZKIT is ready. You've been lulled to sleep like the rest of suburbia. You can wait around for creepers to kick down your door, but when they stagger into town one night, ready to sip someone up like a juice box, I won't be caught slackin' like the rest of you."

"ZKIT?" Katie asked.

"Zombie survival kit." With a grin, Luke shook his head. Glancing to Morgan, Jaime laughed again. "Tell me you're kidding."

"He's not. I've seen it," Luke said.

"What would someone keep in a zombie kit?" Katie asked with genuine intrigue.

"You know, all the normal undead readiness stuff; a 3600 calorie food bar, six pouches of water, a thermal emergency blanket, first aid kit, waterproof matches, some light sticks, a survival tool, an emergency hammer, survival bracelet, a whistle, and last, but not least, two jumbo packs of wild cherry fruit snacks."

More convinced the whole thing was a joke, Katie broke into abrupt laughter. The solemn look on Morgan's face remained.

"Oh, you were serious?" She covered her mouth to stifle the giggle. "I'm sorry."

"Of course I am, Mitchell. I happen to be a bit of an authority on the undead since my childhood and I've been on 'ready go,' for a zombie apocalypse since my teens."

"And by ready, he means he's seen every movie and owns most of the role-playing games that have been made," Jaime chimed in.

"Ready all the same." he smiled. "And no offense intended but what would our innocent little Katie know about fending off the undead?"

She wondered if they would react to her like a radioactive material leak if she ever told them how much experience she actually had on the subject.

"Not much." Katie shrugged. "But I do know this. Wraiths and Creepers are not zombies, and if either of them came after you, I'm certain that whistle and hammer of yours would prove to be pretty useless."

"Now wait just a second." Luke held up his hand. "The hammer might be useless, but I wouldn't be so quick to dismiss the effectiveness of the whistle and fruit snacks."

"Yeah?" Jaime said.

"Absolutely." He extended both arms in front of him like a mummy. "When the Creepers are pouring down into his parent's basement where he's held up, he could 'fend them off by tossing them fruity snacks as he blew the whistle to teach them how to roll over and beg." They all laughed.

"That's awesome." Katie stood, still cracking up. "Thanks for letting me tag along, you guys. I had a good time, but I should be getting home." She put money on the table for her meal.

Luke looked at his watch with disappointment. "But it's only 10:15, why so soon?"

"I promised Leila I'd be home before late. She's a bit on the protective side but that's okay."

"Let me settle the bill and I'll walk you to your car." He pulled out his wallet. All night, he'd been looking forward to being alone with her.

"I'm fine." Katie motioned with her hand. "Besides, they haven't brought your dessert."

Morgan stood, waving to get the server's attention. "Hold up, Mitchell, when the waitress returns, I'll get mine to go. Never know when you might need a little protection."

"Stop, you guys. I appreciate it, but I can handle myself. Just relax and enjoy yourselves. I'll see you Monday."

"Are you sure?" Luke asked. He wanted to insist but would not give Jaime the satisfaction.

"I'm sure. Drive safe and have a good weekend." Katie waved and left. She strolled through the outdoor town center, distracted with thoughts of Luke. After a short procession of cars cleared the stoplight, she crossed the street in the direction of a parking garage several blocks away.

After taking the elevator to the fourth floor, she exited, smiling at a group of younger teen girls full of laughter as they barreled past. As she approached her car, she noticed a suspicious white man standing on the other side of a large concrete support beam.

The man, wearing sunglasses, stepped back into the long shadow of the post. She stopped and looked for the nearest exit. The staircase on the west side of the garage and the elevator behind her, were equal distances away. And the man lurking in the shadow stood between her and the car. Katie wanted her gun but it was stowed in the center console. She hadn't dared bring it inside.

She quickly returned the way she had come. The sound of her hard soled boots on the pavement was answered by much softer soled shoes that quickened when her pace did.

She broke into a full sprint. After realizing the man would overtake her, she ducked around the corner and readied for an attack. When he wheeled around the corner, she blasted him in the sternum with a powerful kick that caught him by complete surprise.

The blow doubled him over and with her hands clasped, Katie slammed both fists across his back. The attacker crumpled to the ground, under the percussion of the powerful strike, but kicked her legs out. She landed on her back a few feet away, but as he wearily got up, ready to fight, she skipped to her feet.

The skilled fighter recovered quickly and led into her. Maneuvering just off line from his attacks, she deflected the strikes as she flowed straight into the path of the on-coming blitzkrieg.

Having closed the distance between them, with a spinning elbow smash—she caught him. Her assailant buckled, clutching at his face. As the man lay on the asphalt, cupping his broken nose, Katie escaped the garage.

Chapter 34

Katie slowed as she drove past the building, looking for a place to park. By the number of cars, there had to be a few hundred people inside. Once again, she found herself on the outside of a full parking lot looking in. And after driving some way down the street, she found an open space and pulled in alongside the curb. For most of her life and years on the run, she'd found comfort in being near crowds like these.

Now, the very thought of their unpredictability with such cramped, close quarters made her more apprehensive than walking down any street or garage alone ever could: just too much to account for—too many things to keep watch of.

Only weeks since an attacker tried to subdue her in the parking garage, the incident remained fresh on her mind. She scanned the street to make sure she wasn't followed. After moments of long hesitation, Katie finally willed herself to go inside and warily exited her car.

She entered the establishment after showing the doorman a perfect fake ID and snaked her way through the uncomfortable throng of people amassed within. Luke had warned her about the popular local hangout, but this was crazy. When she didn't see him anywhere, she took out her phone and called him.

"Katie. Are you here?" he asked on the other end of the line.

"Luke, can you hear me?"

The loud background music washed out the sound of their voices. She became frustrated and hung up. Katie pushed deeper into the raucous mob of reveling club goers and saw someone she knew from work, leaning against a handrail just outside the dance floor.

"Hey, you're Emily, right?"

The woman nodded.

"Katie Mitchell, we work together."

"Right. How are you?" she said with disinterest, as she craned her neck to leer at a couple of jarheads standing nearby.

"Good," Katie replied. "You haven't by any chance seen Luke?"

Emily glanced at her watch. 10:12 p.m. "He was here a few minutes ago, but I saw him leave."

"Thanks," Katie replied. She would be beyond irritated if he'd already left. She easily noticed the 6'3" tall man patiently making his way through the crowd of people between them. When he saw her, his face lit up.

"Hey, you," she said.

"Hope you weren't here too long. I waited for you until I realized I left my headlights on and ran back to my car. So glad you could come."

Luke possessed a ruggedly handsome appearance. The broad shouldered man had a muscular, well-toned physique. Light stubble covered his face. Thoughtful, arresting green eyes made her feel entirely vulnerable, yet she found it difficult to look away. One glance at his summery smile thawed Katie's mood and instantly she forgot why she'd even been annoyed with him in the first place.

"It's fine." She pushed her hair away from her cheek.

"I still wish you would have let me pick you up. It wouldn't have been a problem. Anyway, did you have a hard time finding it?"

"Right where you said it would be, but you didn't tell me this was a club. If I'm honest, this isn't my thing."

"Me either." He took her by the hand. A puzzled look remained on her face as he led her through an anteroom into another section encompassing a very large billiards area. An upscale pool hall was the last thing she expected to see. Away from the smoke-filled, raucous club area, she felt calmer.

"Oregon, how's this? Any better?" He called her by the nickname he'd given her, even now, still uncertain of whether she approved.

"Much." Katie sighed with satisfaction, taking in the ceiling motifs and chandeliers in a place very unlike any ordinary pool hall. She could not believe it had any association with the meat blender she'd just pushed her way through.

"Really? Good. My honor is at stake," he said in genuine relief. "Can I get you a drink?" Luke had no idea Katie was only nineteen. He'd heard her teased at work about her baby face, but nothing more than harmless ribbing. With her maturity and job knowledge, no one thought about her age and he never presumed to ask.

"No, thanks, I shouldn't," Katie said. She'd promised herself long ago she'd never touch the stuff after years of seeing it consume Jonas.

"If beer's not your thing, Ray's Aftershock is real crowd pleaser," Luke said, nodding to bartender, already making a punch alcohol mixture for someone else. She smelled the overpowering scent of coconut rum.

"You don't have to do this," Luke said after seeing her initial hesitation.

"I want to," Katie replied, though she didn't. Ray mixed her a drink and she took it from the bar. She gave it a tentative sip at first, then a bit more.

"Good, no?" the bartender asked.

"Very." She took a much larger sip. Grinning at the man she said, "Thank you."

"You got it." The man nodded.

Luke set his beer down before handing her a pool cue. Leaning across the table to make the break, he glanced at her. "Speaking of which, I do think I'm offended that you thought that was me," he said, referring to the club.

"Sorry." Katie smiled with embarrassment as she watched three striped balls fall into pockets. He missed the subsequent shot.

"Can't believe I missed it." He shook his head. "You have anything like this place back out west?"

"Wouldn't know." Katie stared down the long pool cue, knocking down four in a row, including one most professionals would not attempt. The game brought out a competitive intensity that was obvious on her placid face.

He nodded with impressed amazement. "Wow, look at you. Nice run. You sure you don't play much cuz you're really good."

"Thank you." She made another one.

"What kind of stuff did you do for fun in Oregon?"

"We didn't go out much."

"We?" He locked in on that single word she said. "Was that you and your boyfriend?" he asked.

"Boyfriend? No," Katie responded.

"Who then, your family?"

"No, my—yes." The question unbalanced her and she missed a simple bank shot.

"You don't talk about them at all."

As close as they had grown, of course he would eventually press to know more about her past. She'd long considered going with a story about her parents giving her up as a baby, but loose ends like that could always come back.

"I'm having a great time. You mind if we save that one for another day?"

"Sure. Of course. Sorry."

Three cocktails later, Katie relaxed. Being around Luke always made her feel calm. She trusted him.

"Hey, you want to get out of here?" she asked abruptly.

"Sure." He glanced at his watch. It was 12:35 a.m. and the club would be closing in a few minutes anyway. "Where do you want to go? Not much to do in Loudoun County after one a.m. There's an all-night diner out in Fairfax. It won't take long at this time of morning."

"You could show me your place." Katie hoped that didn't sound too forward.

"Love to. There's someone I've been anxious for you to meet."

"I'll get my car and follow you." Katie reached for her bag, and in an intoxicated, clumsy haste, she fumbled the pack. The crystal containing holy water tumbled from an unsecured side pocket and rolled under the table.

He placed his hand in the small of her back to steady her. "On second thought, my apartment is less than a half mile from here, and it's a nice night. Maybe we should walk."

"Okay." She smiled, and they left.

Chapter 35

After grabbing a brief break-time nap in his car, Dominic returned to the Reston, Virginia, HQ of the dark Albion lobby on his way back to the NOC. When the door to the main entrance opened, the infrared activated thermal sensor controlling the buildings lights came on. In a sleepy fog, he loped across the baroque, high-arching atrium with lunch in hand.

Upon reaching an interior door, he stood in front of a biometric sensor, confirming his identity and granting access. He followed the hall to the breakroom and thought he heard the sound of the automatic door's click at the distant end of the now dark hall outside the breakroom, but couldn't understand why the lights of the corridor did not power on. He glanced to the lunchroom clock. 1:15 a.m. Too early for Morgan to be taking his break. Not to mention the NOC was never left unattended.

"Morgan? Yo." He went over and leaned into the dark hall. As soon as his head broke the plane of the door, the lights came on.

That's weird. Dominic looked down both sides of the long corridor. Seeing nothing, he returned to the coffee machine and poured himself a cup. When he stepped halfway out of the break room, a woman stood in the shadows. He dropped his mug, porcelain crashing on the floor.

"Who are you and how did you get in here?" he asked.

She approached him, stepping into the light. "The one you humans call Katie, where is she?"

"Katie? No one works here by that name. Now you need to leave or I'm calling the police." Dominic removed his cell from his belt and began dialing 911. Without perceiving her movement, the distance between them disappeared. As the

261

entranced man gazed upon her face, she drew his gaze into her eyes—revealing to him, the caliginous, abominable nature within. In them, he saw destruction of countless worlds, lamenting souls, the slaughter of the innocents, and countless other horrific—utterly unspeakable things. A wave of repugnant fear pulsed through him, causing him to retreat to the back of the small breakroom.

"It's their night off."

"Where are they?" she asked with a calm tone.

"I don't know!" he cried. "A few days ago I overheard their plans to go out together tonight. That's all I know. I swear."

"Do you know where they live?"

"I don't know!" Dominic repeated, too fearful to think clearly. He really didn't know where Katie lived but inadvertently lied about Luke. He'd been to the man's condo many times. "Please don't kill me."

Assyria pried into his thoughts, entering through his eyes. He knew exactly where they were. Compelling the weak-minded man would have been as easy but instead she milked him of everything he sought to withhold from her. Finished with the man, leaving him mentally incapacitated, she released the invisible talon grip she had over him.

"I believe you." The sardonic smile departed from her lips. Then, Assyria kissed him. Lips locked, the deadly embrace siphoned his breath, wrenching his soul from his core like flesh torn from bone. A minute later his withered, pruneish carcass slumped to the floor.

Chapter 36

After leaving the bar, on their way to his apartment, Katie and Luke strolled down the sidewalk along the well-lit road. Three powerful cocktails and how safe she felt with the man dulled any thoughts of danger Katie might have otherwise felt. Occasionally, she checked their surroundings during their walk, but her attention was on him.

"My parents were killed in a car crash when I was young," she said in response to the question he'd asked earlier that evening. The moment the awful lie departed from her lips she regretted deceiving him.

"That's awful. I'm so sorry." Luke touched her shoulder.

"It's not like you could have known. It happened when I was a baby. I found my way into the hands of someone who looked after me. He was the only dad I ever knew."

"Where is the man now? Did he move to Virginia with you?" This time, she did not answer. Even in the dark, it was apparent Katie's ever present dimple faded, and he wished he'd left well enough alone.

Clearing a wistful lump from her throat, she asked him, "What about you? Are you from Virginia, I mean originally?"

"Born and raised, unfortunately."

"What do you mean? Seems great here," she said.

"Yeah, I guess it is. I don't know why I've grown so accustomed to saying that.

"Area's changed more than you'd imagine since I was a kid. Back then, everything was either forests or farms. It had a quaint, large county, small town way about itself. Most of that went away with the explosion of technology in the region. That's good and bad I guess, depending on your perspective.

263

"In any case, I spent most of my childhood doing the same thing most small town kids do, dreaming of growing up and moving on. As soon as I graduated from high school, I bounced. Four years of football at the University of Arizona left me with a bum knee that pretty much washed out dreams of playing in the NFL, and I found myself right back here where I started."

"Football? You?" Katie raised her eyebrows in genuine surprise.

"Tight end, started three years."

"Fascinating." She smiled.

Luke wasn't sure why that seemed to surprise her so much. "You know...not all athletes lack intelligence," he said, pretending to take offense.

She whistled playfully, looking toward the sky.

"I double majored in Electrical and Network Engineering, always figuring I couldn't play football forever and when my playing days ended, I needed a solid back up plan. Good thing. A couple of opportunities for IT jobs in Tempe and a third in Chicago just didn't feel right, and I ended up doing what I would never have imagined in a million years."

"Coming home," Katie said.

"You guessed it." He smiled.

After walking several blocks they turned through the park. His apartment building was on the distant end of the large courtyard where a dozen or so people were out and about enjoying the mild evening. It felt pleasant to Katie who started feeling flush with an almost numbing warmness washing over her as the second and third drinks set in.

She glanced at the reflection of the pale moonlight shimmering off the man-made pond. "Can I ask you a question?"

"Sure, of course," he said.

"I don't mean to sound, I don't know—" she paused to gather her thoughts. "What's the story with you and Jaime?"

"What do you mean?"

"It's pretty obvious she's into you. Any history there?"

"Me and Jaime?" He laughed. "Now that's funny."

"Why? You guys should go out. I'm sure you have a lot in common."

"We've known each other for a very long time and I've been there for her through some tough things that happened but that's it."

"You've never even considered it? I think you should. She's very attractive, smart, and independent."

"I guess she is," he said, "but nope. She's a great friend but nothing more. Why? Are you trying to hook us up?"

"Not at all. I just think you're a great guy," she said.

"You're not too bad yourself," he turned to her.

"Thanks," she said, disarmed by Luke's moonlit smile.

"So, you'll be overseas the entire time of company shutdown—a full month?" he asked, referring to the recent decision to furlough its staff beginning in May.

"Four weeks is the plan, but I bought an open-ended ticket in case I decide to return earlier."

"I still can't believe you're really going."

"I am. I could have used the additional money but I guess now is as good a time as any to return. There's something I need to handle."

"Something you need to handle? I thought you said you were just visiting an aunt." There was an unmistakable bite to his tone. It wasn't his intent to sound like he was prying but he'd always had trouble with the story. He didn't doubt she was visiting family, but weeks earlier at lunch, when he'd asked Katie about the trip, she'd almost seemed flustered. It didn't add up, but at the time he decided not to press her.

"It's—very complicated." Katie looked away, not wanting to lie again. She wasn't sure she even could.

"Complicated? Did you really just...?"

"It's not what you think," she interrupted him.

"No? Mind if I ask who you're going with, then?" His tone sounded like that of a frustrated toddler who realized he wouldn't get his way.

"No one. There's not another guy, Luke. If I could go into the whole thing, I would."

They started walking again, but the sudden silence hung between them.

"No matter the reason, going to the other side of the world alone takes big time courage. Are you nervous?"

"I don't think I would put it that way—anxious, more like it. Anyway, I've been through much more difficulty than this."

"I hear you, but I'm still not sure I understand the urgency. Why now? Have you been thinking about this for a long time?" The mere thought of China made him miss her already. He wondered if there was anything he could do to convince her to stay.

"Not to sound like a jerk, I get that you're busy studying for your certs and don't have time for the news, but, Luke, the world's coming undone. The plague, violence, and that's not mentioning what's happening up there." She glanced to the sky. "Who knows how long it will be before it becomes impossible to travel at all."

"That's probably a bit dramatic, but like I said, I hear you." He tried to recover from a bruised ego. "Think anyone would notice a stowaway if I came with?"

"What, like in my suitcase?" In her intoxication, Katie made a noise that sounded more like a snort than a laugh. Luke laughed too.

"You okay?" he teased.

"Yep." She giggled with embarrassment.

When they went inside his apartment, immediately an exuberant yellow Labrador retriever nearly knocked her down.

"Meet Lilly."

"Oh...she's beautiful!" Katie sat on the floor in front of the dog before giving the pooch an affectionate rough scratch on the side of its neck. "We—I used to have a dog."

"Yeah? What happened to it?" Luke asked.

"When I moved here, I left him with a dear friend. He was pretty amazing."

"Which one: the friend or the dog?"

"Both," Katie said. A slight sad smile came over her face.

"I'm sure that was hard."

Brooding, she nodded as Luke sat beside her.

"If you promise not to tell anyone, I'll let you in on a little secret," Luke said.

She continued petting the dog. "Sure, what is it?" Katie asked.

"That's not exactly a promise," he said with a simpering smile.

"Fine, I promise," she replied.

"I have been dreaming about you most of my life."

Katie rolled her eyes and took a deep breath.

"That's absolutely—"

"Amazing, right?" The ridiculous grin on his face was itself almost enough to make her laugh.

"I was going to say, without a doubt, one of the weakest pick-up lines in human history."

"It's true, I swear it!" he replied.

"Just how buzzed do you think I am, Luke? I never took you for that guy."

"Come on. You know I'm not that guy and I'm not lying to you. Truth is, the whole thing would have been very romantic if our first dream kiss hadn't killed me. I guess it's true what they say after all?"

"What?" she asked, referring to the dream.

"First she mates, then she kills." He chuckled.

"With corny come-ons, you're lucky some other girl didn't kill you first." She laughed before socking him hard in the arm.

"Ouch!" The smile on Luke's face dissipated as he rubbed the painful spot.

"I'm sorry. I guess that was kind of hard," Katie said, gently touching his arm. "You know I would never hurt you."

"Wow, *speaking of played out*," he replied.

"Touché, I guess I had that coming, didn't I?"

Luke nodded.

"I'm probably walking right into a dangerous question," Katie smiled with unbelief, "the dreams...you were putting me on right?"

"Nope," he said flatly.

268

"Right. I swear, is there anything a man won't say?"

When Luke's mood suddenly turned serious, she started to wonder. "Okay then, tell me about them," she said.

"I guess they started back when I was five, maybe four. I don't remember much about the earlier ones. They continued off and on throughout my childhood, then, all of a sudden, they stopped. I went years without another one until about eight months ago."

Katie observed his body language as he spoke. Months ago, she'd recognized an obvious tell that always presented itself when he was nervous. And now, when Luke started fidgeting with his hands, she was convinced.

"Go on," she said. "When the dreams resumed, what happened?"

"A mysterious raven-haired girl with porcelain smooth skin and hazel eyes walked towards me on warm black sand bordering cool clear water. She gave me a passionate kiss that literally shook the ground. I was lost in her kiss when I felt something warm on my hands and when I looked down, blood covered me—my blood, from where she had stabbed me in the stomach. I fell to the ground at her feet, helpless and gasping. I reached for her hand but she simply stood over me and watched as I died on the shore."

Pensively, she stared out the window.

"Earth calling Katie, are you out there?"

"Sorry," she said. Deep concern filled her ashen face. She turned toward him.

"Are all the dreams the same? Do they always end up with me killing you?"

"Nope, sometimes you kill Jaime instead." He smiled again but this time she did not.

"Relax, I'm only kidding. No, they're not always the same, and no, I don't always die. The only thing consistent is that they're always strange. There always seems to be an otherworldly quality to them."

"Not sure I follow you, Luke. What do you mean?"

"It's like we're here on Earth—the same, but different, somehow better, well, other than the dying part. It's kind of hard to explain. I just thought it was really cool that I dreamed about you like twenty years before we even met, but I didn't mean to upset you by telling you this stuff. I'm sure it's nothing, forget I ever mentioned it."

What he really wanted to tell her, but knew better, was that he'd fallen in love with her before they ever met. That the real reason he returned to Virginia instead of taking the job offers, was because, somehow, he knew they'd find each other here.

"You're right. I'm sure it's nothing," Katie replied. She didn't believe that for a minute. Premonitions were the kind of things that happened to her, not about her.

He touched her cheek, then leaned in and kissed her. With wide-eyed surprise, her body tensed. But a moment later, she closed her eyes and gave in to the feeling. He lay next to her on the couch. The intoxicating combination of alcohol and his lips pressed to her neck made her dizzy.

"I don't want you to go to China. Stay with me." He looked into her eyes and kissed her again. She felt her passion rising out of control in response to him. She loved Luke and would give anything to be with the man.

"Stop it, I can't!" She put her hands between them, and pushed away. He looked at her as she sprang from the couch and hurried across the room.

"I'm sorry, Katie. I honestly didn't mean to move so fast."

She held up her hand. "I need some air."

He saw the hurt and confused look as she grabbed her pack. Throwing open the door, she dashed outside.

"Luke, you're an idiot!" He cupped his face in his hands. He got up and thought about going after her but fell back onto the couch and waited for the room to stop spinning.

A few minutes later, Katie returned.

"About what just happened—I just got carried away," he said as she came inside. She did not respond as she locked the door behind her and turned off the lights. He watched as she came over to the couch, her silhouette in the moonlit room. She straddled his waist and kissed him.

***

The next morning, Katie stood in the center of her room, in the midst of a headache, either the result of drinking more than she'd realized, or a migraine unlike any she'd had in years. In either case, she looked forward to getting some shuteye on the long flight. Scanning the room for anything that may have been missed, she wondered how anyone could pack enough clothes to last for a month and still travel light.

She sat at her desk to write a note to Leila, letting her know she was leaving. The woman held lecture at George Mason University today, and when she made it home, Katie would be gone. She felt bad knowing Leila would be consumed with worry all the while she was overseas, but there was no time to dwell on that now.

She was finishing when she heard faint knocking at the front door. Katie crept down the stairs, cautiously peering outside before opening the door. Luke stood on the porch.

271

When she saw him, she couldn't decide whether she was excited or still cross with him for the stunt he'd pulled.

Katie looked around, confused by him being there. "Hey, what are you doing here?" she asked.

He went to kiss her, but she coldly turned her face away and his lips found her cheek instead.

"Is everything all right?" she asked.

"Yeah, I thought about it long and hard and I've decided to take you up on the whole stowing away in your suitcase thing." He held up his passport.

"What, are you crazy?" Katie glanced down at the black duffle bag next to his feet. "You're not serious. You hate flying."

"It seems certain friends of mine are under the false impression that I'm afraid to get out and see the world. As your luck would have it, I've never been to China."

"But what happened to plans to go to the Outer Banks with your boys?" she replied, still not entirely convinced.

He shrugged, glancing over his shoulder toward the gray sky. "Changed my mind when I saw the beach forecast: *Overcast with a 70% chance of the creeping-black hand of death.*"

Katie threw her arms around his neck with the enthusiasm of an over excited child.

"Come in then. I've got work to do." She snatched the passport card from him and led him upstairs by the hand.

"This ought to be fun." He followed with a sarcasm-filled smile.

Chapter 37

Luke tipped the taxi driver and gathered his bags from the curb. Twice, he insisted on carrying her pack as well, but she refused. They walked into Reagan National Airport and joined the long queue at the airline ticket counter. His nervousness was outwardly apparent, his face was pale, and whenever the line moved and the people came to a stop, his hands fidgeted at his sides.

After Luke had shown up at Katie's door, she had no choice but to come clean with the real reason she was returning to China—in hopes of finding the parents she'd originally claimed died in a car crash. She felt it necessary to tell him about Jonas being killed but not before finding out about some men in China being among those who were searching for her. She also told him about the relentless killer Dorian, but stopped short of the revelation the man was a creature of supernatural origins.

He entirely agreed with the things Leila had told her: whatever she might learn about her past was not worth the risk. For all Katie knew, he said, they might grab her the moment she walked off the plane. No one would ever hear from her again. She agreed, insisting it was the very thing that necessitated traveling under aliases. Katie would not be reasoned out of it, and refusing to let her face danger alone, he came.

"Luke." Katie whispered into his ear. "You've got to relax or you'll give us up for sure."

He nodded.

"Good afternoon. How may I help you?" the ticket agent asked when they reached the front of the line.

"We booked tickets to Hong Kong, but we just found out that our flight this evening was canceled, so we'd like to catch an earlier flight." Katie slid their pre-printed boarding passes and passport cards across the counter.

"Do you have two seats together up front?" Luke asked.

"Not together. There are a handful of single seats up front, but the flight is almost sold out. The best I can do for two is near the middle of the aircraft. Seats 59A and B."

Luke opened his mouth but Katie cut him off.

"That'll be fine," she replied.

The agent changed their flight information and scanned their digital passport cards. Instantly the Hong Kong stamp appeared on the hologram next to each of their photos.

"Enjoy your flight." The woman handed them their new tickets and returned their IDs.

They made their way through the large crowd in the main concourse, approaching the TSA checkpoints. The couple in front of them was abruptly removed from the line and led away when biometric body scans detected they were both ill.

Luke passed through the checkpoint with no incident.

She followed suit, placing her luggage and backpack on the conveyor before proceeding through the bio scan. Again, the machine displayed a green sensor overhead. But as she glanced to the guard examining her bags under virtual scan, he stopped the belt, staring at the monitor with a quizzical look.

"Problem?" a second TSA Officer standing on the opposite side of the scan asked, holding his hand up in front of Katie.

"Nope, she's good," the first man said after a moment's hesitation. Then he advanced the luggage to the other side.

Katie breathed a silent sigh of relief as she collected her belongings. They did not speak as they advanced their way to the gate, a distant eight concourses away.

When they reached the departure gate, both took a seat along the wall. He turned on his tablet and pulled up a news article.

Katie sat, but did not drop her guard. She was restless—watching the throng of people that came and went through the concourse on the outside possibility they'd been followed. Though she'd never been in an airport, there was a familiarity to the entire moment. The checkpoint—the crowd pressing toward the gate—in fact, now that she thought about it, nearly everything that led up to them being in the airport this evening felt like a repeat.

Almost like it had all happened before, and now she watched the replay. Again, her thoughts turned to Dorian and how the wraith could appear as someone else. It reminded her about the vial that could detect the presence of wraiths and Gwyllgi nearby.

Trying to remember where she'd last seen it, she patted her jacket pockets and felt through her bag's outer compartments. To her dismay, the vial of holy water was gone.

"Leave something?" Luke asked when he noticed her panicked expression.

"Forget it. It's not important," she lied as anxiety swelled.

A few moments later, the airline began the boarding announcements. They checked in at the electronic kiosk and boarded the aircraft.

***

Dorian walked through the terminal. He'd been to her home and read the note Katie left for Leila and now knew about the plans for China.

From there, it hadn't taken him long to figure out where she'd gone. Only two international airports in the local area: Dulles and Reagan, with a half dozen canceled flights to China between them. Only two flights remained, departing only minutes apart.

With those gates at opposite ends of the airport he would not risk the guess that might allow her escape. He stopped and extended his senses toward Katie.

She was here. He felt the distinct electromagnetic current in her rapidly beating heart and headed for her gate. A security agent intercepted him when he lumbered past the security kiosk outside the entrance.

"Sir, I need to see your ticket please."

Dorian said nothing, extending his empty hand in front of the man, mentally compelling the man to see a boarding pass that was not there.

"Thank you." With a glazed-over look, the man stepped aside. "Enjoy your flight."

***

Agent Mark Roulley sprinted through the concourse, weaving in and out of the travelers, en route to Gate N. He slowed, glancing at the flight information on the monitors overhead.

Finding the elusive teen once again proved anything but easy, but after weeks of showing her photo and asking around, he finally located where Katie lived and went to see her.

For a second time, he planned to try and warn her of his strong belief her life was in danger. When he got to the rural

Ashburn home, the front door had been smashed in and several rooms ransacked. At first he didn't see the crumpled note lying on her bedroom floor. When he opened it and read she was leaving town, he went after her.

"This is the final boarding call for flight 3079 to Hong Kong International Airport. Standby passengers Diane and Traci Jennings, please come to the ticket desk."

Roulley approached the ticket counter, stepping in front of two women at the front of the line.

"Diane and Traci?"

"Yes?" the younger of the two women replied with apprehension as she studied the splint on his nose and the still healing bruise surrounding his eye.

"Federal Agent." He displayed his badge. "Catch another flight, you just got bumped."

"What's this all about?" the female behind the counter asked.

"FBI business." He turned toward the gate, flashing his badge again for the security agent standing outside the door and hurried down the gangway toward the aircraft.

***

Katie looked at Luke staring out his window. Lightning pulsed in an enormous shelf cloud that blanketed the distant horizon.

"You know, it's not too late to change your mind." She touched the back of his white knuckled hand. She was fully aware of how much he really hated flying. She also understood the risk he took by accompanying her.

"I'm fine, we'll do this together," he replied unconvincingly.

"You're sweet, Luke." She leaned closer. "I'm really glad you came with me. You shouldn't have but I'm glad you did."

"Women are too complicated." He shook his head.

"I never said otherwise," Katie replied with a warm smile.

A large woman wedged her way up the walk and stopped just in front of their aisle. She hoisted her suitcase and tried to cram it into the nearly full overhead storage bin.

When Katie looked up at the woman, her face lost color.

"Flight attendants, prepare for take-off," sounded through the PA.

"Luke." Katie grabbed his wrist so tight that he winced.

"What?" he asked.

"Déjà vu. Everything we just said, that woman, the flight, everything—it's all wrong!" she replied, wrought with anxiety. An erratic surge caused the lights to flicker and dim.

"What's the big—"

"We've got to get off this plane, or we're all going to die." Katie jumped from her seat and pulled her backpack across her shoulder. She hurried through the aisle, Luke following close behind. Without hesitation, she barreled past the large woman in the walkway and the stewardess behind her.

There, in the opposite row sat Dorian. Only the four seats in the middle section of the flight separated them. When she and Luke gazed upon him, his frigid stare hypnotically held them. Walking toward the nearest cross aisle, the power of his gaze broke and the two made an all-out sprint for the exit. Luke glanced back and saw him running down the opposite aisle, matching them stride for stride.

Luke ran close on her heels. "Go!" he screamed.

The aircraft's engines revved. The flight attendant pulled the cabin door closed. Katie dropped her shoulder and dashed through, fleeing up the gangway back into the airport.

***

Dorian emerged onto the concourse and ran through the crowd until he reached the landing leading to the lower level of the main terminal. He glanced over the rail and saw them running toward the exit.

The crowd screamed in terror when they saw the man hurrying down the stairs, sword in hand.

He crossed the lower lobby, following them as they ran outside toward a cab. When he heard gunshots from the terrace above him, his eyes flittered to the upper level where he saw an armed man he recognized from the plane.

Three other uniformed airport police approached from both directions of the main level of the north concourse. Dorian grabbed a woman standing near him and pulled her along, using her as a shield as he backed toward the main exit. When he reached the door, he pitched a shiny blue metallic sphere toward the center of the terminal and pushed the woman to the floor. Seconds later, a massive blast rippled through the building.

Chapter 38

The cab pulled away from the Arrivals deck when a jarring explosion lit the night sky.

"What was that?" Luke asked, looking back from the cab's rear seat. The airport roared in flames. Then, he saw the killer Katie told him about closing in.

"Go! Go! Go!" he screamed to the taxi driver.

The driver floored the pedal, and they raced along the George Washington Parkway.

As they crossed the Potomac River, startling thunderclaps shook the cab. They had gone little more than three miles before heavy traffic brought them to a virtual standstill. Luke watched for the man through the rear window. When he saw a white box truck weaving in and out of traffic, he knew it was him.

"Faster! He's coming! Can't you go around?"

"Where do you expect me to go, kid? Do you see all of that?" The cabbie pointing to the sea of tail lights along the northern edge of the tidal basin, extending as far as they could see.

"Get out!" Katie screamed. She flung open the door and they ditched the taxi, running among the procession of unmoving vehicles.

Enormous bolts of lightning branched like a fan across the skyline, irradiating the dense, low-flying, tenebrous clouds that dragged over the city like a creeping hand. Storm force swirling winds whisked dead leaves through the air as they ran between the rows of cherry blossom trees lining the Potomac River.

When Luke couldn't run anymore, he stopped and his eyes darted for anything to use as protection. He saw a large fallen tree branch and grabbed it, stepping in front of Katie. Dorian walked toward them, lightning reflecting off the extended blade in his hand.

When Luke saw a pair of pedestrians nearby, he screamed, "Help! Help!"

The couple sprinted toward them. They saw Dorian's sword at his side too late. He slashed them both down.

Katie and Luke slowly backed from the wraith. Dorian had an odd look as he glanced at Luke, holding out the dead branch in front of him to keep the monster at bay.

"Leave us alone! What do you want?" Luke yelled over crashing thunder and wind gusts so strong, they found it difficult to stand.

"Don't play dumb." Dorian glanced at him with loathsome jealousy. "You both know exactly what I want." If he could not possess her, he would see to it no one did.

Katie peered through the rain for an escape. After the thunderous explosion of the nearby airport, impatient drivers on the other side of the grove—believing the city was under attack, stood on their horns desperate to flee the area.

Motorists turned onto the lawns desperate to jump ahead in the endless caravan of crawling vehicles. It was clear help would not come, and it seemed pointless to try and outrun him.

Another street, eighty yards or so away, was blocked off by utility vehicles for street work. Behind them, they were boxed in by the Potomac. She flirted with thoughts of leaping into the river. Automatically, her throat constricted and heart hitched. The water was not an option.

Dorian would intercept and strike them both down as he had the others. After she was dead, no one would be standing between evil and the Artifact. No matter what happened, she could not allow it to fall into his hands. She had to defeat him here, but how? Her sword and firearm remained in her luggage on the plane. Was there another choice?

Hand-to-hand combat. Katie thought she had a chance. Jonas taught her well. But she'd battled the formidable wraith enough times to know that, without a weapon, he would make easy work of her. Almost as if he knew what she was thinking, Dorian did the inexplicable.

"This?" He taunted her by looking at the sword in his hand, with that all too familiar ghastly grin that always adorned his face. "Worried about the odds?" He flipped the weapon into the ground, razor tip lanced into the wet turf, handle pointed toward the sky.

Dorian intended to beat her into humiliating submission. The Artifact was for his master, but Katie was his prize, his slave. He eyed Luke, still holding a downed tree branch. In the wraith's native tongue—a language no human understood, Dorian angrily shouted at him. He snatched the wood from the boy's hand and launched it into the night, sneering as he watched it fly toward the cars.

With an almost smug and peculiar indifference, Luke looked on.

Katie would not give him the chance to reconsider his foolish arrogance. Without another thought, she blitzed the wraith, punching him in his throat. Dorian gurgled in painful disbelief, staggering backwards as Katie pelted him with a seamless stream of jabs, crosses, and a rifling upper cut he could not answer. She blasted him with the sole of her boot.

The powerful kick sent him tumbling backwards to the soft earth. Dorian rose from the grassy knoll, shaking off the wooziness.

With a desperate, eternally pent up fury, Dorian lowered his fangs. He sprang toward her and they battled in the driving rain.

Unlike previous times, with an unbridled aggression, Katie took the fight to him, unwilling to back down. Countless hours of grueling hand-to-hand tactics, martial arts training including Aikido and Jiu-jitsu—most of it with Jonas, and the Kenpo she'd taken up since arriving in Virginia, all came to her in a moment's lucidity.

With his every attack, she found the counter. If she'd realized anything about Dorian from their past— he sensed and gained strength from their fears.

Knowing this, Katie refused to feed the arch-fiend's appetite.

Stronger since their previous confrontations, her attacks came faster and more intense. No longer could he smell the anxiety and terror she'd always exuded in the past.

More than that—he felt a power growing inside her that made *him* fearful. Instead of keeping her for his own use, he'd just kill them both and escape with the box. As soon as Dorian went for his sword, she tackled him.

After a rough tumble, they grappled on the ground, Katie twisting her legs around his neck. He jammed his hand under her chin and in the life or death struggle, the two simultaneously choked each other. Her serpentine thighs constricted around his neck as his own fingers tightened around her throat. With the other hand, Dorian managed to deliver a jarring punch to Katie's midsection that almost made

283

her gasp and almost let go completely. Sensing the advantage sliding from her, he leveled his free palm toward Luke and unleashed a scorching blast of invisible energy that bowled the man over.

The attack, purposed to divert her attention, sent her worried eyes to him. Dorian had the break he needed. He muscled himself onto one knee—still holding her by the throat. His supernatural strength tightened.

Flat on her back, against the ground, Katie felt her windpipe collapsing under the pressure of his stony grip. Grainy interspersed flashes of light faded through rapidly dimming eyesight, making her world begin to turn black.

She drifted across the edge of consciousness and life, dragged to immeasurable depths of a shadowy fathom by malevolent apparitional talons. Her strength waned. He broke free of her leg lock and stretched for his blade. Dorian's fingers wrapped around the hilt and he raised it high.

Helpless, she gazed at the glimmering steel in his hand for what felt like countless moments waiting for the cold blade that would soon mercilessly plunge through her chest.

After centuries of searching, there would be no one to stop the wraiths from obtaining what they'd come to Earth for. The Artifact, safe for so many years, would fall into the hands of darkness. The world would never again be as it was.

Could it all come to this end? Had she not been called? Had she not been chosen by the Artifact? It seemed implausible that throughout the universe, there was not another. She hoped the power the Artifact had drawn her with, would find someone more worthy than she—one possessing the ability to recover and protect it.

As she lay dying, her oxygen deprived brain began to shut down. Rare fond remembrances pressed to the forefront of her mind.

Laughing away a pleasant summer's afternoon on the deck with Jonas, Richard, and Ms. Laura.

Jonas's obvious discomfort for sharing the pull-out bed with an ultra-frisky Chance.

The gentle, assuring smile on her mother's face.

An amorous, heart-palpitating kiss that almost made her surrender, to the only man she'd ever loved.

As she stared beyond his menacing face into the heavens, the dark sky, illuminated by the capitol's lights, a colossal vortex swirled, pulling the nearby clouds into itself—the formation growing larger by the moment.

Following her transfixed gaze, Dorian saw the tip of the spectacular cloud descending toward them. "Incredible," he mouthed as his hold on Katie's throat loosened.

"Let her go and drop it!" a voice shouted from the other side of the trees. "Toss it to the ground, now!"

Agent Roulley loped their way. Injured by the airport explosion, he limped into the clearing and took aim at Dorian. More than thirty yards away, in the rain-filled, gusting winds, he had no line on the man but knew Katie would be dead in seconds. Ignoring the pain in his leg, he ran toward them, shooting. The errant rounds flew past. The instant the wraith glared at him, Agent Roulley found himself wrestling a powerful, invisible force of will that made him lower his weapon. He fought, but it immobilized him. His arms felt heavy as if someone were standing on them.

Her eyes closed when more flashbacks seeped in from a reservoir of painful memories experienced during her short life and the hard fought struggles she and Jonas had overcome. A relentless lifetime hunted along a blood-soaked highway, at the hands of hostility from another realm.

Pursued into the river and nearly swept underwater, snatched from death by Jonas's mighty hand.

The loss of his best friend Herman

A brutal murder of Jonas's mother at the hands of Dorian.

The deaths of Margie and Ken in the diner.

An almost intangible thought whispered to her.

What if there had been other protectors before, but now, she was the only one left? What if she truly was the Artifact's last option—and with her death, the world would fall?

Katie remembered the time Jonas first told her about the wraith and overcome with fear, she asked him: "What if we run and they keep coming?"

Then, she recalled Jonas' response to that same question:

"...then you fight until you can't."

Katie slipped through the very soft still wherein she'd already resolved herself to the sad acceptance of her fate. Not willing to succumb to him—yet another, in the long list of souls Dorian had stolen throughout the centuries, she found and drew upon the only thing she had left—anger, and used it to bring herself back. Refusing to be obedient to death, Katie opened her eyes.

The stench of scorched ozone filled the air. The sword tip hurtled at her. Agent Roulley squeezed off another round. A white flash of blinding light, a concussion of scorching air, struck a tree a few yards away. The surface rocked and blew them to the ground.

When Katie came to, a loud, sharp tone filled her ears, muffling the sound of her racing heart. Her nostrils burned with the smell of charred earth and flesh. As she tried to focus on the chaos around her, the acuity of her mind slowly returned. It became apparent what just happened.

Luke, a few feet from her, sat dazed, gathering his senses. On the other side of the clearing, a man, unmoving, lay on his side. One glimpse at the unconscious man and she recognized him as the same person she'd scuffled with in the parking garage.

Panic set in when she glanced where she had last seen Dorian. He was gone, and her backpack too. Her frantic eyes darted around the tidal basin. She saw a man running toward the street. He whipped his head side to side, like a wounded animal searching for an escape.

When he saw a utility worker, half emerged from a manhole, he ran his way. The wraith grabbed the worker by the head and broke his neck. The lifeless body toppled down the manhole as Dorian descended the ladder. He retreated through the knee-deep waters into the sewer's catacomb.

Chapter 39

"Stay with him!" Katie yelled to Luke to remain with Agent Roulley. Then she tore across the grove in pursuit of Dorian.

"Katie! No!" Luke screamed.

She reached the sewer and skipped down the ladder into turbid, chilly waters rushing past her knees.

What am I doing? This is insane, she said with the sudden realization of how fast the water was moving. The tunnels closed in and everything inside her screamed to flee the watery tomb.

Again she was reminded of the powerlessness she'd felt when battling against the river's current. Wrestling against what felt like a progressing asthma attack, the constricting vice of panic, made her feel cut off from the world above.

Katie turned—glancing at the eight tunnels that branched from this junction. Just as she was about to crumple under the weight of her anxiety, Luke splashed down behind her. She was tempted to scold him but the truth was—she was glad he was there.

She peered into the dark tunnels in front of them. Luke cringed as he slipped around the dead body, trapped between a pipe and the wall, and stopped beside her.

"Are you okay?" he asked when he saw her gingerly holding her ribs in the spot Dorian punched her.

Katie ignored the question. "He went this way." She pointed to the third tunnel from her left.

"How do you know?"

"The water is flowing that way to the Potomac. He'll be looking for the outfall."

They hurried as fast as they could, dragging their feet through viscous muck. She made mental notes of the junctions they passed in an effort to retrace their steps if they had to. So far, eight intersections—each roughly a football field apart. With no discernible way to determine how far they'd come, she estimated a half mile or so.

By the time they passed yet another point with access to the street above, the water level had increased to their thighs. Left of the ladder was a control panel with four lights from left to right: green, yellow, orange, and red. The yellow light flashed slowly. **Water Overflow Level: Danger!**

"It's not getting any lower, so at what point should we begin to worry?" Luke whispered.

"If you haven't already started worrying, then you're late." Katie said without looking at him. She continued to block her fear.

"That's comforting."

"Just stick close to me."

"Count on it."

They struggled farther into the tunnel illuminated by the distantly spaced, oscillating yellow dome lights overhead. They passed two more junctions and a second panel and the indicator switched from a slow intermittent yellow to a more rapid flashing orange. Ahead, Katie saw a silhouette leaning against the wall.

"Dorian!" she screamed as she splashed toward him. He turned to run then suddenly disappeared under the water. The handle of his weapon smacked against something and floated to a calmer area surrounded with old tires, cans, and trash.

Katie grabbed the sword. In front of her, Dorian leaned against the concrete wall. He would have easily regenerated from the gunshot wound to his abdomen but not from the lightning strike that inflicted critical damage upon him. His face was disfigured. One eye hemorrhaged, and nearly all of his blond hair was singed. She went to him and snatched her pack from his almost lifeless, bloody fingers.

"Dorian, you've lost. It's over." Katie said as she pulled the pack's straps over her shoulders.

The wounded wraith laughed, spitting a mouthful of black blood into the water. "All grown up, but in so many ways, you are the same naïve little girl. What is it about humans that you insist on believing good prevails? Surely Jonas taught you better than that. A pity, that even now, you do not realize all is already lost."

He turned toward Luke, the sinister smile leaving his face.

"And you..." Dorian said, "to stand by and let that man shoot me? What were you waiting for? We could have finished this."

"If that is the way it will be, then let's finish it," Katie said, perplexed by what Dorian said to Luke. Didn't matter. Evil such as his could never be reasoned with. She raised the blade to end it.

Hair raising howls pierced the tunnels around them. Katie searched the rising water. Vivid flashes of the recurring dream about the wolves chasing her through the garden maze returned.

She trembled with sudden realization that all these years she had completely misinterpreted her visions.

"Luke, go back. You're in danger!" She looked up at him.

"Wrong again." Luke smiled. "Lover boy isn't in danger, *you are.* He's already dead."

Before Katie's eyes, the wraith witch appeared in his place.

She couldn't fully comprehend what she was seeing. *The pool hall and their walk...all of the things she'd talked to him about. The way he held her in his arms, and for perhaps the first time in her life, she actually believed everything would be okay. Had any of that been with Luke, or was it Assyria, toying with her all along?*

Katie snapped to attention. "What did you do with him?" she screamed.

"Well, I dropped in last night but I missed you when you ran out on him. Naturally, he was very upset about everything that happened. So upset, he came to me, full of desire, seeking everything that you, in your piety denied him. He was so eager to indulge in my passion, I almost felt guilty— almost. Take comfort, child, knowing your boyfriend died with a smile on his face, and *he was delicious.*" A wicked smile dawned on her lips.

"You whore!" Katie raged, launching toward her with a flurry of slashes and strikes in an onslaught of wild, uncontrolled attacks that Assyria nimbly evaded. When Katie saw she could not even hit the evil entity, she paused, breathing heavily, sword forward. "Why are you here?"

"Trapped in the Outlands, your world, for countless centuries, remained invisible to ours. Then, over time, many of us began to witness the vestiges of life. Like beautiful, shimmering lights, your people showed up as bright impressions against the shadows of our rapidly decaying world. At first, we did not believe our eyes, but when we finally realized this universe was real, our ancient hunger was re-kindled. I have spent millennia searching for a way to this side."

"What do you want, witch?" Katie asked with tearful anger, remaining careful to keep her blade between them. Dorian was fast, Assyria faster.

"Only to rule your world, nothing more," the sorceress said.

"Sorry. Election's over. Polls are closed," Katie said coldly.

"A trade then."

"What trade?"

"The Artifact, of course."

"What is it about this thing that everyone wants it? That's it then? You'll take it and leave?"

"...And you," Assyria replied.

"*Me*?"

"Come now. You didn't honestly think it was that simple, did you? The Artifact and your life—for everyone else's." Assyria sneered at Dorian sliding down the wall, closer to the steaming water. Her eyes flicked between the monster and girl. "You child, are *my* reward—promised to *me*."

Promised by whom? Dread wound a suffocating knot within Katie's stomach. "What will become of the box? No one can open it anyway."

"Do not trouble your pretty little head," Assyria replied.

"No deal. Even if I agreed, what assurance would I have you'd honor what you've said?"

"None, but here's one singular truth: if you refuse, our race will ravage your planet and one by one, we will devour your entire species. You will be powerless to stop us."

At that moment, three pair of luminescent eyes peered at Katie from the dark. Gwyllgi crept toward her from the shadowy interconnected tunnels, ready to tear her limb from limb.

What a fool she had been. This trap had been set and she walked straight into it. Katie turned, watching the creatures as they drew closer—readying herself for combat. Her confrontation with Dorian left her battered and weary. She knew she had little left to battle three Gwigs—let alone Assyria, clearly more powerful than any of them. Even worse, these were easily a head larger than the others she'd encountered—

They were sentinels—the conjurer's guards. Katie's mind flashed through every move and counter in a short list of possible outcomes, and with a deep sigh of hopelessness, she let the sword fall from her hand.

Checkmate.

With hesitancy, she waded through the murky water toward Assyria in her final act of self-sacrifice. She hoped to find the courage to die well.

***

Roulley's phone beeped as the power returned from the surge of the lightning strike that nearly killed him. He dialed 911 for back up, but a network flooded with frantic calls regarding the airport explosion produced an all circuits busy tone.

"Unbelievable!" He hit redial several times with the same result. He cursed.

"Federal Agent! I need your help! Help!" He waved his arms in the air.

Several blocks away, Reagan International airport burned. Black smoke from the blaze rose above the cherry blossom treetops of the tidal basin, drifting toward the dark heavens. Terrified sightseers on foot, bike, and automobiles scattered to vacate the city. Roulley started toward the sewer when a hand grabbed his ankle.

"Help me!" a female voice whispered. Startled, he looked down, astonished to see the female still alive.

"I'll get you help, lady." Two people ran toward him from the nearby street.

"What can we do?" the man shouted over the rolling thunder.

"One of you to stay with her, the other go for help. Phone lines are down, so you need to find an officer. Tell him Special Agent Mark Roulley with the FBI is in pursuit of a white male subject, in the sewers under Constitution Avenue. Tell them the male's armed and extremely dangerous. Got it?"

The man nodded. "I'll go, Linda, you stay with her." He ran off in the direction of the Smithsonian.

"I want you to keep trying 911 until you get through. You got a phone?"

The woman shook her head.

"Lady, you've got to be kidding!" he screamed in outrage. "In this day and age, what kind of idiot doesn't have a cell phone?" With a limp, he ran toward the manhole.

Chapter 40

The sewer overflow warning panel made a loud click. The system's orange light shut off, instantly replaced by a rapid flashing red sensor. An alarm reverberated throughout the entire sewer system. Several miles away, the combined sewer overflow opened fully, the waters held at bay discharged into the main junction and raced through the tunnels to the Anacostia, Rock Creek, and the Potomac rivers.

***

When Katie reached Assyria, she stopped, her eyes falling to the water.

"Look at me."

When Katie refused her eyes, the witch grabbed the girl's chin. "I said look at me!"

She raised her eyes until crossing Assyria's gaze. Katie found herself unable to look away from the lifeless Cimmerian eyes as the woman leaned in to kiss her.

Katie felt the same repulsive darkness radiating from the witch that had been growing within her since the night Assyria attacked her in Herman's RV. She fought to break the mental stronghold but was powerless as the woman's icy cold lips touched hers.

An explosive boom echoed through the tunnel. Assyria recoiled, hit in the shoulder by a hollow point round.

Katie fell against the wall, trance broken.

Mark emerged from one of the tunnels. His .45 belched forth a flurry of thunderous ear-popping gun shots, hitting the woman twice more in the chest with the impact of the shells knocking her backward.

Dorian momentarily escaped the rising water after dragging himself upon the base of a low ramp. Katie's eyes shifted quickly to him as she ran to where she dropped the sword and plunged her hands into the water, searching for a hilt. Perceiving the wasted wraith boss to be a lesser threat, she prepared to deal with the Gwyllgi.

The first one sprang from behind. She turned, severing its right paw. The creature made a horrendous, half growling, half snarl, before coming at her again. Her blade skated across his chest in a fluid figure 8. He staggered backwards, unprepared for a continued offensive: a lateral slash took his remaining paw—the next one took his head. The wolf went out in a smoldering ball of dust.
Immediately, two larger beasts pounced at her. One toppled her, shoving her down. The water washed over her head. The one behind her raked his claws across her shoulder blade, and with its jaws, seized the strap of her backpack.

She was whipsawed when the monster thrashed its head back and forth, like a dog violently shaking a chew toy. One of the straps holding the pack on her back tore free and she was flung across the tunnel, where she rolled down the sloping wall into the water.

Right away, the Gwig's partner closed the distance and sprang upon her before she shook off the disorientation. Pinning her, the tenacious predator crashed it's muscular limb through the water, gashing her side.

In one of her worst nightmares, semi-concussed, Katie gasped for air in terror struck hysteria—powerless to fend off the unabated attacks.

Inhaling a lungful of water, her instincts kicked in, and with panic-filled desperation, she stumbled in the water, thrusting her sword upward into his rib cage—a fatal blow that pierced his heart.

As he dissipated, swept away by the current, the one that initially grabbed her backpack, splashed toward her again. When it was in mid-air, Katie covered her head as a survival instinct. She waited for the crushing weight.

Behind her, Mark fired at the creature—a shot that blew a hole in its side, but only infuriated the beast. Its hellish, distressed screams echoed through the sewers. It turned toward him and he fired twice, both shots hitting center mass. A final .45 blast to the head erased the varmint's face and it reeled sideways before a fiery combustion.

Mark quickly reloaded but Assyria pounced on him and bit into his jugular. He turned the fresh clip toward her, firing two errant shots as she held fast to his neck. With a powerful strike, she knocked his gun into the surging torrent.

Mark whipped his body side to side, trying to break free of her bite. He elbowed her ribs, attempting to throw her, but she continued to drain his essence.

Katie staggered forward, plunging the sword deep into Assyria's back. The blade's tip passed harmlessly through her and deep into his left shoulder as she transformed into a swarm of flying locusts. He screamed and slumped into the water. Katie lifted him to his feet and pulled his arm around her shoulder.

Several yards further down, Dorian slumped against the curving wall of the tunnel. The water had risen on the ramp he'd climbed, now reaching his shoulders.

Mark shouted over the blaring alarm. "Stop! I'm taking him into custody."

"No time for that. We need to get back to the junction!" Katie yelled as a fourth Gwyllgi emerged into the tunnel. This one almost seemed reluctant as it slinked to where Assyria had been standing.

As they slogged toward an exit, Katie watched in spellbound horror when the locusts swarmed the wolf creature and then shoved into the mouth of the beast, giving it her power. The creature began violent choking, and thrashed as the insects filled it.

She supported Mark as they waded through the waist-deep water, heading upstream toward the control panel and nearest escape exit. When more ghastly howls echoed through the dark tunnel up ahead, the two stopped.

"We have to find another way out," Mark said. They stood at the main junction, scanning the seven other passages. "Your guess is as good as mine, but I'm pretty sure we're not getting a do-over if we're wrong."

"This one." Katie pointed down one of the darker tunnels several Gwyllgi had emerged from earlier.

"Sure hope you know what you're doing, kid."

They waded through the channel until they saw a pencil-thin slice of light penetrating the darkness. "There!" Katie pointed to the ladder reflecting pops of light coming through the small opening in the manhole.

"You go." He motioned for her to climb first. She spotted a small eye-level ridge jutting from the wall and laid the sword across it. As soon as she started up the ladder, Mark followed. It was a scant eighteen feet to the surface, but with her injuries and fatigue, it may as well have been a hundred. Clinging to the rung by the crook of her elbow, she pushed against the lid but it would not move.

"Can you get it?" he called up to her.

"It's stuck!" In her mind's eye, she perceived the sound of swooshing water racing toward them. She pressed her face to the lid, peering through the finger hole. The noxious smell of exhaust was heavy. There was a car directly above with tire resting atop the lid. Glancing around best she could, she saw a number of emergency vehicles surrounding the one that blocked them in.

"Down here! Help us!" She smashed the heel of palm against the steel manhole cover until her hand became numb.

"No good," she screamed. "I think an ambulance or police car is sitting above us and they can't hear me."

"They might not have heard you, but every last thing in this forsaken tunnel did."

Moments later, an incandescent pair of the Gwyllgi eyes slinked into the chamber -- the one possessed by the locusts, and now, larger than the others.
The creature, invisible in the darkness, made no sound as it waded toward the ladder where Mark braced himself only feet off the ground.

Katie swung her head around, saw the stalker, and sucked in a sharp breath. She jumped off the side of the ladder, grimacing in pain when she landed.

"Katie, no!"

"Keep trying that lid. We're not leaving alive if I don't deal with him now." She retrieved the sword from the ridge in the wall.

The Gwyllgi growled, taking a wide, cautious berth around her. His muscular neck and jaws snapped, frothing saliva dripping from jagged teeth.

"I, so, do not have time for this," she said, clutching at her throbbing hip. The wound hurt so bad she forgot about the sharp ache in her ribcage.

Though Mark was blind in the dark sewer, Katie saw the wraith hound as well as it saw her. She ignored the pain. Knowing she had nothing left, she determined to end the battle fast. With several quick slashes, she assailed the monster without a pause.

The creature drew back, evading her, before grazing her head with its powerful paw. Katie yelped—dazed by the blow that left three thin bloody claw marks on her face.

She crouched, returning her blade to the ready position. Mark barely made her out but didn't need to see to know she was in trouble. He climbed a step higher and braced his back against the manhole and pushed with all of his strength, but the lid remained firmly intact. He placed his eye to the finger hole. Across the street, he saw a cop motioning the motorist to proceed.

"Thank God," he gasped. The car rolled forward and he pushed the lid open, hoping another car wasn't directly behind the first, but what choice did he have? "Katie, come on!"

"Get out. I'm right behind you!" she screamed, not taking her eyes off the wraith hound.

It lunged forward and snapped at her. She stepped to the side, parrying his bite, smashing the hilt of her sword onto its bony head. The monster shook it off, springing at her again.

He swiped, coming within inches of gashing her throat. She spun her sword in a flurried attack that sliced his midsection seconds before cutting off one of the creature's feet. It wailed and stumbled backward on his hind legs.

She sprang toward it, driving the tip of the blade through its sternum. The creature screamed and dropped in front of her before collapsing into a pile of burning cinders.

Katie sprinted across the concrete of the thirty-foot wide tunnel. Halfway to the ladder, she heard swooshing of powerful rushing waters. She turned to see a twenty-foot wall of water about to crash over her. She threw her arms over her face and braced for the impact.

She remained standing, breathing heavy. The water didn't hit. She glanced into the darkness to see the cresting black wave held in suspense over her.

"Are you okay?" Mark screamed, unable to see any of what was happening below.

Somewhere deep within her abdomen, in a sheer force of will, Katie held the water at bay and slowly pushed it back. She edged toward the ladder, never taking her eyes from the wave. Ripples broke free, spilling onto the ground. Doubt began to set in. The wall ebbed toward her.

"I can't hold it anymore," she screamed, and her concentration snapped. She sprang up the ladder, and hurried to the top. Three rungs from the opening, less than two feet from his outstretched hand, one million cubic feet of rushing water crashed headlong into Katie at full force.

Epilogue
One week later

Katie sat in a chair, staring at Luke unmoving in the ICU bed. Tubes ran in and out of his arms and his shallow breath wheezed through a ventilator mask attached to his face. The past few days, she repeatedly reached out her mind to his, but all she heard was jumbled confusion. She felt he was trying to communicate but was trapped among a crowd of voices inside his head.

Her eyes swept to the door. A soft knock, then Agent Roulley limped into the room. A sling covered his left shoulder from when she'd unintentionally run him through with her sword in the sewer. Bandages remained over his splinted nose she'd busted in their parking lot tussle, and lacerations from the debris of the airport explosion covered his face.

Even with all the bruises, he didn't look as rough as Katie felt. The injuries of her multiple battles from Dorian: a rib—maybe two, felt broken, and a sore throat that punished her with every painful swallow. From the Gwyllgi: claw marks on her shoulder, hip, and another thin one on the right side of her face. The abrasions running the length of her arm and sides had all but healed—but not the plum-sized knot on the back of her head.

All those latter injuries received from the rough jostling of the water wall that crashed into her and jettisoned her through the tunnels like a runaway bullet train. Of the eight major outfalls in that quadrant of the sewer, the wave had carried her through the one discharging into a shallower section of the Potomac—absent the jagged rocks awaiting her at the bottom of the others.

Even with all of her injuries, no one would ever need to tell Katie how fortunate she'd been. The Gwyllgi scratches on her back and waist remained raw, but most of the other wounds would heal quickly, just like they always did.

"His parents told me I could come," Mark said. "Have the doctors said anything about his condition?"

"They can't find anything wrong, and yet here he is, fighting for his life." Tears dotted her lower lids. Roulley leaned over the young man and pulled away the flimsy gown from his throat.

Katie launched to her feet with a painful wince. "What are you doing?"
He didn't respond, continuing to examine Luke's neck.

The door swung open and a doctor entered the room. "Good afternoon. I'm Doctor Sydney. I hope I'm not interrupting," he said, face dark with concern, watching the agent standing over his patient. "Excuse me, I need to check his chart."

"Sure," Agent Roulley stepped back. "Any thoughts as to what happened?"

"No idea," he replied. "All we can tell is whatever happened caused his bodily functions to slow dramatically. For the moment, he's stabilized, which is a vast improvement from when he came in a week ago."

"That's great news, right?" Agent Roulley asked.

As Doctor Sydney's eyes moved between them, he seemed reluctant to answer.

"In my position, people turn to me for hope. Sometimes, the news is what friends and families of the patient are praying for, but oftentimes things don't play out that way. No matter the case, I don't feel it helps anyone by sugar coating reality. So, I'll say it like it is.

"We're looking at Mr. Ramsey's situation from every possible angle, and we've never seen anything like it. Without a cure, I am very doubtful his condition will ever improve. I'm very sorry." His sad eyes settled on Katie, then he collected his charts and left the room.

Agent Roulley sat on the arm of a chair a few feet from her. "Listen, I don't want to seem insensitive and I understand you're not in a good place right now, but we have to talk about what happened. The local authorities will speak to you again because you are the last person to see Luke before this coma. We need to get our stories straight. At this point, I'm not sure about . . . What were those things in the sewer? How did that woman—"

"Did you find them?" Katie knew it was a ridiculous question the moment she asked it. In reality, the agent could not answer the question, even if he wanted to. If dead, both Assyria and Dorian would have gone up in a flaming wisp of dust the way most wraiths and Gwyllgi did when they died. In either case, whether dead or gone, she might never be certain.

"No, but half the DC Police department is dragging the Potomac. We'll recover their bodies soon. There's no way either survived that flood."

"I did," she answered.

"All the same, they'll turn up. In fact, as we speak, Metro PD has a team of divers scouring the river off the same bank you washed onto from the tunnels. But until we've got confirmation of dead bodies, it would be good for you to be in protective custody. With me, you'll have peace knowing you're safe."

Katie popped up from the chair and pulled on her jacket, walking toward the door.

"Where you headed, kid?"

Katie turned a stone poker face to him. "You can't protect me, no one can. I'll never be safe. Everyone promises peace, but until the wraiths are dead, there can be no peace. I'm going to save Luke, then find and kill them all," she said and left the room.

Roulley sighed, letting out deep frustration. With every turn of the case, more questions sprang up than answers. The fact the cops hadn't found either body yet wasn't the only thing that troubled him. Neither of two individuals Katie called Dorian and Assyria fit the profile of the killer he'd been searching for—a psychopath who referred to himself as 'The Feaster.'

What was the connection between Dorian, Assyria, and The Feaster to each other, and perhaps even to another set of killers who had ambushed and snatched the Artifact from him and his partner? If those two men had somehow managed to lose control of it too, were they now convinced Katie could lead them to it?

None of it made sense.

He could go after her, but it'd be pointless. All he knew was, for some reason, a number of very dangerous people were desperate to find this woman, and the box. He needed to understand why. He'd keep a close eye on her, whether she liked it or not.

As he limped past Luke's bed, he pulled out his phone and dialed his voicemail. Before the first message played, he heard a low buzzing behind him. Hovering inside the double pane window, a small green locust tapped against the glass.

The Awakening

###

Fiction Author, Michael K. Drummer, born in Chicago, Illinois, and now lives in the Washington, D.C. suburbs with his wife, Trinh. They have three children aged 7-10, as well as three young sponsored children living in Ecuador and Indonesia, and two dogs.

As an avid reader growing up, his fire to become a storyteller was stoked by a number of his favorites: Terry Brooks, Robert Ludlum, Tom Clancy, Tolkien, Robert Jordan, John Milton, Stephen King, Anne Rice, Dean Koontz, Margaret Weiss & Tracy Hickman.

Interests include advocacy to end human trafficking and the oppression of children.

Connect with him online:
Facebook: http://facebook.com/drummerfan
Twitter: http://twitter.com/michaelkdrummer
Website: http://DMSawakening.com

Acknowledgements:

I give thanks to The Lord, through whom, all things are possible.

Special thanks to the following people for their contributions to the Dark Matter Syndrome, book one.

Trinh Drummer: For thoughtful critique and input on the story line.
Lanell and Catherine Drummer: Proofreading and feedback to the story.
Danielle (Dani) Halprin, Debbie Milkowski, Chris Kennedy, Richard Trask, Jeanne Perozich and Mardi Neubauer: Provided feedback and technical expertise.

Very special thanks to
Author, C.J. Ellisson: A wonderful friend and mentor who provided invaluable guidance throughout this process.

Thanks to my friends for lending their names, personalities, or likenesses to this project:

Artist, Kathy Kim —cover model and persona of the story's main character: Katie Mitchell. http://iamsorie.tumblr.com

Mark Roulley – FBI Special Agent, Mark Roulley – Used his name.

Richard Trask – "Sgt. Richard Trask." Lent both his name and his personality.

Cameron Gilbert – aka "Big Sexy." Used both name and nickname.

Ken & Margie James – Names and shades of their personalities.

Dave Ross – Investigative Reporter. Used his name.

Herman Dhaliwal – Borrowed his name and aspects of his personality.

Professional credits:
-To my absolutely amazing editor, Tina Winograd.
-Cover photography and designer, Stephen Campo. www.Campomedias.com

www.ingramcontent.com/pod-product-compliance
Lightning Source LLC
Chambersburg PA
CBHW071246170626
46809CB00001B/95